DEATH ON BOARD

A captivating historical mystery

PAULINE ROWSON

Inspector Ryga Historical Mysteries Book 5

GW00775712

Joffe Books, London
www.joffebooks.com

First published in Great Britain in 2024

Cover art by Dee Dee Book Covers

ISBN: 978-1-83526-467-6

CHAPTER ONE

Monday 7 May, 1951

Ryga surveyed the wreckage of the elegant Harley Street drawing room; whoever had done this had been a soul possessed. Cushions had been upended and tossed on the floor along with books, photographs, candlesticks, broken ornaments, records; even the pictures had been removed from the walls and lay among the debris.

Sergeant Jacobs tutted. 'Looks like wanton destruction for the sake of it.'

'Or a frantic search for something.' Ryga turned to the uniformed Inspector Tanner beside him. 'I understand the occupant is away.'

'Yes. He's on his boat somewhere off the west coast, according to Mrs Marlow, his cleaning lady.'

'So we've no idea what, if anything, has been taken.'

'No. The rest of the house is the same. It's the reason I called the Yard. That and the fact that the occupant is Sir Bernard Crompton.'

Ryga had seen the brass nameplate outside, which revealed that Sir Bernard was a dermatologist.

'Where's Mrs Marlow now?'

1

'In the basement kitchen having a cup of tea. I've left PC Kepple with her. He was first on the scene.'

'And Sir Bernard didn't leave any contact details with her or at the station?'

'No.'

'Secretary or housekeeper?'

The inspector shook his head. 'Mrs Marlow says the secretary left three months ago when Sir Bernard retired, and the housekeeper a month ago. He's putting the house on the market as soon as he returns. He hopes to move to the coast. Mrs Marlow says Sir Bernard hasn't any family, as far as she knows. He's a bachelor.'

Ryga turned to Jacobs. 'Take a look around the ground-floor consulting rooms. See what you can find.'

'Righty-ho, guv.'

'I'll have a word with Mrs Marlow.'

Tanner escorted him to the kitchen, where, among the chaos of cutlery, broken crockery, upended pots and pans, and drawers gaping from the dresser, a plump lady in her early fifties with grey hair and a face like a crumpled brown paper bag sat at the table in the centre of the room, sipping from a china cup she'd obviously managed to salvage. A large earthenware pot was in front of her. Ryga could do with a strong cup of tea himself. He and Jacobs had had little sleep, having had a tip-off that a West End cinema's safe was to be raided, one of a series of robberies at cinemas and theatres over the last two months. The villain, however, had stood them up. Either the tip-off was bogus or chummy had got wise to it. Ryga had called off the surveillance at three in the morning, it being later than when the other robberies had taken place.

PC Kepple stood to attention.

'Who's he?' Mrs Marlow narrowed her eyes at Ryga.

'Scotland Yard,' answered Tanner.

'Blimey. Ain't come across any of you lot before. If you want tea you'll have to take it without milk and sugar. And find yourself a cup that ain't broken.'

'No. I'm fine, thank you,' Ryga answered, changing his mind. He didn't fancy rummaging around on the floor. Sitting, he placed his hat on the table, while Tanner remained standing, leaning against the modern gas cooker. 'You've had a nasty shock, Mrs Marlow.'

'That I have. Sir Bernard will be right angry when he sees all this. And who can blame him? Young hooligans did this, you mark my words. Nothing better to do with their time than destroy decent folk's houses. Sooner they do their National Service the better.'

'Do you know if anything is missing?'

'Only Sir Bernard can tell you that and he ain't here on account of being on his boat somewhere.'

'Does he have a safe?' Judging by the displaced pictures, Ryga felt sure the intruder had thought there was one.

'Ain't never seen him at one, but it could be in the consulting rooms.'

Jacobs would find it if it existed. 'When are you expecting Sir Bernard back, Mrs Marlow?'

'He said he'd write to let me know. I only came in this morning to give the place a spring clean.'

May was possibly a bit later than usual for that but that was no concern of Ryga's. 'Whereabouts did Sir Bernard say he'd be?'

'He didn't. All I know is he went to Scotland a month ago to pick up his boat. Though why he wanted to go all the way up there when there are good enough ones, and boat builders, along the river, I don't know. Still, it's his money and his time.' She sipped her tea. Before Ryga could speak she continued. 'He said he was sailing from Scotland down the west coast to here and on the way looking for where he might retire. I'm to stay on until he moves. Can't you put out one of them notices on the BBC to say he should contact the police?'

'We'll see if one of his former colleagues or friends knows where we can contact him first.'

'Please yourself.'

Jacobs might find an address book.

'Do you want me to tidy up?' she asked, reluctantly. 'Only, this'll be a big job and it'll take a lot of time to put right.'

And she would need extra pay for doing so, thought Ryga. He didn't blame her for that. 'Best to leave things as they are until we can get hold of Sir Bernard and he can check if anything has been stolen. Tell me what happened when you arrived.'

'I've already done that, twice. Once with him—' she nodded towards PC Kepple — 'and then with the inspector there.'

'I'm sorry if this seems unnecessary, Mrs Marlow, but I'd like to hear it myself, and you might recall something you'd forgotten earlier.'

She sniffed as though to say 'unlikely', sat back and folded her arms under her ample, sagging bosom. 'I unlocked that door—'

'This basement one?'

'Yes!' She rolled her eyes and tutted. 'I stepped in here and had the fright of me life when I saw this mess. I ran upstairs into the hall, saw the hall table turned over and the pictures off the wall and went up to the drawing room with me heart pounding fit to burst. I took one look at it and ran like the clappers right into PC Kepple on his beat.'

Ryga had already noted, and Tanner had reported, that there was no sign of a break-in at the front of the house. There wasn't a rear entrance. The basement windows weren't broken, and Tanner had said they were secure.

'The constable come along, took one look and said not to move, he'd report in. I said not likely, I wasn't going to stay in this house alone. I stood on the front steps until he come back. And a time he took, too.' She glared at the constable, who looked stoically ahead. 'Then *he* appeared—' she nodded towards Inspector Tanner — 'and I was told I had to wait for you, so I said to meself, I'm making a cuppa. How many more bobbies are gonna turn up? Do I have to be here all day?'

'Just a few more questions, then you can leave. Does anyone else have a key, either to the front door or the basement?'

'Might have to the front door, but don't ask me who, 'cos I don't know. I doubt they have to this one.'

'Were his consulting room doors closed when you went upstairs?'

'Yes.'

'When was the last time you came to the house, Mrs Marlow?'

'The Friday before Sir Bernard left to fetch his boat. I remember it because our Ronnie come home from school with a black eye and torn trousers. They'd cost me a fortune, so I boxed his ears and told him he'd get no fish and chips, which we always has Fridays. I won't have fighting; I've said time and time—'

'And that was when?' Ryga interjected.

Her face screwed up in thought as she brushed back a stray strand of coarse, grey hair. Then her expression cleared. 'Friday the sixth. Sir Bernard was taking the train to Scotland on the Monday.'

The ninth of April. 'Do you know where in Scotland he was going?'

'No.'

'Has anyone else been in the house since then — a tradesman, for example?' Tanner had already reported that PC Kepple hadn't seen any activity around the house on his shift but he would check with the other beat constable.

'They would have needed a key and no one's asked me to let them in.'

Ryga wondered if Sir Bernard had given a spare front door key to a friend.

'Besides, Sir Bernard is very particular when any work is done,' she added. 'Always wants to be here to make sure they're not slacking.'

But he had trusted his char with a key. 'Have you lost or misplaced your keys at any time?'

'No. They're both on me own key ring along with me house keys. Here, what you saying? That I gave it to someone to come in and do this? Well, I like that! Of all the—'

'No, Mrs Marlow, I'm not saying that, I'm just exploring all the avenues.'

'Then you can explore them on your own. I'm off.' She rose.

'I'm sorry if I offended you,' Ryga soothed, drawing a startled look from the constable, who probably thought apologies were unnecessary from Scotland Yard detectives. But Ryga had learned that it was not only courteous but often the best way to get information from witnesses. It also sometimes lulled them into a false sense of security. Not that he thought Mrs Marlow had any more to tell him. 'We're most grateful for your help. This must be very upsetting for you, and all these questions don't help. You've had a shock.'

Outside a car tooted angrily. 'I have that,' she said, through pursued lips.

'I won't keep you any longer then.' He rose. 'Constable Kepple has your address and we might need to speak to you again, certainly to let you know when we have been able to speak to Sir Bernard. If you could leave your key with us that would be most helpful, and it would avoid us having to disturb you unnecessarily. We might need to return and take photographs and, of course, there are fingerprints to be taken. We'll need yours to eliminate them. Would you be prepared to go with the constable now? Or you can call into the police station later today, if you prefer.'

'I'll find me own way there, 'cos if he walks alongside me everyone will think I've been arrested.' Her small grey eyes scoured the room. 'I don't like to leave the place like this.'

'I know, but it's for the best — for now.'

'You're the guv'nor.' She picked up her capacious bag and her bosom and strode out.

Ryga addressed Kepple. 'You know this beat, Constable. What are your views?' Tanner had told Ryga that he had only just transferred from Surrey and didn't know the area that well or its inhabitants.

The burly young police officer looked taken aback at being asked his opinion. After blinking and swallowing he said, 'First time we've had a break-in around here, sir. It's not as if there were medicines for anyone to steal, Sir Bernard being a skin specialist and retired.'

Ryga knew that being a dermatologist didn't preclude Sir Bernard from having medicines on the premises but being retired probably did. 'Do you know him?'

'I've nodded to him a couple of times — "good afternoon", "nice day", that kind of thing. He seems friendly enough. Drives a Jaguar, which is parked outside, so I suppose he got a taxicab to the station.'

'Anything on the neighbours?'

'This being Harley Street, most of the residents are in the medical profession, decent people. There are a few comings and goings, as you would expect with patients visiting them, but no trouble. There are some flats and offices at the end of the road but nothing untoward with any of them.'

'Let's see if Sergeant Jacobs can throw any light on this.'

They left the basement kitchen and went back up to the ground floor. Jacobs emerged from a room to the right of the hall. 'That was the secretary's office and patient's waiting room.' He indicated the open door. Ryga looked in. Soothing colours, plush seats with the cushions tossed on the floor along with magazines and paintings. The secretary's desk held a typewriter and telephone.

'Nothing in the desk, and no medical records in the filing cabinet,' Jacobs added.

Ryga could see the gaping drawers.

'He must have handed his patient list over to a colleague. Whoever this bloke is, he was looking for something and in a mighty panic to find it.'

'And the consulting room?'

'The same.' Jacobs led the way across the hall to the door opposite. Ryga again peered in. The same soothing colours, a much grander desk and chair, the latter upended, as was the patient's couch and screen. The pictures were again on the floor, two with the glass shattered. 'There are some letters from his fellow consultants and some papers on his membership of the British Association of Dermatologists.'

Ryga could see paperwork scattered around the desk and floor.

'He was also a consultant at the St John's Hospital for Diseases of the Skin in Lisle Street, Soho.' Jacobs referred to his notebook. 'And a consultant at St Thomas' Hospital and Guy's Hospital. Might still be for all that. I heard these medical men never really retire. He might be in touch with one of his colleagues there or at the British Association of Dermatologists in Fitzroy Square. No address book or diary. He must have taken it with him. And nothing on the purchase of his boat.'

'Doesn't surprise me; he'd have needed the documents in order to take possession of it. No safe?'

Jacobs shook his head. 'Windows facing the road — as you can see, guv — are all secure, no sign of being tampered with. Same as the basement ones.'

The luxurious floor-length curtains were still draped back. 'No sign of any spare keys or car keys, I take it?'

'None.'

'Take a look at his car, see if there's anything lying around inside.' Ryga turned to Tanner. 'I'd like to take a quick look around upstairs.'

There, Ryga found the same unholy mess. Sir Bernard's bedroom was plainly decorated and furnished. His clothes — of good quality, as to be expected — were scattered about the floor, the chest of drawers open and emptied, and the double bed stripped of its sheets, blankets and eiderdown, the mattress upturned. In the other two bedrooms there was less chaos because clearly they had been unoccupied, but the cupboard and wardrobe doors were open and the mattresses again upended. The bathroom cabinet had been emptied, leaving some tablet bottles and medicines on the floor. The top floor contained an attic room furnished as a bed-sitting room, which Ryga thought had once been two rooms. There was also a toilet and a bathroom. All was in order because there was nothing in them to ransack. This had clearly been the housekeeper's quarters. He wondered what the intruder had been searching for. Money? Jewellery? Maybe there had been silver, which would have been worth something. Or perhaps Sir Bernard collected priceless small antiques, ornaments or miniatures, and the suspect had been after them. But that didn't answer how he had let himself in, unless Mrs Marlow was no innocent bystander and had given her key to the thief. He hadn't pegged her as crooked, but you never could tell.

Descending the stairs, he said to Tanner, 'Can you ask your officers to talk to the neighbours? Find out if they've seen anyone suspicious hanging around, or heard any unusual noises coming from here over the last month. We can't be specific; it could have been the day Sir Bernard left or last night. Also, make discreet enquiries about Mrs Marlow and her family and contacts. She could be in league with whoever did this.'

Back in the hall, Jacobs broke off his conversation with Kepple on sentry duty at the door.

'Car was unlocked. Nothing in it save some driving gloves, an AA road atlas, spare tyre in the boot and a blanket. I flicked through the AA book to see if he'd marked anywhere in Scotland but there's nothing. No need really, when he travelled up there by train.'

Ryga turned to Tanner. 'We'll lock up and keep the key for now and I'll ask our fingerprint experts to come over and see what they can get. Let me know if anything transpires your end. We'll check with his colleagues.'

In the waiting police car, Ryga instructed the driver to make for Fitzroy Square. 'Jacobs, ask if anyone at the British Association of Dermatologists knows where Sir Bernard is. If you get no joy there, try the hospitals where he worked. See if anyone knows the boat's name, make and who built it. We might be able to track him down that way and inform him of the break-in. Not that he can rush home, unless he leaves the boat moored up somewhere.' Then an idea occurred to him. 'If he's bringing her back here he must have arranged to moor her. I'll ask the River Police to check with the harbour and wharf masters. We could get its name and make that way.'

The driver dropped Jacobs off. Ryga watched as the sergeant pulled up his collar and squared his hat in the slanting rain. He hoped Jacobs would strike lucky at the first port of call; it was too miserable a day to be trudging about. And Jacobs must be as tired and achy as he felt, cramped up in the office of that West End cinema, waiting for their safebreaker to strike. It would have been the fourth time. Perhaps he'd retired on the proceeds he'd already stolen from theatres and cinemas. It was a substantial amount. Or maybe he was just having a rest, or was ill. Ryga had thought the anonymous telephone tip-off had been slightly odd. Cinemas didn't usually do a roaring trade on a Monday, and the other robberies had occurred in the early hours of a Saturday or Sunday when the box office had their best takings. But they couldn't risk ignoring it. Ryga had a feeling the tip-off was from the villain himself having a good laugh at them. Well, they'd see who got the last laugh. Ryga was more determined than ever to get him.

In his office, he put out a request to the River Police to make enquiries about Sir Bernard's possible mooring. He rose and stared through the rain-spattered window, watching two barges crossing the sluggish, dull green-grey Thames towing their lumbering cargo. He wondered what kind of craft Sir Bernard had. He'd be able to afford something a cut above the average. He felt a pang of envy at the thought of cruising down the British west coast. He missed the sea, having spent many years on it prior to and during the very early part of the war, before his merchant ship had been seized by a German raider in forty-one. After the war he'd been fortunate enough to secure a position in the Thames River Police thanks to his mentor in the camp, Detective Superintendent Simmonds, now of the Kent Constabulary. Then promotion and a change of role had beckoned.

Stifling a yawn, he turned back to his desk and, picking up the telephone, called Makepeace in the records office.

'What have we got on Scottish boat builders, those of smaller yachts and gentlemen's motor cruisers?'

'Nothing, but there's bound to be an almanac. If not, I'll get in touch with the Scottish Home Department; they'll give us a list.'

Ryga was tempted to light the gas fire, it being unseasonably cold for May. He felt chilly, more than he used to — a legacy of his POW days — and he was certain the fire would send him to sleep. Tea and a sandwich, courtesy of the tea lady and her trolley, revitalized him. He hoped Jacobs was managing to get a hot drink and something to eat on his enquiries. He forced himself to concentrate on his paperwork and other cases, shutting out Sir Bernard's break-in. It was mid-afternoon when a very wet and weary sergeant shuffled into his office and shook out his coat and hat.

'You need of a cup of tea.' Ryga lifted his phone.

'That I do, my throat's so parched it feels like a carpenter's floor. No one so much as offered me a cuppa, though to be fair they were all rushed off their feet. I never knew there were so many folk with skin problems.' He flopped into the seat across Ryga's desk.

Ryga requested two teas. 'Make that three,' Detective Chief Superintendent Street said, striding in. 'Why haven't you got the heating on, Ryga? It's freezing in here.'

Jacobs sprang up and lit the gas fire.

'How did you get on this morning at the Harley Street break-in?' Street sat and plugged his pipe. He nodded at Jacobs to resume his seat.

Ryga quickly gave his report. Their tea arrived as he finished.

'So we've no idea when the break-in occurred or if anything was stolen. Jacobs?'

'Nothing doing at the hospitals, sir, not for want of trying. Those I managed to speak with haven't heard from Sir Bernard since he retired, and no one knows the name of his boat.'

'I do.' Street struck a match to his pipe. Ryga exchanged a glance with Jacobs. 'It's called the *Patricia Bee*. And I know where it is.' After a couple of satisfactory puffs, Street continued. 'How do I know this? Because early this morning Sir Bernard Crompton was found dead on board.'

Jacobs's jaw dropped. Ryga was troubled. 'Suspicious?'

'Not according to Major Tweed, the chief constable of Cornwall. He telephoned the news to the assistant commissioner two hours ago. Tweed says the doctor has certified death by natural causes and it's down to us to inform his next of kin, Sir Bernard hailing from here. They also need someone to make a formal identification before the inquest. And he asked us to make arrangements for the body, and boat, to be brought back to town.'

'But?' Ryga asked, detecting an undertone in Street's voice.

'The AC and I have discussed the matter and we're in agreement. In light of this break-in we need to make absolutely sure there was no foul play, which means, Ryga, you're to take the nine fifty from Paddington to Penzance tonight.'

CHAPTER TWO

Tuesday 8 May
7.40 a.m.

It was raining when Ryga alighted from the train into a day that smelled of steam and the sea. He'd been fortunate to get a sleeping berth, and while he usually slept well on trains this time he'd struggled. He put it down to a combination of being overtired from the previous night and the fact that the burglary and the sudden death of Sir Bernard insisted on playing merry-go-round in his head. It had to be one of those coincidences, surely — a sentiment that Tweed had voiced most vehemently when he'd learned of Ryga's forthcoming visit, so Street had told him.

Part of him was keen to be here. It was a chance to escape the grime and noise of London and again experience the vast expanse of the sea and all her moods, but another part was reluctant to leave the safebreaking job unfinished. Jacobs would continue working on that. And there was every chance that he could be back in town before chummy pulled his next job.

'Inspector Ryga?' A uniformed officer stepped out of a Humber.

'Yes?'

'The chief constable would like to see you.'

It sounded like a summons. Ryga knew he wasn't to be given the welcome mat. Sure enough, a few minutes later he was shown into an office at the station where a ruddy-faced, stiff-backed, rotund little man glared at him with small, hard eyes.

'I really don't see why you're here,' Tweed launched without any preliminary courtesies. 'It's perfectly clear that Sir Bernard Crompton died a natural death — heart attack or seizure. The inquest on Thursday morning will corroborate that.'

'You have the results of the post-mortem, sir?' Ryga asked, politely.

'There hasn't been one. It's not necessary. The doctor has certified death. There is no crime here for you to investigate. *I* haven't called in the Yard, and our own detectives are perfectly capable of handling the case, *if* there is one, which means you have no business here. My wishes, however, don't seem to count when the assistant commissioner has the ear of the commissioner *and* the home secretary.'

Ryga stifled his surprise. Street hadn't told him that this had gone that high. Obviously Sir Bernard was even more eminent than any of them had thought.

'This is a waste of taxpayers' money. I expect you to leave after the inquest.'

'I might very well be doing so, sir. But first I'd like to see where Sir Bernard died and view the body.'

Tweed clucked disapprovingly. 'No doubt you have to justify your presence and the expense. I have made my views perfectly clear to the assistant commissioner. Still, if the Yard want to squander money, that's their business. Detective Sergeant Pascoe will assist you. He was called to the body and can tell you all you need to know.' He turned, expecting Ryga to follow, which he did, to an office off the public area, where a man in civilian clothes in his late thirties leaped to attention from one of the three desks. He was alone in the room.

14

'Detective Sergeant Pascoe, Inspector Ryga. I expect to be kept fully informed,' Tweed barked at Ryga.

'Of course, sir,' Ryga answered.

With a snort, Tweed marched out.

'Is he always so abrupt?' Ryga asked.

'He's not a Cornishman.'

'Nor am I,' Ryga answered with a smile. 'Does that make a difference?'

'Depends.'

'He thinks I'm wasting my time. What do you think?'

Pascoe's thoughtful gaze told Ryga he was being sized up. He wondered if he'd pass muster.

'Maybe you are, and maybe you're not, sir.'

Ryga was also assessing the sergeant. 'You have doubts about the cause of death?'

'Let's just say there are some odd things.'

'Such as?'

'Best I tell you on the boat, sir, unless you want to view the body first.'

On the train, Ryga had contemplated where to begin his investigation; Pascoe had decided that for him.

'Let's start with the boat. I believe it's currently moored at Mousehole?'

'*Mowzel.*'

'Pardon?'

'You have to get the pronunciation right, sir. Although it looks as though it should be spoken "mouse hole", our Cornish dialect pronounces it "mowzel".' Pascoe's dark brown eyes twinkled. He'd spoken pleasantly, not condescendingly.

'Is Mousehole within walking distance?' Ryga had passed the test. Pascoe had judged him worthy of being corrected in his pronunciation rather than leaving him looking foolish in the eyes of the locals. He was grateful. Pascoe didn't resent his arrival as did Tweed. He could see there was a lot more to the sergeant behind the measured pace of his words and leisurely movement, something Ryga thought Tweed misjudged.

'Depends how far you like to walk.'

'Miles, when I need to,' Ryga answered. He hadn't bought a map at Paddington because he didn't think he would be here long enough to need one. 'But I'd prefer not to this morning.'

'Then we'll take Chief Inspector Jerram's car. He's in charge of the station and would have been here to meet you but Major Tweed insisted on doing so himself. The chief constable doesn't come here often, being based at headquarters at Bodmin.'

Ryga thought Pascoe would like to add, 'Thank goodness.' Tweed had obviously made an exception in his case in order to make his views known.

'The car has been put at our disposal.'

'I'll leave my holdall here. Have you booked me in anywhere?'

'No, sir. I didn't know what your plans were.'

'I don't know them either. Do I need to take my murder case?'

'Not according to Major Tweed, but maybe you should.'

Ryga nodded. This was getting interesting.

Pascoe took a set of keys from his desk drawer and his hat and overcoat from the stand. Intrigued, Ryga followed him out of the station to a Morris. The Humber that had brought him the very short distance here, and the driver, were obviously Tweed's. Perhaps these 'odd things' could be easily explained, though the sergeant looked to be an intelligent, experienced police officer, not one given to flights of fancy or drama.

Soon the town fell behind them as they headed west along the coast. Ryga took in the scenery, although there wasn't much to see save a steely sea and some straggly houses before the harbour of Newlyn approached.

'Tell me what happened, Sergeant. I haven't been given any details.'

'Do you know much about boats and the sea, sir?'

'A fair bit. I was in the Merchant Navy and then the Thames River Police before my current job.'

Pascoe flashed him an admiring look. 'That makes it easier. Major Tweed being a landlubber doesn't really understand.'

'About these "odd things"?'

'To be fair, I haven't told him about them. Nor did I mention all of them to Detective Inspector Giles at Bodmin, who I first reported to on account of our own divisional detective inspector being off sick with a ruptured hernia. I wasn't certain what they meant but the more I thought them over last night, the more I wondered. Then I was told the Yard was on its way. I'd better start at the beginning.'

'Always best to, Pascoe.'

'Well, the *Patricia Bee*, Sir Bernard's craft, was spotted by the Wolf Rock lighthouse keeper. It's a sea-based lighthouse situated between the Isles of Scilly and Porthgwarra — that's the far western point before you get round to Land's End. Porthgwarra is a small, narrow cove with a few houses, boats and a tunnel dug by tin miners from St Just. The craft had cleared Tol-Pedn — that's Cornish for "holed headland".'

'It looks as though I'm going to have to learn a new language.'

'You'll soon pick it up.' Pascoe grinned. 'Tol-Pedn is a granite outcrop and was — still is — referred to by many as St Levan's Land's End after the area around it. There's a coastguard station on Tol-Pedn. The coastguard confirmed the lighthouse keeper's observations. There wasn't anything untoward with the *Patricia Bee*. This was just before six o'clock yesterday morning.' Pascoe broke off to see if Ryga was following him.

'Go on.'

'The craft was making steadily in this direction. The next time the lighthouse keeper looked, it was off the western edge of St Clement's Isle. You'll see the island soon. It's a grand name for a clump of rocks. It's got a monument on it, known as the pepper pot, with the inscription "Lord of the Manor" after a man called Halse who might have owned the island way back in the last century. There it is, sir, just coming into view.'

The rain was beginning to lift, and in the grey sea, Ryga saw a low-lying group of rocks with a slight knoll, and could just make out the square pepper pot on it.

'There are tales of a hermit once living there and local boys often swim out to it. Well, the *Patricia Bee* was drifting, and the keeper was concerned she would go aground. He alerted the Penlee Lifeboat, who went out and hailed the craft. Getting no response, they managed to tie up to it. One of the men, Colin Blayde, boarded her. He found Sir Bernard dead in the aft cabin, although at that stage they didn't know who he was.'

'And this was when?'

'Around six thirty, a little over an hour after high water. They brought her into the harbour and Blayde ran up to the coastguard station at Mousehole and telephoned through to PC Treharne at Newlyn. He covers this area. Blayde also telephoned Dr Bergmann at St Just. There was nothing the doctor could do for the poor man except to certify life was extinct. As it happened, Mrs Bergmann answered the phone and said her husband was on a call in Mousehole at Miss Enys's place up above the harbour. She'd telephone to him there.'

'Where was the harbour master?'

'Over at Sennen. He'd stayed there the night with his brother and didn't get back until the *Patricia Bee* was moored up. PC Treharne cycled to Mousehole, viewed the body and telephoned us at Penzance. Not that he thought it was a suspicious death, but it was one that he considered beyond his jurisdiction to investigate. I drove out, arrived here just after nine. By that time the lifeboat crew and the doctor had gone; only PC Treharne was left to make sure nothing was disturbed. Sir Bernard was dead in the stateroom, aft. No signs of foul play. PC Treharne told me Dr Bergmann had certified death, and that it appeared the man had suffered a heart attack or stroke. I asked Treharne to arrange for the body to be taken to the mortuary in Penzance. He went off to telephone the undertakers at Penzance. We're coming into Mousehole now, sir.'

Tiny terraced cottages crowded the water's edge and twisted up the narrow roads. Before them lay the harbour with a small sandy beach. Framing it were two stone piers, which stretched out and arched so close to each other at the entrance that Ryga wondered anything could sail between them. Clearly they had though, as a number of small craft and fishing boats, some with men tending to their nets, were laid up on the shore and tied up to the piers. It was the splendid motor yacht at the end of the pier, though, that drew Ryga's attention.

'I take it that's the *Patricia Bee*?'

'Yes.' Pascoe silenced the car engine. 'And that's old Silas Able keeping watch over her.'

Ryga could see an elderly man sitting on a bollard smoking a pipe. Beside him was a black-and-white collie.

'Used to be a miner until he had an accident and hurt his back, became a fisherman, then got too old for that, so now he spends his time here, looking after people's boats if they want him to, mending nets and helping with the pilchard catch. That's the main haul here.'

They walked down the pier, where Pascoe nodded a greeting to a handful of fishermen. The place reminded Ryga of the fishing port of Brixham in Devon, where he'd been on an investigation in January. It had been a disturbing case. Not so this one. At least he didn't think so, but then he didn't have all the facts yet, or Pascoe's list of 'odd things'. And there was that break-in.

They drew level with the boat. Silas removed his pipe.

'Anyone been nosing around?' Pascoe asked the old man.

'A few, but nobody's been on board. Now you're here with the man from London, I'll take Jed for a walk.' He touched his cap and strolled off, the dog padding behind him. Ryga didn't bother to ask how the old man knew he was from London.

He peered down at the *Patricia Bee*, taking in with wonder the teak wheelhouse and deck, the new cream canvas stretching over the lockers, the gleaming white wooden hull and shining brass portholes. He had expected something impressive but not as elegant and opulent as this, and that was even before he'd been on board. Makepeace hadn't had any joy finding the boat builders by the time Ryga had left for Penzance but Ryga was bound to get that information on board. It was sad that Sir Bernard had barely had time to enjoy her.

'I'd have thought a boat like this would have had a tender,' he said, eyeing her. There were fixtures for one aft but no boat suspended from them.

'I'd have thought so too, but no one reported seeing one when the *Patricia Bee* was drifting.'

Ryga eyed him shrewdly. 'You think someone took off on it before the boat was seen and boarded?'

'Possibly.'

'One of your "odd things"?'

Pascoe nodded.

'OK, let's go on board.' Ryga climbed nimbly down the iron rungs of the pier-side ladder on to the craft. In another two hours it would be low tide and the boat would rest on the sand.

On deck, Pascoe handed over the keys taken from the dead man, saying, 'Some of these must be to his London home.'

'These two appear to be.' Ryga indicated one to the front door and the other to the basement door. 'Did you know he was burgled?'

'No. Does the major know?' Pascoe looked disturbed.

'My chief at the Yard told him. Major Tweed is of the opinion it has nothing to do with Sir Bernard's death. He could be right. On the other hand . . .'

Pascoe grinned. 'You're getting the hang of things. What was taken from Sir Bernard's house?'

'We don't know. Nothing obvious appeared to have been stolen but there's no one to say what was there to begin with because he lived alone. We're also not sure when the break-in occurred. According to his cleaning lady, Sir Bernard left his home on Monday the ninth of April and she hadn't been inside it from Friday the sixth until yesterday when she found it ransacked.'

'Another "odd thing" to add to my list. It's getting to be quite long.'

'I'll make it even longer,' Ryga said good-humouredly, gazing around the immaculate craft. 'There was no evidence of a forced entry. Mrs Marlow, his charlady, denies leaving her key around for someone to take and copy. But she could have been careless. My instinct tells me she's an honest soul. But I've asked the local CID to question her more deeply and look into her background, and that of her husband and their neighbours. This key is to Crompton's Jaguar. The others must belong to this boat.' He inserted one of them in the wheelhouse door and stepped inside. The smell of new wood and polish greeted him. He drank in the gleaming compass, the spick-and-span controls, the pale cream leather captain's seat and behind it another set into the wood panelling to accommodate two passengers. To the left was a small table used for the navigation charts. The boat builder's name was displayed on a brass plaque behind the table: James B. Parron Limited of Rosneath, Scotland, which tied in with Mrs Marlow telling them Sir Bernard had travelled to Scotland.

'This is splendid,' Ryga uttered in awe. Taking the remaining key, he slotted it into the helm but didn't start the engine. 'Is this exactly as Blayde found it, and with the key in the helm?'

'Yes. And I've no need to doubt him. It was like this when I came on board.' Pascoe was studying Ryga intensely and Ryga knew why; the sergeant was looking to see if he spotted anything else 'odd'. Ryga opened the drawer under the navigation table. It contained some instrumentation — a single-handed brass divider used for measuring the distance between two points on a chart in nautical miles, a parallel ruler, a protractor triangle, two pencils, an eraser and a torch.

'Where are the sea charts? Sir Bernard must have been using them. He couldn't have sailed from Scotland without them.'

'There aren't any.'

'And the logbook?'

'Couldn't find it.'

21

Ryga was mystified. 'And you mentioned this to Detective Inspector Giles?'

'Yes.'

'And he said?'

'"Let the man from the Yard sort it out." Perhaps Sir Bernard gave them to someone, or this other person took them, but that would mean—'

'Two people were on this boat. Hence the missing tender.'

'Yes.'

'We'll ask the boat builders if they supplied one.' And where were the papers confirming ownership and sales invoices? Perhaps in the saloon.

Ryga stepped down into it and soaked up the rich smell of mahogany and leather. The cabin exuded elegance and luxury with its cream seating contrasting with the chest-nut-brown wood panelling and lockers. The brass around the light fittings, mirror and portholes shone. On the table was a half-full bottle of Glenfiddich and a crystal glass beside it, empty. It looked posed as though for an advertisement.

'It all looks too tidy to me,' Pascoe said.

Ryga silently agreed. 'Sir Bernard might have been naturally fastidious.' He couldn't say what the man's habits had been in that direction because of the ransacking in his house. And it wasn't something he had asked Mrs Marlow, not knowing then what would be relevant.

'Did he have a manservant in London?' asked Pascoe.

'Not according to Mrs Marlow. And he'd let his house-keeper go.'

'Who cooked for him, then? And I don't mean in his house, I mean here, on board.'

'Perhaps he liked to cook himself.'

Pascoe looked dubious. 'If he did he was a very neat cook and washed up afterwards.'

'That's not unheard of. I do.'

'You live alone?'

'Yes.' And he'd been glad to after four years living with so many men in the POW camp. But more recently he'd wished for company, and female at that. He thought of two women who had recently impacted on his life: Eva, a professional photographer with a hectic and peripatetic career, and Sonia Shepherd, the former landlady of the Quarryman's Arms on the Isle of Portland in Dorset, where he had also met Eva for the first time. Eva was busily engaged photographing industrial England. He didn't know where Sonia was; he wished he did. She'd taken off abruptly after her criminal husband had unexpectedly reappeared. There was a warrant out for Sam Shepherd's arrest but to date no sightings of him. Sonia had been badly treated and was understandably afraid of him. Ryga wished he knew where she was living. He pushed aside such thoughts and concentrated on what he was here for. 'Maybe Sir Bernard ate out.'

'You could be right, because not only are there basic rations in the galley, but there's also his manner of dress. You'll see for yourself in the stateroom.'

Ryga crossed the narrow passageway leading to the aft. His eyes fell on the bed. 'A dinner jacket? Sir Bernard was wearing evening dress when his body was found?' Ryga had expected him to have been in nautical clothes, or perhaps pyjamas and a dressing gown, given the time of his death.

'One more "odd thing" to add to our list, sir, because as far as I can see he didn't dine with anyone on board on Sunday night, not unless, as I said, he washed up and put everything away. Unusual, I'd say, for a man in his position and on a yacht like this.'

So too would Ryga. 'It's something that backs up the idea that he must have had someone with him, a manservant, to look after him on this trip.'

'Why wouldn't this valet stay and assist the poor man when he was dying?' Pascoe asked. 'He could have made a Mayday call.'

'Maybe he didn't want to get involved. He thought he'd be accused of bringing on the attack. Or perhaps he saw a golden opportunity to help himself to a valuable item on board. We have no idea what was on this boat. Have you got any more "odd things" up your sleeve, Sergeant?'

'I have. There was the way he was lying. His hands were across his chest, indicating he'd clutched his heart on having a severe attack and then slid to the ground. But as I thought about it, I recalled his fists weren't clenched as though in agony. His fingers were splayed out. It looked to me as though . . . well, as though someone had placed them across his chest, laid him out like that. The doctor could have done it, I grant you, and his fingers could naturally have been spread, but his face was wrong. It wasn't grimaced with pain. He was sort of smiling and his eyes were closed. Again, the doctor could have closed them. I haven't spoken to him. But he couldn't have altered the face's expression.'

'Describe exactly how Sir Bernard was dressed when you found him.'

'I took some notes, for the inquest.' Pascoe removed his notebook from inside his coat pocket. 'The jacket, as you can see, is lying face down on the bed. The bed's not been turned down or disturbed in any way. No one had sat on it, or if they did, they smoothed it out. His dickie bow was undone and hanging loose around his neck. He was wearing a cummerbund that was still fastened around his waist. His shirt was clean.'

'Shoes?'

'Black patent leather, also clean. No traces of sand, grit or mud on them and they weren't wet.'

Ryga turned back the crisp white-cotton sheets to reveal a pair of folded blue-silk pyjamas. Leaning down, he sniffed the sheets and then the pillow. There was the faint odour of cologne, which could be hair oil. There were no books or maps on the shelving.

He lifted the dinner jacket. Again Ryga sniffed — no perfume. 'Fetch my murder bag from the wheelhouse, Pascoe.' From it, Ryga retrieved a magnifying glass and studied the outside of the jacket. There were several white hairs and two spots of grease. On the collar were some smaller hairs, which looked more grey than white. Taking his tweezers, Ryga removed them and placed them in a small paper evidence bag. 'You searched his pockets?'

'Yes. In his left trouser pocket were his keys. In the right his wallet, identity card and two pound notes. There was no ration book.'

Ryga raised his eyebrows. 'Curious.'

'Yes, but even more curious is what I found in his dinner jacket pocket.'

'And that was?'

'Five pieces of rock.'

CHAPTER THREE

'Rock?' Ryga repeated, mystified.

'Grey-green in colour, each piece about the size of a half-crown but thicker, with jagged edges. I couldn't think why he had them on his person except that he might have been interested in geology.'

It didn't seem likely to Ryga. But then there was no reason why Sir Bernard shouldn't have been an amateur geologist; Ryga only knew what he and Sergeant Jacobs had gleaned from Mrs Marlow yesterday, and from Jacobs's enquiries with his former colleagues, and that amounted to the fact that Sir Bernard enjoyed sailing. 'Have you mentioned this to anyone?'

'No. I couldn't see how it was relevant. But the more I thought about it, along with the other things, the more it troubled me.'

'I take it you still have them?'

'At the station.'

'Good.' He'd very much like to see them. He also wished to examine this elegant motor cruiser in greater detail. There were certainly some peculiarities here. 'Take a look around the deck, Pascoe, see if there is any evidence of a tender, or any sea charts. I'll poke about here.'

Ryga opened the lockers. Sir Bernard's clothes were mainly casual, of excellent quality and of a nautical leaning — trousers, shirts, jumpers, deck shoes, a pair of plimsolls and two pairs of brogues. There was also a sou'wester and a long oilskin coat for the wet weather and, below them in the same cupboard, a pair of wellington boots. From the size of the clothes, Sir Bernard looked to have been a big man — certainly taller and much broader than him, Ryga thought, holding up the trousers.

He found the hair oil in the washroom, along with shaving tackle, toothbrush, soap, comb, hairbrush and a packet of indigestion tablets. Opening his case, he dusted for prints in both the stateroom and washroom, examined them and carefully photographed them with his small camera. The prints looked to be the same. He suspected Sir Bernard's. If there had been a valet, he'd been very careful not to leave his prints.

In the saloon he found some clear prints on the bottle of whisky and the glass that matched those in Sir Bernard's cabin. Yet he felt there was something not quite right about them, and about the positioning of the objects. He again took photographs with his small camera. Had Sir Bernard sat here, alone, drinking his whisky? It seemed so.

Ryga picked up the glass and sniffed. There was no residue of smell. He ran his finger around the sides and bottom of the glass. Dry. That didn't necessarily mean anything. It was some time since it had been used. He dusted for prints on the tabletop and around the galley; there seemed remarkably few of them.

The for'ard cabin revealed nothing surprising. The bed was unmade. He found bed linen, two blankets, a pillow and towels in the lockers. All looked to be new. There were no clothes and no toiletries in the adjoining washroom. If someone else had been on board they'd cleared out everything and hadn't left any fingerprints.

Ryga wondered who had equipped the boat. It was clear to him that everything was new. Perhaps the boat builder had been commissioned to do that before Sir Bernard took possession. He still couldn't find any paperwork to confirm that.

He went up to the helm, where Pascoe was closely examining for'ard. Opening the drawer under the navigation table, he made a note of the seagoing instruments and dusted for fingerprints. There were some smudged prints on the drawer handle, probably his own, but none on the instrumentation and torch.

Pascoe joined him. 'Aside from the fixtures aft, I can't see any evidence of a tender and there are no lines that might have been fastened to one.'

Ryga told him what he'd done.

'Do you want to check the engine room, sir?'

'Might as well while we're here.'

They did so but it didn't yield anything. It was as Ryga had expected — remarkably pristine. Before leaving he inserted the key in the helm. The boat was petrol powered and there was about half a tank left. More questions occurred to Ryga but he shelved them.

'I'd like to talk to Dr Bergmann. Is his practice far?'

'It's at St Just, a bit more 'n ten miles up country. We should catch him before he goes out on his calls.'

Locking up the boat, they returned to the car and Pascoe was soon weaving his way through a series of twisting, narrow lanes. Ryga hoped they wouldn't meet anything coming in the opposite direction or they'd have a long way to reverse. He breathed a sigh of relief when they came out on to a wider and busier road, but it was short-lived as Pascoe once again dived down more lanes.

'I'd never find my way around here,' Ryga said with feeling.

'The road from Penzance to St Just is the main one, you'd be all right on that. We'll hit it in a moment.'

They did shortly and Ryga relaxed, taking in the bleak, rugged, windswept countryside that intermittently gave way to small fields and pastures. As the road rose and dipped he caught glimpses of the sea and farmhouses. Scattered among the wild landscape were ruined brick buildings and broken, leaning chimneys. It had started raining again, this time more heavily.

'Are there many tin mines left?' he asked.

'Only two. The Catallack Mine south of St Just and another farther north. They did well during the war, and they're not doing too badly now with tin prices high. But it won't last,' Pascoe prophetically claimed. 'Tin and copper prices go up and down like a yo-yo. They'll go down again for certain. That's why the council are so hell-bent on this tourist idea. But it's not the same as giving men a good, steady job. I know it's hard work down the mines, but what can miners do for a load of sightseers?'

Not much, thought Ryga.

'And there's all the other industries attached to mining,' Pascoe continued. 'They'll go to the wall, and that means folk will move out. Can't blame them neither, if there's no work. They've done it before. Went off to the gold mines in Australia and South Africa and sent money back home.'

'Ever been tempted, Sergeant, to move abroad?'

'No, I'm happy here. You?'

'Not abroad. But I'm not sure about staying in London.'

'But your job!' Pascoe exclaimed in shock, almost veering across the road.

'Yes, that's what keeps me there and I love it. Still, who knows?' He missed the sea, not being on it but close to it. He had the river and the docks in London, which both had their charms and idiosyncrasies, but never that sense of space and peace you got with the sea, even when it was wild or dull. Ahead he could see it, a drab blur in the dank day, but it was still magical to him. He would like a small boat to sail along the coast. Perhaps one day.

A sign to their left showed Land's End to be six miles and Sennen four. With a map he'd get a much better feel for this terrain, but did he need to be here that long? The theory that there might have been another person on the *Patricia Bee* didn't mean that someone was guilty of anything, except leaving his master to die alone, and the boat to drift onto the rocks of St Clement's Isle. Those weren't crimes. And if there had been a companion, or valet, then he or she could have disembarked long before the boat had sailed around Mousehole. But those pieces of rock were rather curious, especially given the fact they had been in the dinner jacket. It was possible the dead man could have picked them up from a shore or bay, only that wasn't borne out by his apparel and shoes. He might have been given them by someone, his valet or a guest, and had just popped them in his pocket.

He postponed his thoughts as they came into the small town of St Just, where Pascoe pulled up at the square to allow some traffic to pass. There were a handful of tourists meandering around in see-through plastic mackintoshes over their holiday wear, maps in their hands and dazed looks on their faces. Perhaps they had expected more from the place than granite buildings and twisting narrow streets.

Pascoe indicated to the right into a road of terraced houses. 'That's the police house.'

It was a sturdy double-fronted property.

'Sergeant Marrack has a constable who assists him. He lives in lodgings. Not that they have any trouble here. The miners are chapel. That's it directly ahead.'

Ryga could see the resplendent building with its grand portico entrance.

'Dr Bergmann's house is just around the corner in Chapel Road, sir.'

'Do you know him?'

'No. Sergeant Marrack will though.'

He pulled up outside a house displaying a brass plaque giving the doctor's name and surgery opening times — 8.30 a.m. to 10.30 a.m. and 4.30 p.m. to 7 p.m. It was just on eleven. Pascoe rang the bell and, after a short delay, the door opened to reveal a slender woman in her mid-thirties with a fine-boned, slightly swarthy face and dark shadows under her deep-set brown eyes. Ryga thought her attractive in a mystical, elusive sort of way, or was that his imagination and the Cornish magic beginning to play tricks with him?

Despite holding herself well, her fatigue showed through. Her jet-black hair was drawn off her face. She was dressed simply in a plain navy-blue dress that amplified her elegance. She greeted them politely and pleasantly but her expression turned to concern as Ryga introduced himself and explained why they were there.

'My husband has just finished with his last patient.' There was no trace of Cornish accent but Ryga detected something. He couldn't place it though. 'I'll tell him you are here. Please take a seat in the waiting room.'

She showed them into a chilly, dreary room on the left with posters on the walls advocating vaccinations, the use of handkerchiefs to trap germs, and a request to give blood. An assortment of chairs were placed up against the walls while two more were around a sturdy, scratched wooden table in the centre of the room. It was a marked contrast to Sir Bernard's soothing, opulent waiting room.

Ryga placed his hat beside the small wicker basket on the table containing oblong pieces of white card with numbers in bold. Next to it were a couple of women's magazines, two comics and the April edition of *Family Doctor*, proclaiming to be the first issue of a magazine 'by doctors for the general public who want advice and help with medical matters'. He sat and idly flicked through it, while Pascoe crossed to the unlit electric fire. There was an article on diabetes, one on how to treat a duodenal ulcer and another on the best way to deal with rheumatics.

Before Ryga got any further, an athletic man with dark chiselled features, wild black hair and an abundance of energy swept into the room with an outstretched hand, introducing himself as Dr David Bergmann. Ryga stood to take the dry, firm grasp and returned the pressure as he introduced himself and Pascoe.

'Sarah tells me you wish to speak with me. Do you want to come through to my consulting room or would you prefer to talk here? We shan't be disturbed with the surgery closed.'

'Here will do fine,' Ryga answered, not wishing to take the patient's chair in the medical man's room. It might be tempting fate. He was fit enough, with just a few lingering ailments from his forced captivity. They were nothing.

As with Bergmann's wife, Ryga detected the hint of an accent but couldn't pinpoint it. 'We won't keep you long, Doctor. I'd just like to ask you about the body you examined yesterday on the *Patricia Bee*.'

'Please sit down.'

Ryga resumed his seat. Bergmann took the one opposite while Pascoe, with his notebook and pencil poised, eased himself down on a chair against the wall, facing them.

'What time did you examine the body, Doctor?'

'Around 7.20, or just after, yesterday morning.'

'And your initial thoughts?'

'I could see that nothing had been disturbed in the state-room, so my initial thoughts were he had collapsed suddenly and died almost instantly, which my examination confirmed. There was no indication of foul play, the body wasn't marked or disfigured in any way. But you suspect something — after all, Scotland Yard don't attend deaths on a whim, no matter how eminent the personage.'

'You know who the dead man was then, sir?' Ryga asked, thinking he must have seen the identity card, or word had got around. But Dr Bergmann's answer surprised him.

'Yes. Though I didn't know him personally, I recognized Sir Bernard Crompton as soon as I saw him.'

Pascoe's mouth gaped. 'Why didn't you say?' he asked before Ryga could speak. Nothing slow about the Cornishman there.

'To whom? There was only the lifeboat man and I didn't see any need to tell him.'

'But you could have told Constable Treharne,' Pascoe persisted.

'He wasn't there,' Bergmann answered easily. 'I left before he arrived.'

Pascoe was looking annoyed.

'I told the lifeboat man to tell Constable Treharne that the man was dead, and it was my opinion, from my examination, that he had died of heart failure. I would issue a death certificate to that effect. This is the first contact I've had with the police.'

'But after you'd examined the body you could have contacted us,' Pascoe insisted. Ryga watched Bergmann carefully. He showed no sign of nervousness, nor was his air one of bravado, irritation or anger. He looked tired, like his wife, but that was probably down to the job. And it wasn't surprising that a medical man should know another medical man, especially of Sir Bernard's standing.

'Why should I? I left my message and it was up to the police to contact me if they needed to. As you are now doing. I've hardly had the time to talk to anyone except patients, Sergeant. After my examination of Sir Bernard's body I had to hurry back here, where I had a very full and hectic surgery. I then had several house calls to make. As you know, this is a very large district and it takes me some time to reach my patients. I didn't return here until three o'clock. I then had another full surgery. I'd just got through that when I was called to a very difficult confinement by the midwife in attendance. It was . . .' He took a breath. 'A very sad case. The baby was stillborn and the mother has been taken to Penzance Hospital. She's very poorly. Sir Bernard's death went completely out of my mind.'

'We can understand that,' Ryga said before Pascoe could speak.

'And I've been in surgery all morning.' Bergmann pushed his slender fingers through his unruly hair, making it look even more tousled. His dark eyes swept them both, holding, Ryga thought, an element of sadness. 'I apologize if I should have made a point of telephoning the police, or instructed my wife to do so, but I pronounced death, said I would issue a death certificate and didn't see any need to tell you that I had heard of the dead man and recognized him from medical papers. The living are my concern. There was nothing I could do for Sir Bernard. His death, as far as I ascertained, was due to natural causes, but seeing as you're here, Inspector Ryga, you don't think that is so.' He addressed Ryga with a worried frown.

A telephone rang in the house. Ryga hoped the doctor wouldn't be called away. He heard Mrs Bergmann answering it but couldn't distinguish what was being said. 'Were you surprised to see Sir Bernard here, in Cornwall?'

'Yes and no. I knew he had retired. I read about it in the medical journal, and a colleague of mine at St Thomas' Hospital told me. Sir Bernard was a consultant there and at Guy's, and the St John's Hospital for Diseases of the Skin, but I expect you know that already. He was a dermatologist.'

'Yes.'

'I also knew Sir Bernard was a highly competent sailor. It's no secret. It was one of his passions. He had a boat before the war that he gave over to the Royal Naval Reserve. I believe it was damaged beyond saving. When I saw him on board that new motor cruiser I was shocked, yes, but then it seemed natural he should be on a boat given his retirement and love of the sea. I just didn't expect him to be here in Cornwall, although there is no reason why he shouldn't have been. Do you know why he was here?'

'He'd only just taken possession of his yacht and told his cleaning lady he was sailing it back to London, looking for somewhere to retire while on his way.'

'Oh. I didn't know he was considering moving from London, but then there's no reason why I should.'

'You said one of his passions was sailing — what were the others?'

'His work. He originally intended becoming a surgeon but became interested in skin diseases, particularly occupational ones, including those suffered by miners. He's the author of several papers on the subject, as you'd expect. He was also a skilled clinician and lecturer, much in demand. I'd have thought the lecture circuit abroad would have been his preferred retirement choice rather than settling down in Britain. But, as I said, I didn't know him.'

'His interests didn't extend to geology then?'

34

Bergmann's eyebrows knitted. 'Not that I'm aware of. Why do you ask?'

'Just something we came across.' Ryga got the impression that Bergmann would like to have looked at his wristwatch. 'Have you have been in contact with him recently?'

'No. Our paths are very diverse, not to mention the geographical distance between London and Cornwall.'

'Who would have taken over his practice?'

'I don't know. I'm sure that someone at St John's will be able to tell you that.'

Jacobs was getting that information and anything further he could on Sir Bernard. 'Can you describe how he was lying?'

'On his back on the cabin floor, his arms across his chest.'

'Were his eyes open or closed?'

'Open, I closed them.'

'Did you alter his position?'

'No. I could see he was dead. I checked the pulse in his neck as a matter of routine to confirm it. I lifted the head and felt around the back and the temples for any contusions. There were none. That's all, apart from lifting his arm and replacing it in exactly the same position to test for rigor.'

'Would you say the way he was lying was typical of someone who'd had a heart attack or seizure?'

'Yes.'

'How long do you estimate he had been dead?'

The telephone was ringing again. It was swiftly silenced. Bergmann shifted impatiently and pointedly consulted his watch before answering.

'There was rigor in his jaw and neck but none in his arm. I didn't take the body temperature because I didn't wish to disturb it more than necessary. I know rigor is not the most reliable indicator of time of death, and no doubt you know that too, Inspector — the cold can slow it down, and it was very cold last night, unusually so for the time of year. He'd probably been dead for two to four hours, possibly longer.'

By Ryga's quick calculation that meant Sir Bernard had died between 3.20 and 5.20 on Monday morning, which, according to the lighthouse keeper's testimony of seeing the boat heading towards Penzance at six, then drifting close to St Clement's Isle, could be possible if he had died at the latter time, but not earlier, unless someone else had been piloting it while Sir Bernard lay dead in his cabin. And if he died during that time, why was he still wearing evening dress? Ryga was certain Pascoe was thinking along the same lines and he was grateful the sergeant kept his lips sealed.

'I'm sorry to keep you,' Ryga said. 'I know how busy you must be. Is there anything else you can tell us that might help?'

'I—'

The door opened and Mrs Bergmann entered looking worried. 'I'm sorry to disturb you but that was Sergeant Marrack on the telephone.' Her eyes flicked to Ryga then to her husband. 'He says to come quickly. I told him you were with Inspector Ryga and Sergeant Pascoe and he said that they had better come too. There's been an accident at Priest Cove.'

Bergmann was already on his feet. So too was Ryga.

'What kind of accident?' Bergmann said.

'A fatal one.' Her eyes again darted to Ryga. In them he saw bewilderment. 'Sergeant Marrack has no idea who the man is. He doesn't wish to disturb the body. He says the deceased is wearing a dinner suit.'

CHAPTER FOUR

'There's nothing left of his face to make an identification, sir, and I haven't been through his pockets on account of not wanting to disturb anything,' Sergeant Marrack greeted Ryga as he and Pascoe climbed out of the car. Dr Bergmann's old Austin drew to a halt behind them.

'How did you come to find him, Sergeant?' Ryga asked. He couldn't see the body from where they were standing. Marrack looked shaken. Rain ran off his helmet and down his pale round face. His oilskin cape was soaked.

'I got a telephone call from the coastguard station up there.' Marrack jerked his head towards a tall brick chimney rising above the clifftop. Not far from it, Ryga could see the roof of the coastguard building.

'One of the coastguards was looking around the area with his binoculars. They don't always scour the land — obviously they're more concerned with what's happening out at sea — but he saw something that looked like a body and thought he'd better report it. He didn't have time to come down. And he couldn't neglect his job. He thought it might be someone taken ill. Not many people come to Priest Cove on a day like today.'

Not surprising. The rain was driving off the sea, and the wind was whipping up the waves, sending foam crashing onto the rocks and the shore. Ryga noted three small wooden boats and nets. On their way Pascoe had given him a brief description of the place, although he had admitted he didn't know it well. He'd also apologized for his error in assuming that Treharne had seen Dr Bergmann on board Sir Bernard's boat. An apology that Ryga waived aside. Treharne could have come in for a few sharp words from the sergeant for not being clear in his report, but Ryga already had the measure of the man beside him, who would take full responsibility for the oversight.

'I cycled here,' Marrack continued, nodding a greeting at the doctor. 'I saw the body and rushed up to the coast-guard and asked him to telephone through to Dr Bergmann. I came back to wait for you.'

'Let's see it then.'

Ryga followed Marrack down to the shore and around to their left, away from the large boulders that framed the cove to the right. There was an outcrop of rocks to where they were heading, while the cliff towered above them. It wasn't until they had rounded one large rock that the body came into view.

Ryga steeled himself for what he was about to face. He'd seen some gruesome spectacles in his time in the job, but nothing prepared him for the shock of this one, or the form it took. It was the sound and sight of the disgusting, filthy flies buzzing around the bloody mess of the head that wrenched his mind back to the bodies littering the roadside in Germany on that last forced march before liberation. He drew in his breath, while trying to ease the knot in his stomach and still his thumping heart. He forced himself to unclench his fists, while desperately fighting to keep his eyes on the corpse and the haunting flashbacks at bay. He couldn't and wouldn't betray himself in front of these men. It took every ounce of his willpower to control the nausea and focus on the present. He was a police officer; he could deal with this dispassion-ately. Not without a considerable effort, he brought himself back to the windswept, wet Cornish beach.

Pascoe cleared his throat noisily. Marrack wiped the rain from his chin and swallowed hard. Ryga turned to Bergmann, whose expression showed no emotion. How could the man be so unmoved at the grotesque sight of the body with no face? Tautly he said, 'Could you give us some idea of the possible time of death, Doctor?'

As Bergmann bent down to it, Ryga forced his gaze to stay on the body. He was a slender man, hatless, displaying thinning grey bloodstained hair. Ryga estimated late fifties by his hands, although it was difficult to tell with no face. His black bow tie was still fastened and his dinner jacket was open, showing a dirty, sodden white shirt with blood spatter. His head was facing the huge cliff, his feet out to sea. His arms were outstretched by his side, his hands blueish-pink and veined. A signet ring was on the little finger of his right hand and a wristwatch on the left.

Bergmann lifted one arm and then a leg. They were stiff. 'Rigor is well established, so too is lividity. And from the number of these disgusting creatures—' he waved away some flies — 'I'd say he's been dead about thirty-six hours.'

'That puts it around Sunday midnight,' Ryga replied.

'Thereabouts. It could be a few hours before that or a couple of hours after.'

Pascoe said, 'He can't have lost his balance and fallen because he'd be lying face down, and he doesn't look to have broken any bones.'

'Correct. This man was shot at point-blank range.' Bergmann straightened up. 'Whether he did the deed himself or someone else did it is a matter for you, Inspector, but I can't see any weapon.'

Nor could Ryga. 'Someone could have taken it.'

'Why would they do that?' Pascoe asked, puzzled by the suggestion.

'To sell, perhaps?'

'And leave the poor man lying here? No, I can't see any-one around these parts doing that,' Pascoe affirmed. Marrack nodded agreement.

Ryga would reserve judgement on that. 'Then who would want him dead?'

'Difficult to say until we know who he is,' Pascoe answered. 'He might have ID on him.'

'Want me to go through his pockets?' Bergmann asked.

Ryga nodded. He was grateful to the doctor for offering, but his gratitude was tinged with shame and guilt for not performing the odious task himself. Bergmann's manner annoyed him; it was as though he had no compassion for the individual before them who had met such a brutal end. But then perhaps he had performed this task many times during the war. The doctor was a professional; he was doing what he was trained and paid to do and Ryga scolded himself silently for not acting in the same manner. He put it down to lack of sleep and the haunting memories this corpse had conjured up before telling himself they all had problems to deal with. Mentally he pulled himself together. They had a job to do, and better to get on with it and get out of this wretched weather as soon as possible.

He turned to Marrack. 'Find something to cover that face.' His voice was more terse than usual. Pascoe scratched his neck. Ryga removed some paper bags from his murder case, knowing they would get wet as the rain thickened and the wind strengthened.

Bergmann handed the items to Ryga. Pascoe diligently listed them in his notebook, which was in danger of becoming sodden.

'A set of keys,' Ryga relayed, placing them in a bag. He'd examine all this later out of this dreadful weather. 'A silver monogrammed cigarette case with the initials "R. A."' Inside were six cigarettes of a common brand. He popped that into another bag and quickly into the case at his feet. Bergmann handed him the dead man's wallet, which boasted the same initials. Ryga opened it. In the right-hand compartment he found some pound notes. From the left he withdrew an identity card. Carefully opening it so as not to damage it or let it get blown away, he read out, 'Ralph Ackland—'

'Ackland?'

'You know him?' Ryga asked. This was Bergmann's first show of emotion. He seemed distracted.

'There was an Ackland here during the war. He was a mine inspector from the Ministry of Fuel and Power.'

'Has he been here since the end of the war, on official business?'

'I've no idea. You'll need to ask Mr Logan, the mine licensee, or Captain Strout up at the Catallack Mine.'

Marrack returned with an old piece of sailcloth. 'Best I could find, sir.'

'It will do. Cover his head. Do you know a Ralph Ackland? He's the deceased. Dr Bergmann says he was an inspector of mines during the war.'

'I know the name, but I can't say I ever met him. I was in the army, overseas for a good deal of time. Mrs Marrack could probably tell you more.'

Bergmann was still delving into the man's pockets. 'There's only a handkerchief. Hold on, there's something wrapped in it.' He stood up and handed it across to Ryga who, opening it, found five pieces of rock with jagged edges. A sharp glance at Pascoe stilled any startled statement that might have been about to spring from the sergeant's lips.

Bergmann scrutinized Ryga, who knew he'd connected this find with the question he had asked earlier about Sir Bernard's hobbies possibly including geology. Bergmann also wouldn't have missed the coincidence of both men being dressed in evening attire.

Putting the rock pieces and handkerchief in his murder case and snapping it shut, Ryga addressed the doctor. 'Could you take Sergeant Marrack back to St Just with you? It'll be quicker than you cycling there, Marrack. Bring back the undertaker. I take it there is one in St Just?'

'Chesley and Co. They're builders too but you won't be needing them.'

'Only if the undertaker is otherwise engaged. Then the builders can supply a van to transport the body to Penzance.

We'll stay on here. Try not to be too long. I'd like him moved as quickly as possible.'

'There's a tunnel opening just behind you, sir, if you need to get out of the rain. Was dug by the miners when the mine were operating round these parts.'

Ryga hadn't seen it but he would certainly look for it. Again he addressed Bergmann. 'I'd appreciate it if you would say nothing of this, Doctor. We need to find his next of kin and break the news to them first.'

'I'm not in the habit of gossiping, Inspector.'

'No. We'll need you to make a statement to Sergeant Marrack when you have the time, and there'll be the inquest. Have you been notified about the one on Sir Bernard?'

'Yes, Thursday morning at ten thirty. I'm having to rearrange my surgery,' he said with irritation.

Ryga saw him glance at the body, the head of which Marrack had now covered with the old sailcloth. His blasé manner had gone and in its place was pent-up tension, just as Ryga had seen in the doctor's wife.

'Rum do, this,' Pascoe said, when they were alone. 'Do you think he killed himself?'

'No. For a start there's no gun, although, as we discussed, there is the possibility it could have been taken by someone who didn't wish to report finding the body. But there's also the fact there's no sand on this man's shoes. It's unlikely it's been cleaned off, even given the rain. And how did he get here? There's no car, although that could have been driven away.' Ryga opened his briefcase and withdrew his camera. The bad weather wouldn't make good pictures — they might not come out at all — but he'd do his best.

Pascoe uncovered the face. Ryga suppressed his revulsion but felt relieved that it wasn't as bad as before, and that the memories stayed firmly in the past.

'The pieces of rock are the same as the ones I found in Sir Bernard's pocket,' Pascoe said. 'What do they mean? Are they some kind of secret code?'

42

'No idea. But the two men lived in London. This man's ID card says his address is Abercorn Place, St John's Wood. Yes, I know London is a big place so they might not have known each other, but to coin your phrase, Pascoe, it's another of those odd things.' He took some more pictures then put his camera away.

Pascoe re-covered the face. 'It looks to me as though they might have dined together on Sunday night. Could Sir Bernard have shot this man, and then taken off on his boat? He threw the gun in the sea, but filled with remorse, or in a terrible state, had a seizure?'

'It's a theory but it doesn't solve all your odd things: the tidy boat, the way Sir Bernard was lying, the pieces of rock, the missing charts, logbook, paperwork for the boat and ration book. And why would Sir Bernard kill this man? But we'll postpone all that for now. Let's get out of this rain for a moment while we look at some facts.' They walked to the opening in the cliff face and stepped just inside the narrow entrance in the solid rock. There Ryga continued. 'The personal effects inside his pockets were wet but not sodden. He's above the tideline. Did it rain on Sunday night or Monday?'

'It did on Sunday night then stopped for a while before starting up again late Monday afternoon and all evening. And it was cold.'

'So if he has been lying there since late Sunday night or early Monday morning, the contents of his pockets would have been drenched. I'd also have thought the coastguard, or one of the local fishermen, would have seen him if any of them had come down here to tend to their boat.'

'Sergeant Marrack can make enquiries, but I'm certain they would have reported it.'

'Which means he was killed elsewhere before being placed here.'

'Do you think a boat could have brought him ashore and left him? The tender from the *Patricia Bee*?'

'If there was one. But I still don't think this body has lain there since the early hours of Monday morning when the *Patricia Bee* was found drifting. And those rocks make for slippery and treacherous climbing, so anyone scrambling over them would risk falling, and I doubt anyone could have carried a body across them.'

'But a boat could have landed this side of the cove, where it's sand and shingle.'

'You said there was no evidence on Sir Bernard's trousers or shoes to indicate he'd been walking across the beach.'

'There wasn't, but there might be on his other shoes and clothes.'

'I didn't see any, but admittedly I didn't scrutinize them.' He retrieved his torch from the pocket of his mackintosh and switched it on. The tunnel didn't go very far back. The place gave him the willies. He felt as if the sides and roof were closing in on him. His admiration for miners increased. 'I can't see any evidence of someone having been inside here. No footprints, no dragging of the body. No gun either.' But he'd reserve judgement on that until he could inspect it more thoroughly. 'If Bergmann is right about the time of death then Ackland could have been killed, kept in this tunnel and then dragged out last night or this morning.'

'Wouldn't someone have missed him by now? There might be a wife waiting for him London.'

'If there is she might not be expecting to hear from him for a while if he was down here on business. The Ministry of Fuel and Power will be able to confirm that, if he was still working for them. I'd rather not speak to Mr Logan or Captain Strout until we have more facts. We also need to inform his next of kin. I'll get Sergeant Jacobs round to the address.' Jacobs would have the unenviable task of breaking the tragic news to the family. 'We'll also need to confirm the body is that of Ralph Ackland.'

'No one will be able to verify that from the mess of that face.'

'No. It'll be down to fingerprints, as I suspect will be Sir Bernard's. Take a look around the boats, Pascoe, and that ruined building where the car is parked, in case anything can throw more light on this. I'll have a look around the body.'

He was glad to step outside even though the rain was driving off the sea. With his magnifying glass, which soon got spattered with rain, and steeling his churning stomach, he examined the area around the body more closely for traces of blood, but he couldn't see any. The rain had swept it away. He leaned down and, forcefully shutting out the stench, using one of the handy implements on his trusty penknife, he scraped at some sand and grit. Withdrawing a small brown paper envelope from his case, he deposited the grains in it. The lab would analyse the composition, and if he got some from Sir Bernard's boat it would be interesting to see if they matched.

He was relieved to hear a vehicle approaching and went up to the road to meet the occupants of a black Bedford van. Pascoe joined him with a shake of his head that indicated he had found nothing revealing in his search. Marrack was accompanied by a thin man in his mid-thirties with a cap squashed down on his bullet-shaped head. He introduced himself as the undertaker, Tristan Chesley. Taking a stretcher from the rear of the van, Chesley chatted pleasantly as they made their way to the body. Ryga learned he ran the business with his father, they went back four generations, his brother was a stonemason and his cousin ran the building side of the business, following in his father's and grandfather's footsteps. They knew everyone in St Just and the surrounding areas down to Sennen Cove and across to St Buryan and beyond. 'Then you'll know a man called Ralph Ackland.'

'Of him. Sergeant Marrack told me who the dead man was. Ackland used to come here during the war and lead Captain Strout a pretty dance, moaning about this, that and the other. The men hated him.' Then his expression changed to one of wariness. 'I didn't mean any of them would go so far as to shoot him. He must have killed himself, although I can't think why — still, that's your job to find out. We just bury them.'

Chesley pulled off the sailcloth and tutted. 'Nasty.' It was the closest the undertaker would get to expressing horror, thought Ryga, having seen so much of death. Chesley and Marrack manoeuvred Ackland onto the stretcher. While they carried the body to the van, Ryga took pictures of where it had lain. Then he quickly examined the area underneath as best he could. There was nothing to find.

He told Chesley they would follow him to the mortuary at Penzance. As the van ground its way up the hill, Ryga asked Pascoe to see if he could strap Marrack's bicycle into the boot. 'It will save you lumbering up the hill in this weather.'

'I'll be all right, sir.' But Ryga noted his relief.

'Over the next couple of days, Sergeant, see what you can get from the nearby inhabitants — did any of them see or hear a vehicle heading in this direction between Sunday and this morning? Interview the owners of the small boats on the shore. Also question the coastguards for any sightings of the *Patricia Bee* or a small tender since Sunday.' He gave Marrack a brief description of the vessel and an update on the finding of Sir Bernard's body on board — the reason why he was there. 'There are certain similarities between his death and this one. Either I or Sergeant Pascoe will fill you in on the details later, unless Dr Bergmann tells you first when he makes his statement. If you find anything of note, or if you hear anything about Ralph Ackland, contact me or Sergeant Pascoe at Penzance.'

Marrack said he would, and with the bicycle secured, Pascoe set off up the steep incline with Marrack in the back. At the top, they dropped him and his bicycle off and turned in the opposite direction towards Penzance.

Ryga peered through the window as the inadequate windscreen wiper battled against the elements. Pascoe drove steadily across the bleak countryside in silence, perhaps with his own thoughts, or sensing that Ryga didn't wish to talk. He mulled over the strange occurrences. What had this man done to warrant such a dreadful end? Why here in Cornwall and not London where he lived? If he still worked for the Ministry of Fuel and Power inspecting mines, then why not in Wales, Kent or Sheffield? But then Sir Bernard hadn't been at any of those places, although he must have sailed down the Welsh coast to reach here. This to Ryga's mind pointed in the clear direction of Sir Bernard's death being suspicious. Pascoe's theory of murder followed by a guilt stricken seizure was also a possibility. But why would a retired eminent skin specialist kill a civil servant? And why choose here? And what had the break-in at Harley Street to do with all this?

The town looked drab as they entered its outskirts, a far cry from the so-called tourist hotspot Pascoe said the council were keen to promote. They reached the mortuary and drew up behind Chesley's van. Chesley was inside the cab, smoking a cigarette.

'I'll leave you to oversee things in the mortuary, Pascoe. I can walk to the station from here. I'm sure it's not far.'

Pascoe agreed it wasn't and gave him directions.

Ryga said, 'Make sure the body isn't touched, and if Sir Bernard hasn't already been undressed, see that he stays that way until we can examine both corpses tomorrow morning. I need to report to my chief at the Yard, and to Major Tweed. I'm sure he'll now see the necessity of me remaining to conduct this investigation.'

Pascoe's parting glance said *don't bank on it*.

CHAPTER FIVE

'This really is most trying,' the major snarled down the line at Ryga. He made it sound as though the dead man had got himself killed deliberately to annoy him. Ryga had tackled Tweed before calling Street. Always best to take the nasty medicine first.

'We obviously need to establish if there is a connection between the two men, sir. And I need to report to Detective Chief Superintendent Street at the Yard and instigate enquiries in London.'

'That's just it. I really don't see the need for you to stay here when both men came from London. It's clear to me that whatever caused this latest death, it has its roots there.'

'It could very well have, sir, but I'll have to stay for the inquests anyway.'

Tweed sniffed his disapproval. 'I'll speak to the assistant commissioner at the Yard.' The line went dead.

Ryga jiggled the phone and asked to be connected to Scotland Yard. He shifted in his seat and stamped his cold feet, trying to warm them up. His socks and shoes and the bottom of his trousers were sodden. His mackintosh was dripping pools of water onto the floor. He hadn't thought to light the fire. And he was hungry. He hadn't eaten since breakfast on the train and that had been eight hours ago. No wonder his stomach was making peculiar noises. So much had happened since his arrival that morning, events he'd never have anticipated, food and drink had never occurred to him. Pascoe, too, must be hungry and thirsty. As though his thoughts had conjured him up, the sergeant entered.

'Everything go all right at the mortuary?' asked Ryga.

'Yes. Sir Bernard was still dressed and I gave instructions that he was to remain that way. Ackland too.' He hung up his sodden hat and coat and rubbed his hands together. 'I'll light the fire. And I'll get some tea and biscuits.'

Ryga thanked him warmly. 'Detective Chief Superintendent Street, please,' he said into the mouthpiece when he was finally connected. He wanted to speak to Street before the AC grabbed him with Tweed's version, which would be sparse to say the least as the man had barely listened to a word Ryga had said. And when asked if he'd known Ackland from his visits to the area during the war, Tweed had stiffly replied that he hadn't been here but fighting for his country.

'Oh hello, Chief. There have been some unusual and unforeseen developments here.' Ryga proceeded to update him. He also relayed Tweed's view on the matter.

'Any theories?'

'None that make sense. Sir Bernard could have arranged to meet Ralph Ackland at Priest Cove, he could have shot him then taken off on his yacht, and he could have ditched the gun, and filled with remorse he could have suffered a fatal heart attack or seizure. But that's an awful lot of coulds with no facts to support any of them.'

'And it leaves a lot of questions. Any idea what those pieces of rock mean?'

'None at all.'

'You'll need the Home Office pathologist for the autopsy on Ackland, and while he's there he can conduct one on Sir Bernard to confirm whether or not he had a heart attack or seizure.'

Ryga agreed, although he didn't look forward to the arrival of Dr Plumley — a pompous, prickly, squat little man abrupt to the point of rudeness, much like Tweed. Maybe the pair of them would get on well if they stopped to listen to each other. That was neither here nor there as long as Plumley did his job, but he didn't think Dr Bergmann was going to be too pleased at having his diagnosis and professional capability questioned.

'I'll confirm all this with the AC,' Street said. 'Any changes, I'll let you know. And I'll see how soon Plumley can get down there. Have the local press got wind of it?'

'Not yet but they're bound to soon.'

'Then you might have Fleet Street on your heels *if* they can find their way to Cornwall — and get expenses. I'm reckoning they're much more likely to follow up the London angle. If so, we'll be ready for them.'

Ryga hoped the press would be kept occupied in town.

'I'll put you through to Jacobs and you can give him instructions.'

The line remained quiet for so long that Ryga feared he might have been disconnected, then Jacobs's cockney twang reverberated down the line.

'What's the weather like?' came his usual greeting.

'Wet and windy.'

'Bound to be, you're in Cornwall. I hear you've had a busy day, guv. The chief's just told me you've got another corpse.'

'I have and I need you to perform the sad task of informing Ackland's family — if he has any — of his death.' Ryga relayed the address. 'Identification is impossible, so lift fingerprints from something of the deceased and I'll get them from the body. I'll send the camera film up by police motorcyclist tomorrow, and you can compare prints of Ackland and Sir Bernard with those from items in their house. Have the print boys been round to Sir Bernard's?'

'Yes. But I don't know the full results yet. Inspector Tanner sent over Mrs Marlow's and we have a match on the basement door where she let herself in. We might have to trace the secretary and housekeeper and get theirs in case there are some of their prints left from when they worked there.'

'They've been gone a while, so I doubt it. But no harm in asking. Anything more on the break-in?'

'Nothing. No one saw anyone entering or loitering about in a suspicious manner.'

'Sir Bernard's keys were on him but someone could have copied one of them either before he left for Scotland or while he's been travelling down the coast. Ask DC Crawford to contact the boat builder, James B. Parron Limited of Rosneath, Scotland. I need to know if they fitted out Sir Bernard's boat, the *Patricia Bee*. The tender's missing and indicates a third person is involved. Can Crawford also get the date Sir Bernard took possession of the boat and if he told them about his intended route?'

'Righty-ho.'

Ryga told Jacobs about both men being dressed for dinner and that Ackland was known in the area as a mine inspector. 'I've taken pictures of the body in the cove but the weather was so atrocious that they probably won't be any good. I'll take more at the mortuary tomorrow and you can get them developed.' Ryga wished Eva was here because not only would the pictures have been good but she could have developed them from the back of her Land Rover, which she'd converted into a darkroom. Jacobs could then have sent down the prints they had. But no matter. 'I'll also give the motorcyclist the samples I've taken from around the body and the boat for the lab to analyse. Find out if Ralph Ackland was here in Cornwall on official business and where he was staying. Look for any links between Ackland and Sir Bernard and if either or both had any interest in geology or rocks.'

Ryga explained the curious find of the five rock pieces, to which Jacobs said, 'Odd.'

'Yes, and that word keeps cropping up too frequently for my liking. Anything more on our safebreaker?'

'Nothing.'

Pascoe must have been waiting outside because the moment Ryga replaced the receiver, he entered. Placing the tea and a plate of biscuits in front of Ryga, he said, 'That's the best I can do.'

'It's better than nothing.'

'I think my trousers are beginning to steam.' Pascoe flapped the edges of them in front of the fire.

'You should get yourself a mackintosh.' Eva hated his. She said it made him look like an old man, but Ryga valued its protection from the worst of the British weather. He wished he could say the same for his feet. 'I think I should have brought my wellingtons.'

'I could always find you a pair, sir.'

'And that's another thing, no need to call me "sir". "Guv" or "skipper" will do.'

'OK, guv.'

'And I suggest we take off our wet socks. Neither of us want to catch a cold.' Ryga unzipped his holdall and retrieved a clean pair.

'I'll fetch some from our stores. We always keep spare uniforms and odds and ends in case needed.'

Returning, Pascoe put a chair in front of the fire and draped his and Ryga's socks over it.

'Might as well put our shoes there too,' Ryga said.

Pascoe performed the duty before sitting at one of the two empty desks beside Ryga.

'Who usually sits there?' Ryga asked, biting into a digestive biscuit.

'DC Tremolo. He's on honeymoon.'

'Well, I hope he's picked somewhere sunnier.'

'I doubt it. I've heard it rains a lot in Wales. He'll be back on duty end of next week.'

'And it's just you and Tremolo?'

'There's DC Frost but he's on secondment at Bodmin. He'll be annoyed at missing this and working with you. I wondered if Major Tweed would send him back.'

'He might if this gets complicated.' On the other hand, thought Ryga, Tweed would probably let him flounder so as to prove Scotland Yard were useless. Then again, his and Jacobs's enquiries could very well take him back to town in search of answers — and the killer.

Pascoe said, 'I've arranged for Blayde, the lifeboat man who went on board the *Patricia Bee*, to come in and have his prints taken. And Sergeant Marrack telephoned while you were speaking to the Yard. None of the fishermen who own the boats at Priest Cove have been down there. The weather's not been good enough when the tide's been right. The most recent visit was by Daniel Ilford last Saturday week. No one in the houses closest to the cove claims to have seen or heard a car late at night, but Marrack has still got some folk to talk to, including the farmers around that way. He's also to question the coast-guards for any sightings of *Patricia Bee* or a small tender.'

Ryga told him what Jacobs and Crawford were going to do. 'Let's take a look at Sir Bernard's belongings.'

'Second drawer on the right.'

Ryga made to move.

'No, stay where you are, guv. I'm not precious about where I sit, or my desk. I'm not usually at it long enough to be so. They're in a large brown envelope.'

Ryga withdrew it and emptied the contents next to the typewriter. Pascoe crossed to look at them. There was an expensive wristwatch, no inscription on the back. His leather wallet was of high quality, with the name of the company who had made it inside it. Ryga examined the identity card. 'Nothing unusual in that.' Then he frowned. 'No chequebook.'

Pascoe quickly caught on. 'So how did he get money to pay for food and any other provisions? Would he have taken a large sum of cash with him to last the journey? If so, it's missing.'

'Leaving these two pound notes in his wallet.'

'The valet couldn't bring himself to take them from the body.'

'I think his chequebook was taken for the same reason the ration book, logbook and sea charts were — to prevent anyone tracing his stopover points. Though why, I'm not sure. But all this certainly throws the natural death idea into a cocked hat.' Ryga spread out the rocks. Then, lifting his case onto the desk, he removed the small evidence bag containing the rock pieces taken from Ackland's body.

'They're identical in colour, type and quantity. Only the shapes vary. Any idea where they might have come from?'

'None. Captain Strout might be able to tell us.'

'And give us more information on Ralph Ackland. We'll get to Strout in due course. Let's take a look at the rest of Ackland's personal belongings.' They yielded nothing new. Ryga put the rock pieces into two bags, one he marked '*Sir Bernard*', the other '*Ralph Ackland*'. He popped them, and the other belongings, into his murder case. 'I'll type up the reports on finding the body, you do the one on the search of Sir Bernard's boat and the interview with Dr Bergmann.'

They swapped desks and began work. Shortly after, Chief Inspector Jerram looked in to introduce himself. He made no comment about their socks hanging out to dry, as though he didn't even notice them. He was a spare man in his late forties but looked older. He had that fidgety air about him along with restless eyes and a strain around the mouth that Ryga had seen all too often in the camp and occasionally at work. It showed a man under pressure. He felt some empathy for Jerram, who was probably doing the best he could for an unappreciative chief constable. Men like Tweed, in Ryga's experience, infected others with their cantankerousness and carping to the point of making them jumpy and questioning their own ability, instincts and experience. Well, he wouldn't get the better of Ryga.

After typing up his report he read through PC Treharne's, which backed up Bergmann's statement, in that the doctor hadn't spoken to the constable but had relayed to the lifeboat man that Sir Bernard had died from natural causes. He also read the lifeboat man's statement, which was straightforward and linked in with what Pascoe had told him previously. The helm on the *Patricia Bee* hadn't been tied off to keep it on a set course. Nor had there been a line on the starboard side that could have held the tender in place while the *Patricia Bee* was travelling until this companion was ready to leave the craft. It would have been tricky climbing down on to a tender while the craft was moving but not impossible. The line secured to the *Patricia Bee* could then have been let go. If so, there would have been evidence of it and Pascoe hadn't found any. It would have been a difficult task to reach up from a moving tender and unhook the line from the cleat. Unless it had been fastened to it with a slipped buntline hitch, a quick-release knot that held fast under a load but could come undone quickly and easily with a firm pull on the free end. It was much like the highpoint hitch, which could be very secure yet if tied as a slip knot could also be released quickly and easily with one pull, even after heavy loading. The rope could then have been pulled into the tender and no evidence of it left on deck.

There was no call from the Yard, and Ryga was still hungry and tired. 'Let's call it a day, Pascoe, and come at it fresh in the morning. Our socks are dry, or at least drier.'

'Gladly. Just finished.' Pascoe ripped his report and carbon paper from the typewriter and handed the reports to Ryga. He placed them in the folder to read through later.

'Where are you going to stay, guv? I haven't booked you in anywhere.' Pascoe gathered up the socks and handed Ryga his. 'You're welcome to stay with me and Jean, my sister, or I can book you into the Queen's Hotel.'

But Ryga had another idea. 'What time is the last bus to Mousehole from Penzance?'

'Twenty past ten.'

'Then I've got plenty of time. I want to hear back from Sergeant Jacobs and then I'll return to Mousehole.'

'You're going to stay on board the *Patricia Bee*?'

'For tonight at least. I'm very grateful for your offer, Pascoe, but I'll be all right on the boat using Sir Bernard's rations and I'll make up the bunk in the for'ard cabin.'

'Then come to us for something to eat first.'

'That's very kind of you, but—'

'I insist. You've got to sample some Cornish hospitality,' he added with a gleam in his eyes, meaning, *We're not all as frosty as Major Tweed*. 'After that you can catch the bus on the promenade. We're on the telephone on account of my job. The station can ask Sergeant Jacobs to telephone me.'

'That sounds a splendid idea but only if your sister agrees.'

'I'll call her now but I know what she'll say.'

That he did while Ryga excused himself. It would save Pascoe any embarrassment in case his sister asked awkward questions about him or needed persuading into letting him share their meal.

He chatted to the desk sergeant for a moment but Pascoe was finished in an instant. 'Jean says she'd be delighted for you to join us.'

'Then she can have some meat off my ration book in exchange.'

'Won't hear of it, guv. You're our guest,' Pascoe added to the curious gaze of the desk sergeant.

Pascoe gave instructions that when a message came for Detective Inspector Ryga from Sergeant Jacobs, or anyone else, they should telephone him at his home.

'It's not a police house,' Pascoe explained as they walked the wet streets to his home. 'My mother had to give that up when dad died in thirty-six; he was a sergeant. I was a constable then. Mum moved to a rented house and let out rooms to police constables. It gave her an income and she was used to the shifts.'

'Have you always been stationed here?'

'Yes, even during the war. I intended to volunteer for the armed services, but I postponed it having met Rita, my wife, and then the police became a reserved occupation, as of course you'd know. There was, sadly, a lot of crime, and so many new rules and regulations that it was hard to know if you were coming or going, not to mention the shortage of men. I married Rita and we moved in with my mother. Rita was killed in June forty-one when the town was bombed. She was on her way to the factory where she was doing war work. I was on shift at the time. Our daughter, Rosie, was with my mother. She was two years old.'

They stepped around a stray dog rummaging in the bins for food. There was nothing Ryga could say.

'My mother took in evacuees. Then she sadly died and Jean, my sister, who lost her husband at Torbrook, moved back to Penzance from Plymouth and we took up in another place, a smaller house. Jean looks after me and Rosie. Here we are.'

Ryga was glad they had reached their destination before Pascoe could ask him about his war. He didn't like to talk about it. Not only because there were things that he'd rather not recall but also because he saw no point in going over it. There was also the fact that when some people learned he'd been a prisoner of war, they were insensitive and stupid enough to say he'd had it easy.

Jean was an attractive, lively woman in her early thirties with a shapely figure, curly dark hair, a pleasant smile and the same deep-set brown eyes as her brother. The terraced house climbing the hill was modest, clean and welcoming. She took his hat and coat and showed him through to the sitting room, while Pascoe went upstairs to say goodnight to his daughter. Here, as in Brixham on his last investigation outside of London, Ryga felt the longing for roots like this, a family. He thought of Eva, but couldn't see her settling down to domestic bliss, and there was no reason why she should. They were close, and part of him would have liked it to be more, but he wasn't sure how strongly Eva felt. There was a restlessness about her, and her career took her away a great deal.

He washed his hands in the scullery to the rear of the house, adjoining the kitchen, where the smell of food reinforced his hunger pangs. His mind turned to thoughts of Sonia and her young son, Steven, and he again felt a stab of regret that he hadn't done more for her. He'd just returned to the sitting room, where a table was laid for their meal, when the telephone rang. Jean entered to answer it.

'It's Detective Chief Superintendent Street.' She handed over the receiver.

'The AC has agreed for you to stay on and investigate both deaths. In fact he insists, despite what Major Tweed says. Dr Plumley is driving down tomorrow. He'll conduct both autopsies on Thursday. He'll stay down for the inquests. Can you arrange for them to be held on Friday? He has a weekend engagement that he says he has no intention of missing.'

'I'll see if the coroner will oblige,' Ryga answered somewhat tongue in cheek. 'Anything from Sergeant Jacobs?'

'Not yet.'

Ryga passed the news on to Pascoe, who said he would see that accommodation was arranged for the pathologist, and that he'd make arrangements with the mortuary for Dr Plumley to conduct the two autopsies on Thursday. Pascoe assured him that the coroner, Mr Gregory, was a very reasonable man and wouldn't see any problem with moving the inquests.

They tucked into a very tasty shepherd's pie, which Ryga and Pascoe washed down with a light ale. They talked pleasantly about the local area, and Pascoe found a map, which, when the table was cleared, Ryga studied as Pascoe pointed out where they had driven that day and where the body had been found. He also pointed out the Catallack Mine. Ryga asked if he could keep the map while he was there.

'Of course.'

The phone rang. This time it was Jacobs.

'Do you want the good news or the bad?' the sergeant greeted him.

'There's good?'

'Yes, if you count the fact there was no family here and no wife to learn of her husband's death.'

'So she's in Cornwall?'

'She might be in spirit but certainly not in body. She left this world ten years ago.'

'Ah.'

'The porter at Abercorn Mansions, Melton, let me in with his master key. He told me that Mr Ackland left the apartment on Friday evening carrying a small brown suitcase, saying he'd be back Tuesday morning. He didn't mention where he was going. He lived alone, often went out in the evenings, came back late, sometimes in the early hours of the morning. He's never seen him with a lady friend nor has he entertained one in his apartment, as far as he knows. When he doesn't go out he has his meals sent up — it's a serviced flat. We'll talk to the chef tomorrow but if Ackland had ordered meals for two it doesn't mean to say it was for a lady. And, yes, he was a civil servant, quite high up, though Melton's not sure what rank or what he did. I haven't had time to talk to anyone at the Ministry of Fuel and Power. Melton says that Ackland went off every morning regular as clockwork, Monday to Friday, carrying his umbrella and wearing his bowler hat.'

The line crackled. Ryga hoped they wouldn't be cut off before Jacobs came to the bad news.

'Ackland never indulged in small talk, was mean with his money — he rarely gave tips and when he did they were meagre — was just as close with his smiles and didn't mix with the other residents. He didn't drive — that is, he didn't own a car. Melton hailed a taxi for him on Friday evening. He heard him tell the taxi driver to take him to Paddington.'

'Which means he was heading for Cornwall on the overnight train.'

'Could have alighted at Exeter or Plymouth.'

'And ended up in Cornwall? I doubt it, but I'll check at the railway station.'

'There are a couple of photographs of him in the flat. Melton says Ackland was lean, about six feet tall, with thin grey hair.'

'Which matches the body in Priest Cove, although Ackland can't be the only lean man of that height with thin grey hair in Britain.'

'Well, I've got a hairbrush with a fine set of prints on, two books, a bottle of whisky—'

'Which brand?'

'Glenfiddich.'

'The same as on Sir Bernard's boat.'

'It's a popular brand.'

Another crackle. Ryga held the phone from his ear. Then put it back. 'You still there, Jacobs?'

'Yes. I've taken some surface prints but I'll have to return, and here's the bad news and the reason why I never got to the Ministry of Fuel and Power: Ackland's apartment has been ransacked.'

CHAPTER SIX

It was just after ten when Ryga alighted from the bus at Mousehole. There had been three people on it and they'd got off at Newlyn. He had enjoyed the short journey left alone with his thoughts by a considerate or tired conductor.

The quayside was deserted. The door of the Ship Inn opened, someone shouted goodnight and the landlord's booming voice called last orders. By the light of his torch Ryga made his way to the *Patricia Bee*. The wind had eased and it had ceased raining but it was a cold night, much like the previous one, which made him wonder if the low temperature had slowed the rigor in Ackland's body and he'd actually been dead longer than Dr Bergmann had said. Perhaps Dr Plumley could place the time of death more accurately.

Why ransack both dead men's properties? Pascoe had mused aloud. It was the same question Jacobs had put to Ryga. He mulled it over. Was it the same intruder who had struck twice? If so, he had both of the dead men's keys and yet the keys had been found on the bodies. That indicated the intruder had had access to those keys at some stage in order to make an impression and have them copied. Either that or he had stolen spares. The intruder had also had enough time on his hands to tip both places upside down, and for what? Had he found it?

The porter hadn't seen or heard anything suspicious, and had told Jacobs that there had been no strangers in the building over the weekend. But he hadn't been at his desk the entire time — there were lunch breaks, and emergencies to attend to in the other residents' apartments. And he didn't work through the night. The neighbours, and others on the same floor, hadn't witnessed or heard anything untoward either.

As Ryga came to a halt by the boat he considered the idea that it might have been wanton vandalism, but only for a second. The front doors would have shown evidence of having been forced — unless it had been a very experienced thief who had a bunch of expert skeleton keys — and a vandal wouldn't lock the premises behind him after creating such destruction.

Jacobs had verified with the porter that Mrs Marlow didn't clean for Ackland, so the chance of her key having been taken and copied were ruled out as far as Ackland was concerned.

'Who are you? What are you doing here?'

Ryga spun round but could see nothing of the woman whose flashlight was blinding him. 'Do you mind pointing that elsewhere?' He reached for his warrant card. 'Inspector Ryga, Scotland Yard.' He thrust it towards her. The torch was lowered as she scrutinized his identification. It was his turn to swing his beam on her. She was in her fifties with short, straight brown hair flecked with grey. Her overlarge black mackintosh swamped her scrawny frame and her left ankle was heavily bandaged. In her right hand was a stout wooden stick. She looked up at him as he slightly lowered his torch.

'Why are Scotland Yard here? The owner of this craft died of natural causes,' she declared with no trace of a Cornish accent.

'Who told you that, Mrs . . . ?'

'Enys. Marjorie, and it's Miss. Constable Treharne told me. He asked me if I'd seen this boat through my telescope out at sea on Monday morning. I hadn't because I wasn't looking through it. I'd foolishly twisted my ankle, slipped on a step in the garden. Dr Bergmann was with me. Good job he was too. His wife telephoned to say he was needed here. I saw your torchlight and thought a local no-good had decided to help himself to any spoils. Came to investigate. I was sick to the back teeth of being cooped up indoors. Ankle or no ankle, I needed fresh air. Thought I'd look over my boat; it's down by the shore. What do you intend on doing with her?' she demanded, ending her deluge of words.

'That's not been decided yet.'

'You're staying on board?' Her eyes narrowed at his holdall.

'I am, Miss Enys.'

'Huh!' She made to move off then turned back. 'Come up to the house tomorrow morning. I'll give you breakfast. Gulls Nest. Stupid name but it was my mother's choice. Raginnis Hill, the big white house at the top on your right. Eight o'clock.'

He made to decline but she was already hobbling away. She reminded him of Eva with her no-nonsense approach.

He climbed down the ladder onto the boat. The tide was on its way out but there was still sufficient water underneath it to keep it afloat. Opening the wheelhouse, he inserted the key into the helm and the engine throbbed into life. He didn't think the sound would wake anyone as the houses were some distance away and the prevailing wind would carry the noise in the opposite direction. He let it run for a while to get warmth and light, unpacked his shaving tackle, soap and small towel, put them in the spare washroom and returned to the galley, where he made a cup of tea. He took it up to the wheelhouse.

Glimmering lights showed from Mousehole. His thoughts returned to Sir Bernard and his voyage here. Tomorrow DC Crawford would hopefully come back with more information from the boat builder and they might be able to plot Sir Bernard's progress and discover if there had been someone on board with him. Had Ralph Ackland been staying on board this boat since his arrival on Saturday morning in Penzance until the time of his murder? If he had, Sir Bernard had cleaned it most thoroughly because there was no trace of the man, unless one or more of the prints Ryga had taken earlier that morning matched Ackland's. But where were Ackland's clothes and his suitcase? Had Sir Bernard tossed them overboard after killing him?

Ryga finished his tea and silenced the engine. He hoped to sleep and expected to. He was dog-tired, and was used to the sounds of the sea from his time in the Merchant Navy. But though the mattress was an expensive one, he nevertheless felt the wood of the bunk beneath it. With that came the haunting memories of the prison camp, of sleeping on a hard wooden bunk with rough, thin blankets over him, shivering in the cold. In his restless sleep the wind screaming through the halyards became the guards' whistles, the slapping ropes their marching boots and the howling sounds the moaning of men. He tried to shut it out, but every time he managed to drift off to sleep he was back in the prison camp. Then came those flies. He shot up, in a sweat. Determined not to let them and the memories defeat him, he tried again to sleep, urging himself to think of anything but that wretched war. There was Eva with her long, fair hair and her way of looking at him as though she could see into his mind. And Sonia, so different to Eva, with her dark looks and her quiet strength and yet vulnerability. Her love and tenderness towards her young son, Steven. A good lad, and bright. God, Ryga hoped that wretch of a father wasn't anywhere near them. He should do more to locate them.

His mind swirled round but eventually he drifted off. Nevertheless, he rose long before the dawn, with an aching back, a headache and a tremor that he couldn't stifle with a strong cup of tea. He flexed his trembling fingers, wishing he could run them over a keyboard. He found relief and peace in music, and Eva's gift to him of access to the Guildhall School of Music at any time he wished was one of the most wonderful things anyone had ever done for him, not counting the kindness, courage and help some of his fellow prisoners had bestowed on him.

He poured out another cup of tea and took it up on deck. A few deep breaths of the cold, brisk, salty sea air helped. The tide was up, giving him a good view of the harbour, and from the bow he could gaze out to sea. He stayed there for some time watching the dawn rise. Slowly, the space and beauty of the choppy waves calmed him. He hadn't expected the nightmares to return while on board such a luxurious craft.

After yet another strong cup of tea, a cold wash and a shave he felt better, even though his muggy head through lack of sleep and nightmares remained. He'd cope with that. He set out with vigour for a walk around Mousehole, which he enjoyed. The little town was primarily still asleep, but as with all villages and towns, he came across the milkman and his horse. The horse could tell him nothing, sadly, nor could the milkman, who had been the other side of Mousehole at the time of all the fuss with the *Patricia Bee*. He struck out for Raginnis Hill, stopping off now and again on the steep incline to gaze down at the harbour. It made a pretty picture in the steely morning with its sandy shore, rocky approach and arched piers. In the distance he could make out a projection of land. He wondered if it was Lizard Point. There was a coaster far out to sea, its black smoke curling in the breeze.

Small terraced cottages on his right gave way to bigger detached houses, set above the road with nothing opposite them, giving even more splendid views over the harbour. This in turn gave way to hedgerows on both sides of the narrow lane. He wondered if he had missed Gulls Nest, as from Pascoe's map he'd consulted that morning, he thought he'd soon be in the small hamlet of Raginnis itself. Then he saw it. Set above the level of the road was a large, majestic, three-bayed white house. He was a little put out to see the guesthouse sign, only because he didn't fancy sharing breakfast with holidaymakers and having to make polite conversation. Perhaps he could decline if that was on offer.

He climbed the stone steps to the entrance. In one of the wide bay windows on the ground floor, facing a square of garden framed with shrubs, was a couple in their early sixties, eating their breakfast.

He pressed the doorbell and stood back. The door was answered promptly by Miss Enys, who greeted him pleasantly. She didn't look quite so formidable in the light of day without the raincoat. As he wiped his feet on the mat and removed his hat she said, 'I'll give instructions to Edna for your breakfast. Tea or coffee?'

'Tea, please.'

'Hang up your hat and coat. Stay here.' He did, smiling to himself at her command while glancing around. On the small table to his left, just past the coat stand, were some leaflets about the local area. Pinned to the wall on a cork board were the rules of the house and a map showing the coast up as far as St Just. He inspected it to the clatter of knives and forks and the rattle of crockery. He could see Priest Cove just below Cape Cornwall and then the small inlet of Porth Nanven, Bosavern and Kelynack to the south of St Just, which looked to be just farm buildings and an isolated cottage or two. He'd already considered walking along the clifftop to Priest Cove and then on to the Catallack Mine that morning to seek out Captain Strout, but that could take too long and, as Major Tweed was certain to remind him, he wasn't here on holiday.

Miss Enys reappeared and gestured him to the stairs.

'Follow me. It's all right, I'm not going to lead you astray,' she teased. 'Don't worry about them,' she tossed over her shoulder as she limped her way up the staircase holding on to the banister with one hand and her stick with the other. 'The Varleys will be off as soon as they've had their breakfast, which they've nearly finished, then you can have yours in peace.'

He was glad of that. She hadn't asked him what he wished to eat.

'My sitting room is at the front, above the breakfast room. I've got a bedroom and bathroom off it. The rest of the rooms, three of them, I let out to holidaymakers, or in the winter to anyone who wants lodgings, although in this neck of the woods they're few and far between. I don't mind. It gives me a break. Edna lives in. She has a small room and bathroom at the back; the guests all share another bathroom.'

They turned onto the landing and she limped her way into a pleasant sitting room, haphazardly furnished in worn chintz and stripes. To the right of a small table in the bay window was an impressive telescope. 'I thought you might like to look through it. It's a pity I didn't see the *Patricia Bee* on Monday morning. If I hadn't been chasing off a fox in the garden I would have done. Pedrick has a telescope. He might have seen her. Ask him.'

'Miss Enys,' a man's voice called softly from the landing.

'That's Mr Fallows, my other guest. He doesn't have breakfast. I think that's to avoid the Varleys. Can't say I blame him. Nice couple, from Bristol. He's a retired civil servant, she's a fusspot, they talk a lot. I'll see what he wants.'

After she'd hobbled out, Ryga crossed to the telescope, making a mental note to find out who Pedrick was and where he lived. He might have seen a tender leaving the *Patricia Bee*. Focusing the instrument, he could see the beautiful craft in the harbour, and beside it, sitting on a bollard, was Silas with his dog. On the quayside was the postman talking to a tall, gaunt, stooping man in an old green corduroy jacket and brown worsted trousers that were far too short for his spindly legs. They turned towards the harbour, and by the direction of their gaze and gesticulations, Ryga deemed they were talking about the *Patricia Bee*. A baker's van trundled past.

He looked across to St Clement's Isle and could clearly pick out the pepper pot. Next he surveyed the sea in the direction from which Sir Bernard's boat had been travelling. There was little to give him confirmation of what might have happened but he could clearly see that it was possible for someone to have left the *Patricia Bee* on a small tender on the starboard side of the craft, away from prying eyes from the shore, on or around sunrise. The man could have rowed to St Clement's Isle and sheltered on the other side of it until the *Patricia Bee* had been taken into Mousehole. Then he could have rowed into Mousehole, abandoned the tender and headed on foot for Newlyn and Penzance. That was, if there had been someone else on board.

Ryga scoured the harbour. A rumble of voices came from the hallway. There were tenders but none looked to be pristine and new, as Sir Bernard's would have been. It could have been abandoned elsewhere along the coast. And it could have had an outboard engine, which meant he could have motored on to Newlyn or Penzance or even back to Land's End, Sennen Cove or any of the other coves up the west coast, including Priest Cove.

He heard the front door close and saw a wiry man strike out down the driveway. Mr Fallows, he presumed, dressed for a hike with his sturdy boots, jacket and cap, his trousers tucked into thick socks, and carrying a small rucksack and a hefty walking stick. He turned in the direction of Mousehole. More voices came to him from the landing, a high-pitched female one and a quieter, slightly nervy man's, along with Miss Enys's sharper tones, bidding them to wait a moment. She put her head round the door, saying, 'The dining room is free now. Make your way down to it. I'll join you in a moment. I can smell your breakfast.'

So could Ryga and he was looking forward to it. He didn't know when next he'd get a chance to eat. Even the thought that he was to go to the mortuary to view both bodies didn't put him off his food. He nodded a greeting to the Varleys, who eyed him curiously. As he descended the stairs he heard Miss Enys say 'London', and surmised they were discussing him and his purpose there. He wondered if they had seen anything of the *Patricia Bee* Monday morning from their bedroom window, if it was situated at the front. Or perhaps Mr Fallows had.

The dining room was spacious, pleasantly furnished and boasted a spectacular view down into the harbour and out to sea. A pretty, dark-haired woman wearing a pink-and-white gingham apron over a simple blue dress entered, carrying a small teapot.

'I'll clear that table in a moment. Will you sit here, sir?' She indicated one by the right-hand wall behind the door. Placing the teapot on it she said, 'Miss Enys says you're a detective from London, is that right?'

'I am, and you're also from London,' Ryga said, sitting. He recognized the accent.

'Tottenham. Evacuated during the war and stayed. Not much point going back; my mum and dad got killed in the Blitz. Besides, I'm getting married soon,' she proudly added.

'Congratulations.'

'To the postman, Ted Shannon.'

'Is that the man I saw in the harbour, good-looking with his cap at an angle, talking to a tall, stooping man with trousers at half-mast?'

She laughed. 'Yes, that'll be Ted and the other is Mr Pedrick. He's an astronomer and Ted, my fiancé, is interested in the stars.'

'Where does Mr Pedrick live?'

'Up along the Parade, just past the coastguard station.'

'And you and your fiancé will be staying in Mousehole?'

'No, we'll probably move to Newlyn.'

'Edna, Mr Ryga would like his breakfast now and not tomorrow.' Miss Enys had appeared quite suddenly behind the young woman.

'Sorry, miss.' She winked at Ryga and marched off.

Ryga laughed. 'Nice girl.'

'Yes. She came here as a straggly little cockney evacuee, aged eight. I shall miss her when she goes.' The usual brisk tone was softened by a sad note. Then crisply she said, 'I'll leave you to eat your breakfast in peace, *when it arrives.*'

'It's here now, miss, no need to get in a tizz.' Edna had arrived bearing a tray of steaming hot food. 'That ankle has made her moody,' she confided when her mistress was out of sight. 'She's always sharpish, I should know, but good-natured underneath it. She's been snapping and snarling at me though. Still, can't blame her. Can't be much fun being laid up when she's usually so active.'

Ryga agreed. 'Do Mr and Mrs Varley sleep at the front of the house?'

'They do but they didn't see that gentleman's boat. That's why you're asking, isn't it?'

There were no flies on Edna. 'It is.'

'They were snoring their heads off when I went down to help Miss Enys with her fall in the garden. I sleep at the back and had only just got up when I heard her call out. I rushed down in my dressing gown, thinking I might need Mr Fallows to help me with her, but I didn't like to disturb him, not without Miss Enys's say-so. His room's in the front too. We've got another guest room but that's at the back and no one's in it anyway. Miss Enys managed to lean on me and I got her in a chair in the kitchen and telephoned to the doctor. Lucky she didn't break anything. I'll leave you to eat or she'll be telling me off.' With a smile she swayed her way back to the kitchen.

He tucked into his breakfast, thinking he must pay for it. He didn't expect to get it free. Times were hard enough with rationing and shortages, although the Enys household seemed to be doing well, judging by the eggs and bacon he was enjoying. Perhaps he should take that coastal walk to keep off the extra pounds with all this hearty Cornish food. He was just having his second cup of tea when Miss Enys reappeared, Edna following her.

'I'll have a cup of tea, Edna.'

'Righty-ho, miss.' She cleared Ryga's place. He refused more tea, on the grounds that he was now awash with it, and complimented her on a splendid breakfast. Miss Enys eased herself onto the seat opposite Ryga with a wince and stretched out her lame leg.

'How did you end up here in Cornwall?' he asked.

'My lack of regional dialect gives me away, eh? Being Scotland Yard, you'd be bound to work that out.' She sniffed. 'My father was in the army, so my sister and I were educated in

Surrey while he served overseas. We both attended a secretarial course in London. After that I worked as an agency secretary until I decided I could run a business better than most of the companies I was working for, so I set up my own agency.'

He could well imagine. She struck him as being very efficient.

'I specialized in providing secretaries and domestic staff. It did very well until the war. I closed it January 1941. My father was ill and the woman who did for him was hopeless. I came here to look after him, sacking the useless woman. He died in the June of that year and left me this house. Thank you, Edna.' She broke off as the tea was placed in front of her. 'I threw myself into the war work here. Area billeting officer. The guesthouse came afterwards. It helps eke out the finances and gives me company. But you're not interested in my life story. I'd offer you a bed if I thought you'd be here long. I've got a vacant room. But I shouldn't have thought your enquiries would take up much time. The owner of that boat must have been very rich and important to bring Scotland Yard down. I hope he didn't make money on the back of others' suffering during the war.'

'He didn't.' Ryga saw no point in holding back on the information about the two dead men when it was bound to be in the newspaper shortly, and there were the inquests on Friday, if the coroner agreed the date.

'The *Patricia Bee* belonged to Sir Bernard Crompton. He was an eminent dermatologist in Harley Street.'

'He was a long way from home.'

'He'd retired and had only just bought the craft from a boat builder in Scotland. She was on her maiden voyage to London. His cleaning lady said he was looking at areas along the coast where he might retire.'

'Was he was piloting her alone?'

'It seems so.'

'Must have had a good knowledge of seamanship. Do you doubt his death was from natural causes? Did Dr Bergmann get it wrong? Or perhaps that lanky constable did.'

'I'm looking into that, but we do have another death that could be connected with Sir Bernard. Yesterday a man's body was discovered in Priest Cove. He'd been shot.'

She gazed at him with narrowed eyes.

'He was also from London and we've been given to understand he was a regular visitor to these parts on account of his job. He was a mine inspector with the Ministry of Fuel and Power.'

'You surely don't mean Ralph Ackland?'

'I do. You knew him?' He wasn't surprised; it was a close-knit community and she had been the area billeting officer. She might have come across him while performing her duties.

'Oh, I knew him, all right.' Her bitter tone surprised him. 'In fact, I knew him very well. Ralph Ackland was my brother-in-law, and what's more, I despised him.'

CHAPTER SEVEN

'How sure are you that it's him?' she curtly demanded.

Ryga, rapidly recovering from his shock at this unexpected news, said, 'He had ID on him but we'll confirm it through fingerprints.'

'Then you won't want me to identify him?'

'His injuries are such that a physical identification is impossible.' He studied her, curious. She showed no horror or distress, but then by her own admission she had hated her late brother-in-law. Ryga would very much like to know why.

'How did he die?'

'We don't know for certain, but it appears he was shot in the head.' It was as though they were discussing a newspaper article.

'Did he shoot himself?' But she swiftly continued before he could answer. 'No, impossible — he'd never do that.'

Edna arrived to clear the table, her expression one of subdued excitement, which indicated to Ryga she'd heard every word they'd spoken. She made to clear the table but Miss Enys sharply dismissed her. 'Leave this. Carry on with your other duties.'

That looked about the last thing Edna wished to do. She was bursting with curiosity and would dearly have loved to have plonked her shapely backside on one of the chairs at the table. Reluctantly, she sidled away. Ryga suspected not far and not out of earshot. It didn't matter much because he was certain Miss Enys would tell her the news, and no doubt Edna's fiancé, the postman, would fill in the gaps. He'd be sure to pick up all the gossip on his round.

'Why are you so certain he wouldn't shoot himself?' Ryga asked, eager to get a feel for the victim.

'Because he was vain and arrogant,' came her smart retort. 'He was an odious man. I'm not going to pretend I felt otherwise. I won't have any truck with this nonsense of not speaking ill of the dead, especially where that vile creature is concerned.'

Ryga wondered if she had shot him.

'I never understood what my sister, Phyllis, saw in him, but then she was afraid of being left on the shelf like me. Foolishly, she grabbed the first proposal she got. Oh, Ralph wasn't arrogant in a loud, bullish sort of way, Inspector, quite the opposite — he never raised his voice to her or anyone. You might even have thought him timid on first encounter, but that would have been a grave misjudgement. He excelled at looking humble and being polite, pretending to be kind, but he was venomous, cunning and manipulative.'

She took a breath and stared out of the window. He remained silent. How reliable was her judgement, he wondered. Her hatred was overwhelmingly powerful.

She put her cold eyes back on Ryga. 'He killed my sister. Yes, you can look surprised and sceptical but it's what I firmly believe. He wore her down, made her question herself. He belittled her at every opportunity. He slowly sucked the life out of her, picking up on everything she did or said with that gentle smirk and quiet voice that made me want to hit him, until she lost all confidence.'

'She told you this?'

'Didn't have to. I saw the change in her. In the end she couldn't make a single decision. He did everything, right down to telling her what to wear and when and where to go. She had no friends and barely left the house before she became too ill to go anywhere or do anything.'

'Did you see her often?'

'I tried to when I was living in London, running my agency. But once I was down here I never saw her at all. Before I came, during the Blitz, I urged her to join me, but she said that Ralph needed her there. He didn't. He was never at home. They had a maid but she left just before my sister died. The bombs terrified my sister, and who can blame her? She couldn't escape Ralph. Our father died on the sixth of June 1941, Phyllis fourteen days later.' Her knuckles whitened as she gripped her stick. Ryga could hear Edna clattering about in the kitchen. 'I had no idea she was that ill. I'd tried to call her a couple of times but the lines were often down, and when I did get through there was no answer. I wrote. She didn't reply. Then a telegram came from Ralph to say she'd died and the funeral was the following week.'

Ryga thought that callous. Was this a true picture of Ralph Ackland or was it coloured by Miss Enys's distress over her sister's death?

'I went up to town for the funeral, although the journey was hellish, as you can imagine in wartime. I wasn't permitted to stay in their apartment. I had to put up in a lodging house.' Her voice was harsh with acrimony. 'Ralph and I were the only mourners. I don't know if there were others who would have come and he put them off or didn't invite them. When I challenged him about it he said the war made it very difficult for people to attend and her friends had dispersed to other places because of it. I bit my tongue. It was, after all, my sister's pathetic funeral.'

She was visibly moved by the memory. She had given Ryga a motive for murder, and yet he was certain that if she had killed her brother-in-law for his treatment of her sister, and for shutting her out of her sister's life and death, then she would have come right out and told him, unashamed, and unafraid of the consequences — certainly life imprisonment if not the death penalty.

She resumed. 'Ralph gave me a box containing my sister's jewellery. Some of it had been our mother's, and there were some photographs. He'd dispensed with her clothes and there were no letters or diaries. I took the box, told him what I thought of him and said I wished to never see him again. I came home.'

'And did you see him again?' Ryga asked, wondering if she might say she did, at Priest Cove.

'Unfortunately, yes. During the war at Tregarris House — that's Jory Logan's place, it's just south of St Just. Jory has the licence to the Catallack Mine from Colonel Cavendish-Dorrian, who owns the land. I was there in my official capacity as area billeting officer. It's a big rambling house with stables. I had evacuees staying there along with a handful of the Bevin Boys working in the mines. Ralph was there in connection with the ministry. His job was to make sure the mines were producing as much tin as they could and that the Bevin Boys were being put to maximum use. Many of the poor conscripted souls hadn't been brought up with that kind of hard labour, sweating in the bowels of the earth, and they loathed it. Some took off. They might have ended up fighting the war elsewhere in the forces. Ralph asked how I was. I told him to go to hell, and I sincerely hope he has.'

A clock chimed the half hour. 'Did Mr Ackland know Sir Bernard Crompton?'

She shrugged.

'Can you give me your movements for Sunday night, Miss Enys?'

Her head whipped round. A hard look crossed her face. 'You think I killed him.'

'Did you?' he asked quietly.

'I'd like to have done, several times, when I saw how he had changed my sister. But I didn't. There was enough death all around us. Whoever did kill him must have had a very strong reason for doing so, which means Ralph had destroyed another soul. I heartily hope you never get the person who did it.'

Ryga thought they might not if it was Sir Bernard Crompton. But he couldn't think of a motive for Crompton killing Ackland. From what they had discovered to date, Sir Bernard seemed to have been robust enough to resist any quiet intimidation by Ackland, although one idea did occur to Ryga. He'd consider that later. And there was that ransacking of both men's homes to take into account.

'Your movements, Miss Enys?' he gently prompted. 'I know about Monday morning and your ankle.'

'I was here all day. I don't attend church or chapel. Edna has Sundays off and I don't serve dinner on a Sunday. I have a cold spread. I made the Varleys' cocoa at half past eight. They drank it in the guest lounge and then retired for the night at about nine. Mr Fallows was in his room. I washed up the cups and then went up and read for a while before going to bed.'

He recalled she'd told him she kept a boat in the harbour, but it would have been dark and difficult, if not impossible, for her to have navigated it around the coast to meet with Ackland. And he didn't think she had done so.

'Do you have a car?'

'Yes. It's that pre-war boneshaker parked across the road. You think I went to meet Ralph? Well, I didn't.'

Even if she had, why would he have worn evening dress? He wouldn't have dined at Gulls Nest if she had hated him as much as she claimed, and Ryga believed she did. And the Varleys and Mr Fallows would have seen or heard him.

'Can you tell me anything of his background? Does he have any relatives? Friends?'

'I sincerely doubt the latter,' she scoffed. 'And there are no relatives. His parents died years ago. I believe there was a brother but he never spoke of him. Phyllis told me that Ralph had mentioned him once and said that they were not to speak of him again. Ralph would only get upset and angry. At their wedding there was me, my father and a man Ralph worked with who acted as his best man, but that was years ago. His father was a civil servant. Ralph went to a minor public school and passed the civil service entrance examination. That's all I know and all I want to know about that despicable creature. Others will tell you more. I suppose you'll need to talk to Captain Strout and Jory Logan, although Jory didn't know Ackland as well as the captain, him being away during the war.' Her expression softened for a moment. 'Take my car, unless you have one.'

'I don't.'

'Then take it. The buses aren't always reliable. No, I insist, it's no good to me at the moment. You'll have to put some petrol in it though.' She hauled herself up with a wince.

He wanted to refuse, but conceded it would be of great assistance. He could go straight to the mine rather than return to Penzance. 'Thank you.'

'I'll get the keys. They're in my coat pocket in the hall.'

Ryga followed her out. 'Would you mind if I telephoned Sergeant Pascoe at Penzance? I'll pay for the call.'

'Help yourself.' She waved at the instrument on the hall table.

'Do you have a photograph of Ralph Ackland?'

'Yes, of their wedding. I would have destroyed it but for the fact Phyllis is in it. I'll ask Edna to fetch it for you. It's upstairs in my bedroom.' She hobbled away and a few minutes later they both appeared while Ryga was waiting for the operator to connect him to the police station. With an excited glance at Ryga, Edna ran up the stairs.

Miss Enys said, 'I told Edna about Ralph. I hope that was all right. It'll be all over Penwith soon anyway.'

'Yes, that's fine . . . Hello, it's Inspector Ryga.'

'I'll leave you to your call.'

'Is Sergeant Pascoe there . . . ? Pascoe, there's been a development. I'm at Miss Enys's in Mousehole. Ralph Ackland was her late brother-in-law. I'll tell you about it when I get back. I'm going over to the mine. Miss Enys is loaning me her car. Can you get over to the railway station and establish if anyone answering Ackland's description got off the Paddington train? And try and find out where he went from there. Also, can you ask the coroner to move the inquests, and handle the mortuary on your own? Take both men's fingerprints and, with the help of the attendant, undress both men and take pictures of them before and after. Do you have a camera?' Ryga's was on him in his murder case. 'Good. Bring their clothes and shoes back to the station.'

He rang off. Edna appeared at the top of the stairs; she'd obviously been waiting for him to finish his call. Ryga took the photograph from her. They looked a happy couple. Phyllis resembled her sister in the shape of her face and her mouth. Her eyes seemed to be dancing and Ralph Ackland was looking distinguished. He could see nothing of the personality Miss Enys had described, but he'd met men like him before who, on the surface, looked harmless and yet underneath were cruel. But he needed others' views of Ackland before he fully accepted what she had told him.

Miss Enys stepped into the hall. 'They married in November 1923.'

'May I keep this for a while?'

'Do as you wish,' she said wearily. He could see this news had quite altered her. The spark he'd witnessed before had been extinguished.

'I'll let you have your car keys back later today.'

It was as though she hadn't heard him.

Ryga paid her for the call and the breakfast, which he insisted was only right. Opposite the house he unlocked her Ford and drove a short distance in the direction of Raginnis, where he pulled over into a rough lay-by and consulted the AA road map that he found in the glove compartment, along with a pair of women's driving gloves. He recalled Pascoe's route to St Just yesterday along narrow lanes and then across country on the main road, which, from the map, he saw was the A3071. There was an alternative route on a B road that would take him along the coast to Land's End and then up to St Just. It would give him a good feel of the coast, not to mention spectacular views, but it was twice the mileage. Could he justify that?

He switched on the ignition and tapped the fuel gauge. Miss Enys was correct — there wasn't much petrol in the tank. As he would have to find a garage, the decision on which route to take was made for him. He headed towards Newlyn, stopping off to pick up his murder case from the boat and have a brief word with Silas, mainly about the weather. But he also asked him to keep an eye on the *Patricia Bee* and to note anyone who became nosy about her or attempted to board her. He showed Silas the photograph of Ralph Ackland and asked if he had seen him before or knew him. The answer on both counts was in the negative.

After Newlyn, Ryga picked up the same road they had taken the previous day. He consoled himself with the decision that he'd take the longer coastal road back.

Halfway to St Just, he pulled off the road onto a track and stopped the engine some yards along it. The only inhabitants were a bunch of scraggy, talkative sheep. He didn't for a moment believe that Miss Enys had killed her brother-in-law, or that she had entertained him before taking him to Priest Cove and shooting him in the face, but as her car was at his disposal, and because he was a police officer who couldn't take anything on trust, he would search it.

Methodically, he started with the front passenger seat. There he found white hairs which could be anyone's and not necessarily Ralph Ackland's, but if she had taken him to a supposed dinner engagement, hence the evening dress, then perhaps they were the dead man's. He put the hairs in an evidence bag.

The front seats tilted forward to allow passengers to climb into the back, and he ran his hand along the creases, manipulating them forward then back, but nothing was lodged in or under them. Next he searched the boot, where he found a rug, a tyre jack, a spare tyre, spare plugs, rags, a box of assorted tools — with no blood on them — and a pair of old, stout walking shoes, which he examined carefully. There were grains of sand and small stones lodged in the soles, but that wasn't surprising given that Miss Enys would have used them to walk around the Mousehole shore to her boat. Nevertheless, he took some scrapings.

He continued on his journey as the clouds gathered. At St Just he asked directions to the Catallack Mine and ten minutes later parked the car as close as possible to the outcrop of brick buildings high on the clifftop. In the now howling wind and battering rain, he hurried towards a broad-shouldered man in a long oilskin with a sou'wester rammed over his craggy face. He was talking to a short man with an oilcloth draped around his shoulders and a sodden cap on his lean head. Their gesticulations and expressions showed there was a problem and some disagreement about how to tackle it.

'Captain Strout?'

'Aye?' the man in the long oilskin snapped at Ryga. 'What do you want now? If you men from the ministry didn't show up so often with your moaning, we might get more work done. Hasn't anyone told you the war's over and the mine's no longer any of your business?'

Ryga quickly corrected him on who he was with a show of his warrant card.

Strout waved away the man with the oilcloth. 'If it's about Ackland, I heard he's dead. I couldn't stand the fellow when he were alive and I don't care for him now he's dead, and I don't mind who knows it, Scotland Yard or no.'

Another person of the same opinion as Miss Enys, but it had to be for a different reason. Ryga was becoming more intrigued by the minute. He wondered if Strout might provide an even more damning character assessment. He followed him to one of the small brick buildings, where the captain shook out his sou'wester, scattering the raindrops over the dusty floor and furniture.

'I'm only surprised no one hasn't killed him afore now.' He gestured Ryga into a battered, grime-covered chair in the messy room crammed with implements, wooden boxes and with paperwork strewn on a rough table. Ryga thought it impolite to remain standing despite the fact his mackintosh would be covered with dust and dirt. He wouldn't sacrifice his hat though and kept it on his lap.

'What was wrong with him?'

Strout snorted. 'What were right with him?' He plonked himself down in the other chair, which only had one arm. There was a harassed air about him and a sorrow behind the tired eyes that Ryga had seen before in men resigned to their fate and about to give up. 'I know we hate all men from the ministry but with him it was more than that. He had no idea what it was like to work down the mine. Wouldn't even go down to see. Always carping on about this, that and the other. You'd have thought he owned the ruddy place, but then he believed he did and reminded us often enough when it were nationalized. And Mr Logan weren't here to remind him that he had the licence. He was in the Far East, a prisoner of war, and we all now know how badly they were treated.'

Strout was right. Ryga had suffered along with many others who had fared much worse than him, but what they had learned about the treatment of captured servicemen and civilian women after the fall of Singapore was appalling.

'And there was Ackland, safe and comfortable, lording it over us all, a puny, upstart civil servant who came down here as often as he could to avoid the bombs in London.' Strout made to spit then refrained. 'He were always preaching at us to do our bit. Us! What bit did he ever do, I'd like to know. Now he's dead. I felt like pushing him down the mine shaft myself many a time. How did he die?'

'He was shot.'

Strout's eyes narrowed and he rubbed his nose. 'I heard he was found in Priest Cove.'

'He was. And have you heard anything else about his death?'

'No. And I wouldn't tell you if I had.' Strout held up his large hand to staunch Ryga's reply. 'And before you go spouting off about it being my duty to speak out and against the law to withhold information, let me tell you this: he had it coming to him a long time ago. Now it's finally caught up with him, and not before time. When you find who did it, let me know and I'll shake him by the hand. But I hope and pray you never do catch him.'

Strout's views echoed Miss Enys's then, and his emotions where Ackland was concerned were equally strong. Had Ackland really been as devilish as the two of them claimed?

'Was he due at the mine last weekend or this week?'

'No. Mr Logan would have told me if he had been.'

'When was the last time you saw Mr Ackland?'

Strout pinched his nose. 'Dunno. About seven months ago. November.'

'Where did he stay when he came down here?' Ryga wondered if he'd had a regular hotel he'd used and his clothes were in that room.

'I don't know.' Strout rose. 'Now, I got work to do and I'm not going to waste any more time talking about someone I cared nothing for.' With that he opened the door, letting in the squally rain, and waltzed out before Ryga could protest.

It was clear that Strout knew a great deal more about Ackland and his visits here. It was also obvious that he wasn't going to speak. Was Strout capable of murder? Yes, thought Ryga as he dashed to the car, but his motive couldn't have been because Ackland was from the ministry. That wasn't nearly enough to shoot a man in the head, although some had been shot for a lot less. He shuddered, shutting out the memories.

He wondered where Strout had been at the time of the murder. Would he have had a gun in his possession? Strout, being a miner, would know something of the composition and possible origin of the pieces of rock found in the dead men's pockets, but why were they there? Did Strout also know Sir Bernard? He hadn't had the chance to ask him that or the other questions that buzzed around his brain. Could Strout pilot a boat? Possibly.

He would return to question the mine captain more thoroughly. He also needed to speak to Mr Logan. Despite the fact Logan hadn't been here during the war when Ackland's visits had been frequent, Logan would have had contact with him since the end of the war, and Ryga was curious to hear Logan's character assessment of the dead man. Before that, he wanted to see what Jacobs had come up with from Ackland's employer. And there was someone else he wanted to speak with. His experience told him that there were three people in a village who seemed to know everything and everyone — the postman, the post office mistress and the milkman. But in this case there was one other — not the local police officer, but his wife. Ryga made for St Just.

CHAPTER EIGHT

'Sergeant Marrack isn't due back for another hour for his dinner, Mr Ryga, but you're welcome to wait in the parlour for him.' Mrs Marrack greeted him in a front room of the terraced house that served as the public office.

'It's you I wanted to talk to, if you could spare me the time. It's about Mr Ackland.'

'Ah, I heard he was dead.'

'I take it you knew him, from his visits here during the war.'

'I did. My father worked at the Catallack Mine. You'd better come through and have a cup of tea.'

'I don't wish to put you to any trouble.'

'Not at all, Mr Ryga.'

He followed the generously proportioned woman into the hallway and down it to a room on their right, a cosy parlour.

'Now, sit yourself down. The kettle's already boiled. I won't be long. If the counter bell goes, ignore it. I'll see to it. Oh, and don't mind Smudge, he's harmless and a bit deaf.' The Jack Russell looked up from his comfortable position in front of the coal fire, eyed Ryga, then yawned, deeming him to be of little interest.

Ryga did as requested, taking the seat at the table. The room was comfortably furnished and clean. His eyes travelled to the mantelpiece, where there was an array of photographs. One was a picture of two girls, one about seven, the other Ryga thought about nine or ten, along with a boy of about the same age. There was also one of a young man about eighteen, and the others were of Sergeant Marrack in police uniform and the Marracks in their wedding finery.

'There now.' Mrs Marrack entered carrying a tray on which were a colourful knitted tea cosy over a teapot, two china cups and saucers and a plate of biscuits. She poured him out a cup of tea. 'Help yourself to sugar and a biscuit.'

He politely declined both.

She settled herself opposite and studied him with kindly, toffee-coloured eyes. 'Sergeant Marrack and I talked about the death of Mr Ackland last night. He didn't know him, being away at war a great deal of time. He was a reservist so got called up immediately when war broke out. He was shocked at Mr Ackland's death but I wasn't. I suppose that sounds wicked to you.' She patted her grey-streaked hair piled up in a bun, her round, open face solemn. 'I'm sorry to have to say this, Mr Ryga, but Mr Ackland was universally disliked, and not without reason.'

Ryga had already judged her to be sensible. He also believed her to be unbiased. Ackland, it seemed, had no redeeming qualities. 'Please continue and be frank. I'm trying to understand the man.'

She sipped her tea, then carefully replaced the cup. 'Well, as I said, my father worked at the Catallack Mine. He was a foreman there. He died in 1945. There was a lot of pressure to get more tin out of the mines and the strain of the work built up in him, so much so that the moment the war was over he had a stroke and died. The mine had lost a lot of men who had been called up, or who took the chance of getting away from the mines. Many of the Bevin Boys who were drafted in from forty-three onwards, and later the

POWs, hated it. You can understand that, them not being brought up with mining in their blood.'

Ryga would have loathed to work in the bowels of the earth and had the greatest respect for miners of all kinds. He swallowed some tea.

'My father used to say, *Here's that man from the ministry again. Can't he leave us be? Always badgering us, nitpicking and moaning.* He became known behind his back as Mr Awkward or Mr Awful. He was such a regular visitor that everyone thought he was here for a holiday and was trying to avoid the bombs in London.'

What Strout had said. 'Can you remember when Mr Ackland last visited here?'

'I can't say, Mr Ryga. Captain Strout will know, or Mr Logan, who has the licence. He wasn't here during the war but he'll know if Mr Ackland has been since.'

'Did you meet Mr Ackland?'

'I did, on four occasions, and I can't say I took to him. He was a cold, spiteful man. He looked down his nose at everyone. He'd either make some nasty remark, or cut you dead when you spoke to him. You'd say something pleasant like, "Nice day, isn't it, Mr Ackland?" and he'd look at you as though you'd no business to utter a word, that you were nothing more than an insect to be squashed. Other times I'd see him turn his head away when someone was addressing him, and then just walk off.' She shook her head sadly. 'He'd do that with Miss Wargrove. She had a terrible time with him. I caught her crying once. Mr Ackland had been that nasty to her. Then she pulled herself together and said she wouldn't let him get the better of her. She's a strong young lady. I wonder what she'll think of his death.'

'Miss Wargrove?'

'She's the council geologist.'

She would know about rocks then. 'Do you know Miss Enys?'

Mrs Marrack gave a tinkling laugh, a mischievous glint filling her eyes. 'Everyone knows Miss Enys, and there's a fair few who still tremble when they see her coming. She'd have no nonsense during the war; she got things done. The previous billeting lady was a demon, and it was a mess around here with all the evacuees and people being choosy over taking in some of those poor little mites, but Miss Enys soon sorted them out. That's one of the evacuees I took in, in that picture with my two daughters.' She indicated the one on the mantelpiece. 'Norman Barnworth. Lovely boy. He stayed the longest and writes to us regularly. He's twenty-one now and in the navy,' she declared proudly as if Norman were her son. 'My daughter Alice, the eldest, is married to a nice young man, a baker, who lives in Penzance. She's expecting a baby. Our first grandchild.'

'Congratulations.'

'And my other daughter, Karen, is eighteen, works in a dress shop in Penzance and is courting a fisherman. The young man there on his own is Roy Canton. He was a Bevin Boy who billeted with us. He's married now and in the police force in Sheffield. He still keeps in touch.'

She drank some more tea. 'But you don't want to hear about my family. Miss Enys practically took over Tregarris House, where there were evacuees and Bevin Boys. Poor Mrs Logan wasn't the most organized of souls, bless her. Nice young woman, but very dreamy and out of her depth, and so upset when Mr Logan went missing. Then we heard he'd been captured by the Japanese. We were pleased to know he was safe.' Her face fell. 'But that was before we learned how dreadful it had been and how cruelly they treated prisoners of war. When he eventually got back — it took a long time for them all to come home — he was a shell of the man we'd known. Then just when things were beginning to look better for him and Mrs Logan, with a baby on the way, the poor little mite, a boy, was born not quite right. He died a few months after that, in 1948. Mrs Logan never got over it. She died a year later. It nearly sent Mr Logan over the edge. Captain Strout takes a lot on his shoulders at the mine to help out but I'm not sure how long the mine will last.'

'Did you know that Mr Ackland was Miss Enys's brother-in-law?'

'I did. She was at Tregarris House when he was staying there once and I heard them having words. She said she never wanted to see or speak to him again and that if ever they were in the same room she would leave it. It's a pity Mrs Knowles is no longer with us. She was the Logans' house-keeper. She died a year after Mrs Logan. Mrs Knowles ran the house all through the war because Mrs Logan returned to London. She thought she'd be happier there with her friends, though being in London with all the bombs was the last place I'd have wanted to be. But then Charlotte Logan was from London and it was strange for her to be all the way down here, her not knowing anyone. They'd only just been married when Mr Logan went off to war.'

'I understand that Colonel Cavendish-Dorrian owns the land. Would Ackland have known him? Would he have stayed with him?'

'He might have known him but he wouldn't have stayed with him. The colonel lives in London. He used to own a lot of land around here. He's sold much of it now, along with the cottages — something to do with death duties.'

The counter bell pinged. She rose. 'I'd better see who that is.'

'And I'll be going. Thank you for your help.'

'You're welcome. Anything else you need, just let us know. I'll tell Sergeant Marrack to report back to you later.'

He left her to attend to an elderly lady who had lost her cat and who Mrs Marrack obviously knew very well. By the conversation he overheard before leaving, the lost cat was a regular occurrence. And possibly an excuse for a bit of a chat and company.

Keeping the promise he had made to himself earlier, Ryga took the longer coastal road back to Mousehole, noting the mileage from the mine down to Priest Cove where he pulled up. It was only a mile — no distance at all for some-one to walk and kill Ackland, but that didn't explain what Ackland would be doing there in evening dress.

He climbed out. The heavy rain had ceased and a sliver of light stretched out along the darker rim of the horizon. A steamer was plunging her way a couple of miles out, her smoke rising from the funnel. The seagulls wheeled noisily overhead and he watched them dive down to the water, skirt it with their breasts and bob up again to wheel in above the waves.

He breathed in the crisp, clean air with its salt tang from the leaden sea as though trying to cleanse his senses of a man who had evoked such strong negative feelings and animosity, even from such a kindly woman as Mrs Marrack. Looking up in awe at the immovable cliffs and then at the vast expanse and power of the sea that had caused such rock formations, he thought of those five small pieces of rock in both men's pockets. They surely had to mean something.

He crossed to the gaping hole of the tunnel. Stepping inside, he switched on his torch and began a close scrutiny, venturing as far as he dared inside. The walls and ceiling looked solid enough but he shuddered as again, like the previous day, he felt them pressing down on him. He examined the ground, while conscious of any movement behind him, suppressing an irresistible urge to keep looking over his shoulder to make sure that no one would shut him in. They couldn't, of course — it just felt like it.

He turned to face the entrance, feeling better because behind him now was a solid wall. He couldn't see any marks on the ground to say that the body had lain there and had been dragged out but reason told him it must have been, because despite the weather and no fishermen having been down to the cove, he felt sure it would have been discovered before the coastguard had spotted it the day before. But who would do that? The killer most probably needing the body to be found. Why? Out of conscience? Perhaps. Or because he wished to confuse the time of death? Maybe. The alternative was that Ackland had been brought here by car or boat — and probably the first because the coastguard would have seen a boat — and dumped early Tuesday morning. On the other hand, perhaps someone had inadvertently stumbled over the corpse in this tunnel and didn't wish to report it to the police, but also didn't wish the remains to rot there. A smuggler? Possibly. The tunnel could be used to hide contraband, although he could see no evidence of that either.

He returned to the car and drove along the coast, stopping off at an inn at Sennen Cove for a half pint of bitter and a sandwich. As a matter of routine he enquired if the landlord or landlady had seen Ackland, giving his description. He didn't expect a positive reply so he wasn't disappointed when they shook their heads. Nor did they know him. As he was leaving, he saw a bedraggled figure trudging along the road. Recognizing him as the man he'd seen leaving Miss Enys's that morning, Ryga pulled over and, leaning across, wound down the window.

'Can I give you a lift back to Mousehole? This is Miss Enys's car — she's loaned it to me. I saw you leave her guest-house this morning. You're Mr Fallows, aren't you?'

Fallows's worried expression cleared. 'I am and that's very kind of you. I'm whacked, not to mention wet through. Not the best day for hiking.' He climbed in. 'You're the detective from Scotland Yard, Miss Enys told me about you this morning. She said you're here about the man found dead on that lovely boat in the harbour.'

'Did you see it Monday morning at sea?'

'No. By the time I drew the curtains it was in the harbour. That was just on seven. I didn't even hear the doctor's car arrive earlier after Miss Enys had her fall. I told Edna she should have woken me and I'd have helped, but Miss Enys being proud and independent wouldn't have liked it. I slept like a top — it's this Cornish sea air.'

Ryga wished he could have said the same. 'Sadly there's been another death, a body has been found in Priest Cove. We're treating it as suspicious.'

'Is there a connection between the two?'

'It's too early to say.'

'Of course.'

It wasn't Ryga's place to tell Fallows that the dead man was related to Miss Enys. She could do that if she so wished.

'How long are you staying, Mr Fallows?'

'Only a few more days, then it's back to the pea-soupers.'

'You work in London?'

'No, but I live there. I have a small legacy and my health's not too good. I've been thinking about moving. Cornwall seemed as good a place but I've decided it's too far away. I'd like something closer to town — Margate perhaps or Southend-on-Sea. Not as spectacular as here but at least you can see the ocean — and smell it, of course.'

Ryga knew exactly what he meant. He wondered if Fallows was ex-navy but didn't ask, fearing it would spark talk of the war — the last thing he wished to discuss. Instead they talked about the weather, Cornwall and the tourists, which took them to Mousehole, where Ryga spotted a man studying the *Patricia Bee*. It was the same one he'd seen talking to the postman that morning from Miss Enys's house who Edna had told him was Mr Pedrick. He was hatless and his hair was wet and awry. 'Do you mind if I drop you off here, Mr Fallows? Only, there's someone I'd like to talk to.'

'Of course not.'

'Could you tell Miss Enys that I'll return her car later today and that I'm very grateful to her for the use of it?'

'Will do, and thanks for the lift.'

Parking the car, Ryga hurried towards Pedrick. There was no sign of Silas. He'd been told the old man always kept watch, but then Silas was only human.

'It's Mr Pedrick, isn't it? I'm Detective Inspector Ryga from Scotland Yard.'

Pedrick gave a small cry and looked alarmed.

Ryga judged him to be about mid-fifties, although from the lines on his face and his frightened, watery eyes he could have been older. 'I've been informed that you have a telescope, sir. I wondered if you were looking out to sea on Monday morning and saw this craft, the *Patricia Bee*.'

'No. I didn't see anything,' he gabbled. 'Why should I have done?'

He looked desperate to get away.

'I just wondered.'

'Well, I wasn't looking.' He scratched the side of his face, which Ryga could see was already sore as though he'd been in the sun or suffered from a rash. Seeing Ryga's gaze, he snatched his hand away and wiped it down the side of his shabby jacket. 'I have an article to write for the Penzance Astronomy Society.' And with that he scuttled off, almost stumbling in his haste to get away. Clearly he was a nervous man. Was that just eccentricity or was there more to Pedrick's study of the boat and his manner? Perhaps he had seen something out to sea on Monday morning and, whatever it was, he was afraid to say.

Ryga pondered over this and what he had learned about Ralph Ackland as he made his way to Penzance. He was keen to hear what Pascoe thought of it. Perhaps the sergeant had discovered where Ackland had been staying or Jacobs would find out from the ministry, because if Ackland hadn't come down here on official business, then someone had invited him. That someone had either disguised his hatred of the man with the intention of killing him or had been a friend, and from what Ryga had so far learned, Ackland had none in this locality, save perhaps one man — a fellow Londoner, Sir Bernard Crompton.

CHAPTER NINE

'Well, Ackland got off that train from Paddington on Saturday morning, all right,' Pascoe greeted Ryga. 'The ticket collector and porter both remember a man answering to his description alighting just after 8.20 a.m. He was carrying a brown suitcase, wearing a black overcoat and a dark grey hat, but neither man saw where he went or if he got in a car outside. Ackland didn't speak and there didn't seem to be anything troubling him.'

Ryga took DC Tremolo's vacant seat. He could see two bundles of clothes and two pairs of dress shoes on the other desk. He'd come to them in a moment.

'I asked the two taxi drivers if they had picked him up as a fare but they hadn't. One took a woman to Newlyn, the other a man in his forties to the hospital. There were two other cars waiting for passengers; both taxi drivers recognized the cars and told me who they belonged to. And I've interviewed the vehicle owners. They didn't pick up Ackland either. I've also spoken to their passengers — one an elderly man returning from Exeter, and the other a young woman staying with her aunt for a few days. They didn't see where Ackland went. He could have walked into the town, or someone picked him up from one of the side streets. The duty beat constables don't remember seeing him.'

Ryga rose and crossed to the large map of Penzance on the wall. The railway station was clearly marked and was very close to the harbour. 'Could he have walked to the harbour and been picked up by boat?'

'Not the *Patricia Bee*. It wasn't in the harbour.'

'Have we checked?'

'No, but it was heading in this direction when it was spotted by the coastguard, not going away from here.'

'That was on Monday morning. It could have come into Penzance late on Friday evening, or even in the early hours of Saturday, picked up Ackland then motored back to a bay or cove beyond Mousehole.'

'Not Priest Cove. The coastguard would have seen the boat.'

'There are other bays, coves and harbours. Yes, I know it sounds unlikely,' Ryga quickly added to Pascoe's sceptical gaze, 'but we need to ask the harbour master. If it wasn't the *Patricia Bee* then Ackland could have been met by some other boat owner. Get a list of any visitors to the harbour for that period, and while you're at it, a list of all the regulars. What did the coroner say about the inquests?'

'He's happy to hold them both on Friday, Sir Bernard's at ten thirty followed immediately by Ackland's. I've notified everyone who needs to be there. Dr Bergmann wasn't very happy about his day being disrupted as he'll have to attend both, but that can't be helped. The coroner said he'd liked to discuss both inquests with you before the first one, and would see you at the court at ten o'clock.'

'Good. That will give me the opportunity to ask him to hear the basic details and adjourn them pending further enquiries.'

'I've booked Dr Plumley into the Queen's Hotel, and while I was there I established that Ralph Ackland, or anyone fitting his description, didn't book in there. I can't see him having booked into any smaller hotels or boarding houses, but the beat constables are going to ask around.'

Ryga told Pascoe what he had discovered. It drew an amazed expression and a sad shake of his head. 'Not a glowing epitaph. We might end up having several suspects.'

'And there might be more in London, not to mention your theory of Sir Bernard being the killer. Anything strike you about his clothes or Ackland's?' Ryga crossed to the desk. Pascoe joined him.

Ryga could see immediately that both men's were of a high quality, but Sir Bernard's were superior and from a Savile Row tailor, as he had expected. His shoes were also handmade.

'No exceptional marks on either of them. No grit or sand on Sir Bernard's shoes as I remarked when I first saw them,' Pascoe said. 'Some on Ackland's, probably from the cove. No salt rings or stains on Ackland's shoes or around the hem of his trousers, so the tide hadn't reached him. There's blood on the front of the shirt, as we saw yesterday, but when the mortuary attendant and I moved the body to undress it we also found blood on the top of his back collar and his head.'

'Which indicates he was struck from behind at some stage. I explored that tunnel again, and although I couldn't see any evidence he was kept there before being dragged out onto the shore, my instinct tells me he was.' Ryga picked up Ackland's wristwatch. It was a common make, nothing special.

Pascoe said, 'The signet ring only has his initials on it. Nine-carat gold. His cufflinks are pewter whereas Sir Bernard's are silver. Underwear for both men, as you can see, are silk, as are the socks.'

The telephone rang and Pascoe answered it. Handing over the receiver, he said, 'Sergeant Jacobs, guv,' and made the sign for a drink. Ryga nodded and swivelled into Pascoe's seat. After Jacobs's usual greeting about the weather he got down to business.

'First, Sir Bernard,' Jacobs began. 'We've spoken to his bank manager, who was very frosty and said he couldn't possibly divulge anything about his account without authorization from Sir Bernard's solicitor or a warrant. Sir Bernard also has a safe deposit box there. I've requested a warrant because the solicitor is on holiday in France. His secretary says he'll be back Monday week. She was able to tell us though that Sir Bernard had made a will, and although she wouldn't be specific, she said the bulk of his estate goes to a couple of hospitals, one being the St John's Hospital for Diseases of the Skin. There are a couple of bequests, one to his former secretary, Miss Angela Tamley, and the other to Miss Joyce Pickford, his former housekeeper. Miss Tamley lives in Norfolk and Mrs Pickford in Northern Ireland, but she doesn't have their addresses to hand or won't say, which is irritating. I pressed her but nothing doing. We're trying to get in touch with them via the local police network to get their fingerprints. There's no next of kin as far as she is aware, or relatives.'

Ryga caught the sound of voices outside.

'DC Crawford went over to St John's and dug deeper than I did yesterday. He reported back that Sir Bernard was well respected and very clever. He could be blunt though, and sharpish. Some people found him downright rude but everyone forgave him because apparently what he didn't know about skin diseases wasn't worth knowing. He acted as an adviser on dermatology to the army during the war. Couldn't have the army laid up with itchy skin and blotchy feet,' Jacobs said cheerfully. 'It's amazing what I've learned from Crawford about skin diseases caused by chemicals in army clothing. Crompton went to North Africa and the Mediterranean, where the sun caused problems, and continued to practise on and off at Harley Street when not engaged by the army abroad.'

'Did he ever advise at the mines, Cornwall in particular?' Ryga thought of Pedrick scratching his face. Bergmann had also mentioned that Sir Bernard had an interest in occupational skin diseases, including those experienced by miners. Not that he thought Pedrick had been a miner, but he didn't know that for certain.

'Crawford says not. After the war Sir Bernard resumed his private practice as well as his work at the skin clinics in the London hospitals.'

'Anything more on the break-in?'

97

Pascoe entered with a mug of tea and placed it in front of Ryga. He indicated for Pascoe to remain.

'Inspector Tanner hasn't unearthed anything dodgy on Mrs Marlow or her husband and children. I don't think she gave anyone the key, or any of their acquaintances took it to copy. Not sure they're bright enough to do that. She cleans for others who, on the surface, have far more valuable things to steal. And there's nothing reported on them.'

'What about Sir Bernard's boat?' Ryga sipped his tea.

'Crawford finally managed to get hold of the boat builders. There was no tender supplied with the *Patricia Bee* because they were behind schedule building it. Someone at the company had made a pig's ear of ordering the right amount of timber. Sir Bernard said he couldn't hang around for it. He'd put into harbours and ports. The boat builders would have to arrange to transport and fit the tender in due course.'

'Did he say where he would be keeping the boat in London?'

'No. He told them he'd notify them when he got back to town. He didn't know when that would be. The River Police say that none of the wharf or harbour masters know anything about a berth or mooring for Sir Bernard. He looked over the boat on Wednesday the eleventh of April—'

'Having travelled up to Scotland on the overnight train on Monday the ninth of April. Arriving there on Tuesday the tenth. Do we know where he stayed?'

'Yes, the Fairlight Hotel in Gourock. The local police have made enquiries. Sir Bernard has stayed there a few times, obviously while checking on the progress of his boat. He was well known to the staff. Always alone. He booked in for three nights — Tuesday, Wednesday and Thursday. Caught the ferry across to Rosneath on Wednesday, where he looked over the craft. Everything was in order.'

'Was it fully furnished? By that, I mean did it come equipped with bed linen, towels, crockery, et cetera?'

'Yes. Sir Bernard asked the boat builders to purchase some food and cleaning supplies to be put on board. He returned on Thursday and took the boat out on a familiarization trip. He formally took possession of the *Patricia Bee* on Friday the thirteenth — not a good omen, eh?'

'He obviously wasn't superstitious.'

'Maybe he should have been. The man at the boat builders told Crawford that Sir Bernard was a very competent sailor and handling the craft was like second nature to him. Sir Bernard told them he'd put in at Troon for his first trip, which he did. Crawford has spoken to the harbour master there. The *Patricia Bee* arrived on Friday the thirteenth and stayed for one night. He doesn't know where it went from there but he says Sir Bernard was alone.'

'I'll get some charts and see if we can plot his onward route. Is that it on Sir Bernard?'

'Yes. Have you got anything your end?'

'Not much on Sir Bernard but some interesting information on Ackland.' Ryga gave him a digest of what he'd learned.

'That fits with what we've got. Ackland bought a return ticket on Friday at Paddington to Penzance and got a berth on the 9.50 p.m. night train. We're still trying to trace the taxi driver who took him to the railway station in case Ackland made some small talk, but in light of what you've just told me, and what the porter, Melton, has already told us, that seems unlikely. The ministry have confirmed that he wasn't due to visit Cornwall or anywhere else. I interviewed his guv'nor myself, who said he was shocked at Ackland's death, but I can tell you this, guv, there was a glimmer in his eyes when he said it. Ackland was due to retire. I think I'll return tomorrow and dig a bit deeper now I know what you've discovered down there. So far we haven't discovered any link between Sir Bernard and Ackland. He could have been a patient, I suppose. If we can get hold of the secretary, we'll ask her. And Crawford will find out who took over Sir Bernard's patient list.'

'Ask Ackland's guv'nor if he ever spoke about Sir Bernard or expressed an interest in geology. Was he friendly with anyone in particular in the office? Did any of them know Mrs Ackland? Also, was there anything unusual or significant in his reports about the Catallack Mine?'

'Righty-ho.'

'I'll get the film cartridges containing the dead men's prints, and my samples, up to you tonight. They should be with you by midnight.'

'I'll get the boys working on them first thing.'

Ringing off, Ryga instructed Pascoe to arrange for a police motorcyclist to collect the film cartridges — both his and the one Pascoe had — and to despatch them to Scotland Yard. While Pascoe organized this, Ryga sipped his tea and considered what Jacobs had told him.

'The motorcyclist is coming over now,' Pascoe said, replacing the receiver.

'Did you get the gist of my conversation with Jacobs?'

'Yes. It sounds as though Sir Bernard was sailing her single-handed.'

'I'd have agreed if it weren't for that missing logbook, the sea charts and those blessed pieces of rock.' Ryga consulted his watch. He rose and grabbed his hat and coat. 'Leave everything for the motorcyclist with the desk sergeant. Miss Wargrove, the council geologist, might still be in her office. Bring those rock pieces with you, Pascoe.'

The council offices were only next door. They were out of luck though. Miss Wargrove had left for the day. Ryga could have requested her home address but there wasn't any urgency to speak to her. Besides, she might not have gone home but on to an appointment. Ryga would hopefully speak to her in the morning.

'Let's call at the Queen's Hotel. I'll introduce you to Dr Plumley.'

Ten minutes later, in a quiet corner of the deserted lounge, they found the pathologist taking tea. Ryga introduced Pascoe, who got a curt nod in return. Ryga thought Plumley looked tired. He wasn't a young man and the long road journey must have been exhausting even if the traffic had been light. Conducting two in-depth autopsies would be arduous even for a fit, younger medical man, and from Plumley's heavily ringed eyes and florid complexion, Ryga was concerned that it might be too much for him. He didn't say that though. It would be certain to ruffle his feathers.

'I won't keep you long, Doctor,' Ryga politely said. 'I'll update you as to the circumstances behind the deaths of the two men in question.' He did so succinctly. Plumley made some notes in a small notebook.

'Did you know Sir Bernard Crompton?' asked Ryga.

'No.'

'But you've heard of him in your profession, perhaps other medical men discussing him?'

'We don't gossip, Inspector.'

'Of course not, I just wondered if you'd heard of his reputation, which by all accounts was formidable.'

'It might have been, but I haven't come across him.'

So much for that. 'I'd like to know if Sir Bernard had been suffering from any ailment that would have required medication. Also, if you could look for evidence of either man having been drugged.'

'Of course,' he crisply replied with a sour expression, as though it were obvious he would have done so anyway. But Ryga had wanted to make certain.

Plumley bid them a curt farewell and outside Pascoe said, 'It's a good job he's dealing with corpses and not the living. I'd be terrified of seeing him if I were ill.'

'I don't think you'd dare be,' Ryga rejoined with a smile.

They returned to the station, where Pascoe attended to some outstanding CID matters and Ryga wrote up his reports. He refused Pascoe's offer of a meal, not wishing to intrude on Jean's hospitality a second night. He'd get some fish and chips. He couldn't find a chip shop open though, and he didn't fancy traipsing around the town looking for somewhere else to eat. Instead, he set off for Mousehole with the intention of making do with what he had on board, which wasn't much. First though, he'd return the car to Miss Enys.

He found her recovered from her initial shock but paler than on their first meeting. The Varleys were enjoying a meal and Mr Fallows was in his room, she informed Ryga after showing him into the guests' lounge.

'We've discovered that your brother-in-law caught the sleeper from Paddington on Friday night and alighted at Penzance on Saturday morning. We're trying to establish where he went from there.' He watched her carefully.

She held his gaze. 'He didn't come here.'

'No one saw him get in a car outside the railway station. And he didn't take a taxi. We're wondering if he met someone farther away from the station. Do you know who that might be?'

'No.'

'Captain Strout says he wasn't due to visit the mine and the ministry have confirmed that. Can you think of any other reason why he should come to Cornwall?'

'No.'

'Mr Ackland's apartment has been ransacked. Have you any idea who might have done that?'

'None whatsoever. I wouldn't have thought there wasn't anything to steal, he was so tight-fisted.'

Ryga heard Edna's cheerful voice chatting to the Varleys. He said, 'The post-mortem is being conducted tomorrow, and the inquests on both Sir Bernard and Mr Ackland are on Friday at ten thirty. Formal identification will be made from fingerprints, but you will be called upon to confirm that Ralph Ackland was your brother-in-law. Would you like me, or an officer, to drive you to Penzance on account of your ankle?'

'No, thank you. I'll manage.'

Ryga thanked her for the use of her car and made his way thoughtfully down to the harbour. Had she a hand in her brother-in-law's murder? Could she have levelled a gun at him and shot him in the face? She was made of strong stuff.

The *Patricia Bee* was how he had left her; nothing looked untoward. At the sight of the bunk in the for'ard cabin, the memory of the previous night flooded through him. He felt the atmosphere oppressive rather than opulent. The boat was cold and empty despite its luxury. Ryga had initially looked forward to being alone on board with some quietude; that now was the last thing he desired. He longed for company.

He locked up and struck out down the pier to the Ship Inn. There were a handful of men inside. The conversation halted as he entered, and he drew some curious looks, but the chatter quickly resumed when the landlady greeted him warmly, as though he were a regular. He didn't need to introduce himself; she knew who he was, and took him under her wing by asking if he'd eaten. He said he hadn't but he was fine, upon which she insisted he have some steak and kidney pie she had left over from their dinner, although she said it would be a case of 'hunt the steak' in it.

Fifteen minutes later he was sitting in her cosy parlour in front of the coal fire tucking into pie and vegetables with half a pint of bitter in front of him. He was very grateful to her.

'Think nothing of it, sir,' she said, clearing away his plate. 'You looked right peaky when you came in but now you've got some colour back. I'll fetch you the other half. Smoke if you like.'

He said he didn't. He hadn't realized the boat and those memories had taken a toll on his appearance.

The landlord brought his beer and settled himself down at the table with Ryga. 'It's quiet out there now. The missus can handle it.'

'You're a Londoner?'

'Born and raised in Battersea. Married a Cornish lass in thirty-three and never went back. Miss it sometimes.'

They spent a pleasant half an hour talking about the football, fishing, London and the Festival of Britain, which the landlord said he and his wife hoped to visit in Plymouth when the exhibition ship visited there.

Before Ryga left, he asked him about Mr Pedrick. 'I saw him looking at the *Patricia Bee* earlier. Not that there's anything wrong in that — she's a fine craft — but Mr Pedrick seemed very anxious and distracted.'

'That's just his way. He's a bag of nerves, has been ever since the Great War. Shell shock. He used to live in London but when the bombing started he came down here. His nerves couldn't stand it.'

'Was that war responsible for the redness on his face? It's like a rash.'

'I don't know. He doesn't mention it and it's not my place to ask.'

'Does he work?'

'Only a couple of days a week, up at the hospital in Penzance, as an orderly. Used to work in one of the London hospitals.'

Ryga immediately wondered if it had been one where Sir Bernard had been a consultant. Even if it was, it didn't mean their paths had crossed.

'He writes articles on astronomy. Nice man, not sociable or talkative though.' It was said as though that were a defect.

Ryga took his farewells after again expressing his gratitude for the meal, beer and company. The landlady urged him to come in any time.

On the boat he turned on the engine and ran it for a while, made himself a cup of tea, sat down and went through his notes and the reports. The major thing that stood out was how despised Ackland had been. Hatred could have been a strong enough motive for luring him here and killing him, but why now? As Strout had intimated, there had been more cause for murdering the man during the war than now, six years after its cessation. And more opportunity to do so.

He retired for the night, steeling himself for the nightmares and haunting memories. And they came. Frustrated and annoyed, he rose, dragged a blanket from the bunk and slept on the couch in the saloon. It wasn't very comfortable, and it took him a long time to get off to sleep. When he did his dreams were still of the war.

CHAPTER TEN

Thursday 10 May

He rose early, disgusted with himself for his haunting dreams, and resolved to get a grip on this case and himself once and for all. His usual level-headedness seemed to have vanished in the Cornish mist that enveloped the boat.

He shaved, washed and dressed. Taking the navigational aids from the drawer at the helm, he locked up and struck out on foot along the coast to Penzance. A good brisk walk, no matter what the weather, was what he needed. It was only about three miles and at a steady pace would take him about an hour. He cleared his mind of the case as best he could and threw himself into the enjoyment of the walk in the damp silence of the morning mist, punctuated by the occasional grinding of a car's gears, a couple of barking dogs and a few workmen who greeted him pleasantly. He couldn't make out St Clement's Isle or even the shore in places. Newlyn Harbour was still and quiet as he walked through it. Then came a stretch of coast before the houses of Penzance. He found a café, ordered tea and a cooked breakfast.

Fortified and feeling a good deal better, he made his way to the railway station and from there surveyed the streets, considering which way Ackland might have gone and where he might have been picked up. The harbour was still a possibility. Pascoe was to make enquiries there today.

Ryga walked down to Wharf Road, where, keeping the sea on his left, he familiarized himself with the houses, shops and inns on his right. Had Ackland stayed at any of the latter or in a house along here? The local beat constables hadn't found any evidence of that yet, although there was nothing to stop anyone from lying to them. Somewhere along the line though, someone must have seen Ackland. He would issue a statement to the press asking for anyone with information to come forward. It would bring people out like a rash, and much of what they reported would be useless, but sometimes in among them was that nugget of information that could help. Nuggets made him think of the stones found in both men's pockets. If he could grasp the significance of those, maybe it would unlock the key to the case. He hoped that Miss Wargrove might enlighten him.

He walked as far as the swing bridge, where the buildings on his right petered out. Ahead were the docks. He turned and walked briskly back in the opposite direction along Chyandour Cliff with the sea on his right. Several roads branched off to his left and Ackland could have gone down any one of them, but as Ryga turned back he thought from his reconnaissance of the area the most likely possibility was that he had been picked up by car or by boat at the harbour.

An idea occurred to him. Maybe Ackland had expected the boat that was to meet him to be the *Patricia Bee* because he'd received an invitation from Sir Bernard, or someone purporting to be Sir Bernard, to join him at Penzance. Ackland had been lured down here for the sole purpose of murder. But why? And by whom? That was what he was here to find out and so far he wasn't doing too well. Then he corrected his thinking. He hadn't been here for Ackland's murder, he just happened to be on the spot, and the body had just happened to be found at that time. Was that in itself a coincidence though? It was still very early in an investigation to have all the answers, or any of them.

At the station, Pascoe had left him a message to say he would purchase some sea charts and return with them later. There was also a message to say the local reporter had asked for a statement about the body found in Priest Cove. Ryga prepared one and, after updating Chief Inspector Jerram, instructed the desk sergeant to send the statement over to the local newspaper. That done, he called Sergeant Jacobs.

'What's the weather like?' came Jacobs's standard greeting.

'Misty.'

'We've got rain.'

'Lucky you. I hoped I'd catch you before you went out. I want you to instigate enquiries at the Central Telegraph Office. Find out if Ackland received a telegram recently, especially from Cornwall. It might have been delivered to him at work, but also check with the porter at Abercorn Mansions and ask him if Ackland received a letter in the last two weeks — if so, does he recall the postmark? Did he receive any telephone calls from Cornwall? Check that with the telephone exchange too.'

Leaving the navigational aids and his murder case on Pascoe's desk, Ryga made his way to the council building next door, where he was informed that Miss Wargrove was in her office.

She was a delightful surprise. Far from being the wild, weather-beaten, middle-aged woman his imagination had conjured up, she was in her mid-thirties, auburn-haired with pale freckled skin, a pretty round face and a firm handshake. Her hazel eyes held his in a confident and enquiring manner with just a hint of amusement as though she'd read his mind. Perhaps his expression had betrayed him; although as a policeman he tried hard not to show emotion, he was only human. He had to stop thinking in stereotypes, Ryga silently scolded himself. He'd always prided himself on keeping an open mind but it was getting decidedly soggy on this investigation.

She offered him refreshment — which he politely refused — and gestured him into the seat across her desk, piled high with maps and charts, stones and rocks. A stiff breeze was coming in through the open window, blowing away the last remnants of the mist.

'I'm investigating the death of a man found in Priest Cove on Tuesday.'

She looked bewildered. 'I thought he was found dead on his boat?'

'That was Sir Bernard Crompton, an eminent skin specialist. Did you know him?'

'No. Never heard of him.'

'The man found in Priest Cove is Ralph Ackland.'

'My goodness!' She blinked hard. 'Ackland. Are you sure?'

'Yes.' Although he was still awaiting confirmation of fingerprints. 'I believe you knew him.'

'I did, more's the pity. I'm sorry if that sounds callous.'

It was no more than Ryga had come to expect. 'Were you expecting him to visit, Miss Wargrove?'

'No, and neither was Captain Strout or he would have told me.'

'Then Mr Ackland must have been here in a private capacity. You look doubtful about that — why?'

'Because I can't think of anyone who would *want* to invite him. He was universally loathed in these parts.'

'Including by yourself?'

'Yes.'

'Why?' Ryga asked. Mrs Marrack had already told him that Ackland had made Miss Wargrove cry, after which she had been determined to stand up to him. She considered her response before answering.

'He was arrogant, vindictive and pompous. Not just to me but to everyone. I know one shouldn't speak ill of the dead and all that stuff, but I think you'll be hard pressed to find anyone in these parts who has a good word to say about him.'

That was certainly proving correct.

'He was a mine inspector with the Ministry of Fuel and Power, as you probably already know. And when he came here he made his presence felt in an odious way.'

'To you in particular, Miss Wargrove?'

'Oh yes. I was in a position he thought best served by the male of the species. Not that he so much as mentioned it, but there are other ways to make you feel humiliated and hurt.'

Miss Enys's words came back to Ryga of how Ackland had treated her sister. 'Please go on. I need to understand him.'

'In order to get his killer? I hope you never do,' she said with force.

Another one.

'I know that's wicked of me to say, and wrong, but it's what anyone around here who came across him will tell you. He went about as though he despised everyone. He never said as much outright, or was openly coarse or rude, but he had a silent sneer about him.'

Ryga had met that type before. It still wasn't unusual to find a certain class of person who thought detectives were tradesmen or lower. And some people considered themselves to be above the law.

'It didn't help that he didn't have any idea about the mines, which wouldn't have mattered a jot if he had admitted it. But he never *tried* to understand, and he never went down. If he had done so, even if he had shown how much he hated it, or was afraid, the men would have been more generous and respectful towards him. They'd have understood that.'

She was certainly backing up what Strout had told him. He'd come back to how Ackland had treated her later. 'Can you tell me more about his role here?'

'He'd come down from London fairly regularly, especially during the war, less so after it and only a couple of times since the mines have been denationalized and handed back to the owners and licensees. During the war we had several mines and quarries operating, the latter also his responsibility. Many of those have ceased now. He used to receive regular reports from the captains, which were copied to my superior, Mr Heeley, and to me. Mr Heeley died three years ago and I was promoted.'

She paused for a moment before resuming. Ryga got the impression she had liked Mr Heeley.

'Sometimes Mr Heeley would go with Mr Ackland. Other times Mr Ackland would go alone. A car was always put at his disposal and, of course, the petrol ration was granted from the government. I went with him only once, when Mr Heeley was indisposed. It's a journey I'll never forget. Mr Ackland never said a single word to me. At first I tried to make conversation but it was as though I didn't exist. I was hurt. He made me feel so small and insignificant.'

Again into Ryga's head flashed Miss Enys's words about her sister.

'Then I got angry, but I bit my tongue because I had the feeling that was exactly what he wanted, so that he could complain about me and have me removed from my job. It was all right if I sat in on the meetings and took notes like a dutiful secretary, but as soon as Mr Heeley asked my views as a geologist, or I had a geological point to raise, Mr Ackland would look right through me and defer to Mr Heeley, even though Mr Heeley was full of praise for me and reiterated why I was there and in the job. I'd been doing it since 1940 when the then council geologist, Michael Rowberry, became an adviser to the army in North Africa and was sadly killed on active service.'

'Do you come from a mining background? I'm genuinely interested, not questioning your abilities.'

'I can see that. And yes, I do. My grandfather was a Cornish miner who took himself and his family off to Australia in 1851. The mines over there were just opening as ours were in decline and our miners had the expertise Australia needed. My grandfather did well. My father was educated and became a mining engineer. I studied geology and came to England for the first time in 1935. I never went back.'

Hence that hint of an accent he'd picked up behind the slight Cornish burr.

'I met my fiancé here. Sadly, he was killed in the Spanish Civil War.' She broke off and bit her nail. 'I decided to stay. I love it here and I was fortunate enough to get a position as assistant to Mr Heeley. As my work was deemed vital to the war effort, advising on the mines and quarries and the building of airfields, I didn't get called up. Now I advise on road and house building, in addition to still giving advice to the remaining mines and quarries, but they're getting few and far between. Both industries won't survive here for much longer, especially the mines — there's a world capacity surplus and a drop in commercial demand. America will soon have enough for their strategic and stockpiling initiative — an act they passed in 1946,' she explained to Ryga's baffled look. 'It's to stockpile the minerals they need. And Russia started exporting tin for the first time last year. The market will soon be flooded, prices will fall and the mines will go. Tourism is supposed to take their place. It's deemed that the geology of our coast will be of interest to walkers, of whom we get quite a few already, and to amateur as well as professional geologists.'

'It's the rocks that I'm particularly interested in — not for myself,' Ryga quickly added. 'It's connected with my investigation. What's the composition at Priest Cove?'

She eyed him curiously. 'Mainly granite, which varies from a greyish colour to pink or orange towards the north at the contact with the Mylor Slate Formation. Minerals within the granite include quartz, and can also include rutile, zircon and apatite; these are typically best observed using a microscope.'

'How about these?' Ryga removed the two envelopes from his mackintosh pocket and emptied them separately on her desk. 'Would these have come from Priest Cove?'

She picked up a magnifying glass and sat forward, examining them. A door slammed and footsteps clipped past the room.

'They could have done, they're granite with apatite. See the greenish strands?' He did. 'But they could also have come from the St Austell district.'

'Could they easily be picked up off the shore or would someone have had to chip them from a rock?'

'Both. A geologist's hammer can do the latter. Hold on.' She rose and crossed to a cabinet, where she retrieved an implement and put it in front of him. He could see that it had a flat square head on one end of the small shaft, and a chisel on the other.

She said, 'The edge of the flat head is used to deliver a blow to a rock with the intention of splitting it. The chisel is used to clear loose material and vegetation, or to clear exposures. Sometimes it can be used to pry open fissures, but you risk damaging the material then. Some rocks can be easily split, like slate or shale, to reveal a fossil.'

A lethal weapon in the wrong hands. But Ackland had been shot, not bludgeoned.

She resumed her seat. 'These specimens could have come from the shore at Priest Cove or one of the other coves along that coast. Alternatively, someone could have chipped away at the granite and prised these out.' She turned one of them over. 'It's possible that one large piece was broken up into these ten pieces.'

That meant it was someone who knew the area, and how to break up rock. A miner perhaps? Strout? Or a geologist. Her? 'Can you think of any reason why two dead men might have these in their pockets?'

She raised her eyebrows. 'Did they? No, I can't.' Then she added thoughtfully, 'Unless they thought them to be valuable.'

'Are they?'

'Apatite can be used as a gem but that's rare. And it would be blue apatite, not granite with a trace of apatite in it. No, these rocks aren't valuable in either monetary or geological terms — not even artistically; they're too small. But I'm not an artist.'

Had the two men been conned into believing a rich source of apatite had been found in Priest Cove and with investment could be mined to make both wealthy? But he couldn't see Ackland parting with his money from what he had learned about him. And he didn't think Sir Bernard would have been duped either.

She looked at her wristwatch. 'I'm sorry, I have to go. I'm due at the Catallack Mine in half an hour to see Captain Strout about a possible new vein. Hence my wearing trousers.'

Ryga had never seen Eva in anything but trousers. 'I hope I haven't held you up,' he said, rising.

'Not at all.' She grabbed her coat from the stand and Ryga opened the door for her.

'Did you know Mr Ackland was Miss Enys's brother-in-law?'

'Yes. I was at Tregarris House with Mr Ackland when Miss Enys showed up. This was in wartime. I was taken aback when he greeted her by her Christian name. Afterwards, she told me about her sister and how much she despised Mr Ackland. She said he had bullied her sister into an early grave. And I can believe that.' They descended the stairs. 'Jory can't stand him either — that's Mr Logan, he's the licensee.' Her expression clouded over. 'I don't think he'll have it for much longer though, not solely because the mine won't be making enough money for him or the shareholders, despite Captain Strout's possible new vein, but because . . .' She paused outside. 'Mr Logan's had it tough, what with the war, then losing his child and wife. His heart's gone out of it and out of this area.'

'I'd like to talk to him.'

'I'll take you over there now if you wish, but I expect you have a car.'

'I don't, as it happens.'

'Then climb in.'

She was a competent driver. The car, a Morris, was a little more comfortable than Miss Enys's old Ford. On their way across the pitted landscape that was now becoming familiar to him, she gave a running commentary of where the old mine shafts were situated and the geological make-up of the area. He asked if she went up to London to report to the ministry.

'I do but not as often as I used to during the war. In fact, I haven't been up there for some months.'

He wondered if that were true. There had been a slight hesitation in her voice.

'Did Mr Ackland ever mention Sir Bernard Crompton?'

'Not to me.'

They turned onto a rutted track. Ryga noted they were about a mile from the Catallack Mine. Ahead, a metallic sea stretched out before them. After about a quarter of a mile, she branched off right and drove along a weed-strewn drive towards a squarely built stone house, set on the clifftop facing out to sea. In the distance to the right, he saw the tall chimney of the mine.

She drew to a halt behind a battered Rover with a dented bumper and skew-whiff number plate. 'That's Jory's but it doesn't mean he's in. He often walks to the mine. This house is far too big for one person and Jory hates it now that Charlotte's gone. He has a char, Lizzie, who's a miner's wife, and Mrs Masterman, a farmer's wife, cooks for him of a couple of times a week and plates meals for him, but he doesn't eat enough.'

Ryga noted her concern for Logan, which he felt was more than professional.

'Most of the rooms are shut up.'

The weather-worn oak door opened to reveal a thin man with a harrowed face. His expression darkened at the sight of Ryga, and Miss Wargrove quickly introduced him. Logan's expression relaxed. He stretched out a hand. 'I thought you might be someone from the ministry, or from that wretched mining committee. You're here about Ackland, I take it.'

His dark eyes were restless and haunted. His face, like his frame, was lean with deep lines etched on it. Ryga found it difficult to put an age on him. He was most probably mid-thirties but he looked about twenty years older.

'If you can spare me a moment, sir.'

Miss Wargrove intervened. 'I'll head over to the mine. I'll see you there, Jory. If you'd like to bring Inspector Ryga with you when you've finished, I'll take him back to Penzance, unless there's somewhere else you need to be, Inspector.'

'If it's no trouble.'

'None whatsoever,' she answered brightly, climbing back in the car.

Logan said, 'Come in, Inspector, and I'll tell you how much I loathed Ralph Ackland.'

CHAPTER ELEVEN

Ryga thought he could write the script by now. It came as no surprise when Logan announced, 'He was pompous, condescending, rude and a bully.'

They were seated in a spacious room with a magnificent view out to the Atlantic and a wilderness of a garden in between the house and the clifftop. The furniture was old and worn, the wallpaper faded and torn in places, the rugs, once good, bore only faint traces of their once bold patterns. It was as though the room had given up on its occupant long ago. Ryga felt tense as he faced a man who had gone through the same harrowing experience as he had in a POW camp. But Logan's had been so much worse, given what they had learned since the end of the war about the atrocities inflicted on prisoners by the Japanese.

Logan reached for the cigarette box on a side table. Ryga noticed two fingers of his right hand were missing. He refused the offer of a cigarette. Logan lit up with a lighter taken from the pocket of his sturdy, grubby trousers and drew on the cigarette, exhaling jerkily, as though he wasn't used to smoking.

'When did you last see him, sir?' Ryga asked.

'November. I hoped it would be the last time and my wish has been granted.' The expression that crossed his battered features sent a cold chill down Ryga's spine.

'Was he due here this week, or over the weekend in connection with the mines?' Ryga knew he hadn't been but he wanted to see Logan's reaction.

'Not that I was informed of, but I wouldn't have put it past the blighter to spring a surprise visit. Although the mines have been handed back to us, there are still various government development boards and committees who dish out grants, and Ackland wrangled his way onto them. I'd like to tell them all to go to hell, but that means cutting off their funds and my fellow directors don't care for that.' He puffed at his cigarette. 'I'm thinking of chucking the whole thing in anyway. In fact, I told them that on Monday. I got sympathetic nods and comments about it being too soon after my wife's death, I'm still grieving and all that guff, but I tell you I'm sick of it all.' He leaped up and paced to the window. His restlessness was disturbing. It was though he wished to push back the walls. Ryga could see he was at the end of his tether, and despite what Logan had told his fellow directors, he clearly was still grieving for his wife and child.

He turned. 'I don't think the mine will be viable for much longer anyway, and I told the board that. They think the high prices will continue, but the market's been flooded and things are changing. The next dividends won't be what they've come to expect. They think I'm being pessimistic, but I'm not. Just realistic.' He strode back and stood before Ryga, shifting his feet as though he wished to rush off. He had barely smoked his cigarette, yet he stubbed it out in the ashtray with force. Straightening up, he stared at Ryga with eyes that didn't see him. 'It's not the same, nothing is.'

Ryga knew instantly what Logan meant. Hadn't he experienced it himself on his return to England? He rarely talked about it. In fact, he didn't think he ever had, save only once, briefly, to Eva. Before he knew it, he was saying,

'You cling on to the life you had before; it's the one thing that helps to keep you going — the dreams, the wishes, the thoughts that one day it will end and you'll be back to where you were. But when you return, the world you left behind has changed and so have you.'

'You know!' Logan's head whipped up and he stared at Ryga with a mixture of awe and wariness.

'Yes.'

'Where?'

'Germany. Four years. I had it better than you.'

'It was still tough though.'

Ryga nodded.

Logan took a breath. 'Were you married?'

'No.'

Logan threw himself into the chair. 'Being cut off from the news, and everything that was happening here on the home front, meant you had no conception of what people were experiencing. No idea of how things had changed. Returning was far more disorientating than I had ever expected. Were you a police officer before?'

'No. I was in the Merchant Navy. Our ship was seized by a German raider in forty-one. After the war I was fortunate to be released from the Merchant to join the police. I had a very good sponsor.' George Simmonds, a fellow prisoner and senior police officer. Simmonds and his wife had also found it difficult to adjust, as Ryga had witnessed in Kent on a recent investigation.

'So you started a completely different life and career. Did it help?'

'Yes. I miss the sea, but I love my job.'

'Even if it means catching innocent people and seeing them hanged.' Logan scowled.

Ryga regarded him steadily. Had he killed Ackland? Was he about to confess? But why would he murder Ackland? 'I catch those who have broken the law. My job is to get to the truth and ensure that all the evidence points to the guilty party, not the innocent. Sentencing is the judge's duty.'

118

Ryga held Logan's tormented eyes. A blackbird broke into full song. That hadn't changed, thank the Lord. The tension eased a little.

Logan took out another cigarette but he didn't light it. 'When I returned I couldn't focus on anything. Work or my marriage. Poor Charlotte, my wife, she had a terrible time with me. You see, I'd idealized her. In my mind I'd painted a picture of a woman who didn't exist. She was so different when I came home, and so was I. Instead of the confident, well-built man she'd waved off, there was a skeleton of a human being. Nervous, distrustful, exhausted. Strout saw that. He's a gem of a man, Inspector.' His expression softened before the hardness returned. 'I was a wreck. I decided to go to one of those Civil Resettlement Units the War Office had set up.'

'I read about them. They did some good work. I was fortunate that the Thames River Police helped me to readjust.' Ryga left unsaid that he still at times found it hard to shake off the nightmares, such as those recently experienced on Sir Bernard's boat. He didn't need to tell Logan that. He could see the man suffered the same.

'Dr Bergmann first mentioned them to me,' Logan continued. 'I shied away from it, thinking it would be a camp, but it wasn't. It was in a country house in Devon. There was no queuing for food, we were waited on hand and foot. There was no distinction between officers and ranks. There were vocational courses, talks, and a medical officer on hand and others to talk to, if you wanted to. It gave me time to try and gather myself together. I returned here, and Charlotte and I tried to pick up the pieces of our lives and marriage. We were delighted when we found she was having a baby. It had taken me a while to function as a man again. Then she had two miscarriages, but the third time things went well. That was until the child was born. It died six months later, then Charlotte went too.' He suddenly sat up. 'But you haven't come here to talk about my life and problems. I can't tell you anything about who killed Ackland.'

119

Ryga wasn't so sure about that. 'Did you know Sir Bernard Crompton?'

'I don't think so.'

'You don't seem so sure.'

'The name sounds familiar.' He rubbed a hand across his forehead.

'He was an eminent dermatologist with a practice in Harley Street.'

'I might have seen his nameplate then. Our company's head office is at the end of Harley Street.'

'You didn't know he was cruising around Cornwall on his boat?'

'No reason why I should.'

'Where were you over the weekend, Mr Logan?'

'Is that when Ackland was killed?'

Ryga didn't answer.

'I went to the mine on Saturday morning then I caught the night train up to London at 8.45 p.m. for the board meeting on Monday, and the night train back that day at 9.50 p.m., getting into Penzance on Tuesday morning.'

Ryga could easily verify that. He reached into his coat pocket and withdrew one of the paper envelopes labelled 'Ackland' and laid the rock pieces out on the table. 'Do you recognize these, sir?'

Logan stared down at the stones. 'Granite and with what looks like apatite in them.'

'Do you know where they might have come from?'

'Around here somewhere. Miss Wargrove will know, but then you must have already asked her.'

'Any idea why they should be in Mr Ackland's pocket?'

'Were they?' He spoke as though he couldn't care less and Ryga thought he couldn't. 'I need to get over to the mine. We can talk in the car if you have any further questions but I've nothing more to add about Ackland, except to say he was a hideous man, and no one is the worse for him having departed this world, not like some who deserved to live.'

But Ryga had changed his mind about going back to Penzance with Miss Wargrove. 'I'll walk back to St Just. It's not far. There's something I need to discuss with Sergeant Marrack.' There wasn't specifically, but Marrack might have more information for him from his enquiries. It wasn't that though. Ryga needed air and exercise to clear his head and lift the depression that Logan had caused in him.

Maybe Logan saw this. He shrugged. 'Please yourself.'

Outside, Ryga stretched out his hand. Logan took it in a firm grasp, and as they connected, their shared experiences flew between them like an electric current. Ryga felt Logan's pain. He felt his anger, bewilderment and frustration. Despite what Logan had said, the Civil Resettlement Unit hadn't worked its magic. Ryga knew nothing could for some people.

As he set off for St Just he sincerely hoped that Jory Logan hadn't killed Ackland, but he was very much afraid he had. The thought tormented him as he trudged the countryside to St Just, barely noticing a thing around him. Despite what he had told Logan about his job being only to catch lawbreakers, not to sentence them, he didn't want to be the one to arrest Logan and see him imprisoned once again, or hanged. He would derive no satisfaction from solving the case if that were so. Perhaps Logan would be classed as being mentally unbalanced, but even then he would be locked away in an asylum, and that wasn't right for a man who had suffered as he had.

Ryga felt sorry for him. No, it was more than that. This kind of sorrow burrowed deep into the pit of his stomach. It caused his body to stiffen as though with rage, not pity. Yes, anger for what the man had endured and was still enduring. But anger was no use to anyone, especially to oneself. He'd learned that in the camp. It couldn't be focused on anyone or any one thing. It was too big for that. But if you let it, it would fester inside you and poison everything and everyone you touched. Had Logan focused his anger on something tangible, an individual? Ackland? How would Logan have seen Ackland? Sneering, superior, condescending. A man without empathy and understanding. One who had led a comfortable life in war-torn Britain, who had taken Logan's hospitality, had escaped from the London bombs, had never experienced a moment's pain, doubt, anguish, fear. Oh yes, Logan had evidently felt anger towards Ackland. Enough to shoot him in the face? Ryga thought so.

His spirits lifted when he was greeted by the cheerful Mrs Marrack and her husband, who was just finishing his dinner. Ryga hastily waved Marrack back into his seat and to continue with his pudding, apologizing for disturbing him. He refused Mrs Marrack's offer of something to eat but settled for a cup of tea, which, despite his wishes, was accompanied by a large slice of cake. And it was welcome. He ate while Marrack quickly polished off his rhubarb pie and custard, after which he reported back. All his news was negative. No one had seen or heard a car or a boat approach Priest Cove. The coastguards hadn't spotted the *Patricia Bee* out to sea.

Ryga told the sergeant and Mrs Marrack that he had spoken to Captain Strout, Miss Wargrove and Mr Logan, and all claimed to have no idea why Ackland had come to Cornwall. He saw Mrs Marrack study him curiously. He suspected she wanted to ask him what he had made of Logan. He would, but not yet; he still needed to digest his feelings where that man was concerned.

He caught the bus to Penzance, where he headed for the railway station. Thirty-five minutes later he had confirmation that Jory Logan had bought a ticket for Paddington for the Saturday night outward journey on the 8.45, returning on Monday night on the 9.50. Ryga's relief told him that he was desperate for this killer not to be Logan. The ticket collector had seen Logan arrive around quarter to ten, then board the train on Saturday. But Ryga had to check with the sleeping-berth attendant that Logan had stayed on board that train and not alighted elsewhere and returned to Priest Cove to kill Ackland, and had then been driven up to London by an accomplice or taken his own car.

It was now late afternoon and he made his way to the mortuary, hoping that Dr Plumley had completed his work. He had, just. He looked pink, tired and irritable. As he washed his hands, he tersely delivered his report.

'Sir Bernard Crompton had some hardening of the arteries, arthritis in his right shoulder and hands, and an enlarged prostate. Other than that, he was generally in good health.' Plumley wiped his hands on the towel. 'There was no obvious evidence he'd been drugged. I've sent tissue and blood samples for analysis, but it will only confirm that his death was due to natural causes.'

'If his heart was sound, why should he suddenly die?'

'People do.'

'Of what?' Ryga persisted.

'A brain seizure, which I am unable to detect, despite studying that organ and dissecting it.'

Ryga held Plumley's cold stare. 'Could he have been frightened to death?' he asked.

'He had normal cardiac findings, so he did not suffer a heart attack induced by shock or terror. Nor was he shot, strangled or bludgeoned, and if that disappoints you, Inspector, then I can't help it. There is no murder there for you. Not so your second corpse, which is obviously murder even to the lay man.' Plumley consulted his pocket watch. Ryga almost expected him to say 'seven minutes and counting'.

'Ackland was shot at point-blank range — that is, less than three feet. The bullet entered just above the nose and was embedded in the skull. I've dug it out for you. It's over there.' He tossed his head at a dish by the side of the slab where Ackland's covered body lay. 'You can send it up to the ballistic expert at the Yard but I'd say it's from a Webley Mark VI revolver. I've seen enough of them in my time to recognize one.'

Ryga knew that Plumley had served as a young medic in the Great War when Webleys were used by British army officers. He'd also served as a doctor in the last war when Enfields replaced Webleys.

'To be shot at such close quarters means he must have known his killer and was taken by surprise,' Ryga said.

'He knew nothing about it.' Plumley stretched his plump arms into his suit jacket. 'He was already dead.'

Ryga's head spun.

Plumley continued. 'Although it appears on the surface that his death was caused by the bullet wound, I examined the face and head in detail. I found blunt-force trauma at the back of the skull, which might or might not have been the fatal blow, but which would certainly have rendered him unconscious. He was then bludgeoned in the face, and that would certainly have killed him, after which he was shot.'

'But why shoot him if he was already dead?'

'That's for you to find out, Inspector.' Plumley made for the mortuary door.

'Can you tell me what kind of weapon was used?'

'A stick, iron bar, hammer? Difficult to make out but delivered with fury.'

Ryga shuddered. His mind flew to the implement Miss Wargrove had shown him that morning, the type geologists used.

'Was he restrained at any time?'

'There's no evidence of that on his wrists or ankles. He might have been gagged, though the facial wounds are too extensive to say if he was. He was a fairly fit man. No fractures save those in his skull, and no major operations as far as I can see. And he wasn't drugged or poisoned. You can wait for the test results but they'll only confirm what I've told you.'

'Time of death?'

'For Sir Bernard, the early hours of Monday. For Ackland, a little more difficult as his cadaver was exposed to the elements for some time. I'd say he was killed late Sunday night or the early hours of Monday.' He pushed open the door. 'You'll have my full reports tomorrow. I'll see you at the inquests.'

CHAPTER TWELVE

Ryga found Pascoe with the local newspaper in front of him. 'Your press statement's in, guv. We might get a response. And I've got those sea charts. I've also got some interesting information from the harbour master.'

Ryga took the envelopes containing the rock pieces from his mackintosh and hung it up as Pascoe continued.

'The *Patricia Bee* didn't put in at Penzance Harbour or Newlyn on Friday, Saturday or Sunday, but one boat did, here in Penzance. The owner of it we know. Miss Enys.'

'When?'

'Saturday, very early morning. The harbour master said she must have come in just after high water to have moored up along the quayside. That would have been between 3.29 a.m. and 4.30 a.m.'

'That's a very early morning sail. Even if she had arrived at the latter time, it's still an hour before sunrise. Could she really have managed that? What was the weather like on Saturday morning?'

'Calm, dry and clear. Miss Enys has a small outboard on her boat. And, according to the harbour master, she's a very good sailor. She often puts in here. She knows the harbours and coves like the back of her hand.'

'Including Priest Cove,' Ryga mused.

'Must do. She paid harbour dues for the day, although the harbour master didn't recall seeing her again. The boat wasn't there on high water in the afternoon at 3.58 p.m.'

'She didn't tell me this when I said Ackland had arrived at Penzance on Saturday morning on the Paddington express. I can't see Ackland getting into her small boat, not from what I've heard about him. Not only because he didn't think much of his sister-in-law, nor she of him, but because it would have been beneath his dignity.'

'Perhaps he wasn't given any choice. She threatened or blackmailed him into getting aboard.'

Ryga looked doubtful.

'I suppose it is dubious,' Pascoe admitted. 'Because nobody I spoke to saw a man get on her boat. And even if he did, where was he all the time that boat was in the harbour? And where was she? Her boat only has a small cuddy for limited shelter, she couldn't just have been sitting on board for hours. The harbour master said he'd ask around for any-one who might have seen her or anyone fitting Ackland's description.'

Ryga told him about his interview with Miss Wargrove and subsequently with Jory Logan, without mentioning the emotions Logan had stirred in him. He finished with relaying Plumley's results on the autopsies.

'Two people must have had a hand in Ackland's death,' Pascoe proclaimed. 'Because why would one person take the trouble to bludgeon him and then shoot him? It's usually the other way around, if at all, and only because the killer thinks he'll hide the identity of the corpse, which he won't because of fingerprints. Which reminds me, the desk sergeant took a message from Sergeant Jacobs. He has the results of the fingerprints we sent up.'

Ryga rose and reached across to the phone on Pascoe's desk. The sergeant made to move but Ryga indicated for him to stay put. He asked to be connected to the Yard. While he waited, Pascoe continued.

'I suppose the person who fired the gun might not have known Ackland was already dead.'

'Surely he could have seen that from the extent of the wounds.'

'Not if it was dark, and according to Dr Plumley's estimated time of death it would have been.'

'He could have used a torch.' Ryga's mind flicked to the tunnel behind where the body had been found.

'Perhaps the killer did shoot him after bludgeoning him to make sure he *was* dead. A belt-and-braces job, and a vicious one at that.'

'Or, as you suggested, it was two people. The first struck Ackland and ran off in a terrible state. He confessed what he had done to the second person, who went to make sure the job was finished, and to try and disguise the blows to the face and retrieve the murder weapon, which the first person had dropped in his or her panic.'

'Her? Surely a woman couldn't have done that to his face?' Pascoe said, astonished.

'I think one could, if she was in a state of fury. Yes, I'll hold,' Ryga said into the receiver. 'Miss Enys has a motive. She blames Ackland for the death of her sister. She's also walking with the aid of a very stout stick, on account of her ankle injury, which could have been used to strike him, according to Plumley. And I'd like to know if she has a Webley. She told me her father was in the army, so it's possible. But why would she wait until now to kill him when her sister has been dead for ten years?'

'Perhaps it was the first real opportunity she had. She'd planned it for some time. She managed to lure him down here on some pretext.'

'It would have to be a very strong one to get him here.'

'Money's a powerful incentive.'

'Those pieces of rocks? Yes, I'm still holding.' Ryga again addressed the voice on the other end of the telephone. 'If that's so, then she, or someone she's in league with, needed to involve Sir Bernard.'

'He could have been used as bait to draw Ackland here.'

Ryga had already considered that, hence his earlier instructions to Jacobs at the Yard to find out if a telegram or letter had been sent to Ackland from Cornwall, or a call put through the telephone exchange. 'Alternatively, Sir Bernard could have lured Ackland here with the purpose of killing him, but where's his motive? And how does it fit in with both men's properties being ransacked? Then there's Captain Strout, who also despised Ackland, but he's had ample opportunity to dispose of him over the years, and possibly without any comeback by making it look like an accident at the mine. Logan didn't know Ackland until a few years ago, but in that short time he came to hate him. It's possible his experiences in the war have brutalized him, or he's suffering from a complete mental breakdown after the tragedy of losing his wife and child, but why would he lash out so violently against Ackland?'

'He could have shot him to protect the real killer. Strout.'

'Ah, Jacobs is that you?'

'It is indeed, guv. But only just. I'm on my way out shortly. We've got another tip-off on those safe jobs, this time from a reliable source, Charlie Shrub. He's heard that our safecracking chummy might try a cinema in Charing Cross Road. Which one of the three though, we don't know, so we've brought in extra men and posted them at each. My money's on the Astoria as that has the same make of safe as two of the theatre jobs. And the basement ballroom means it'll be carrying extra money. It's where I'll be holed up for the night.'

'Well, the best of luck with it. And don't go tripping the light fandango and break a leg.'

Jacobs chuckled.

Ryga half wished he was still on that job in London; that way his nightmares wouldn't have returned and he wouldn't be faced with the dilemma of apprehending someone for murder who he had no wish to arrest. But a police officer, he silently scolded himself, couldn't afford sentiments like that. 'Tell me what you've got.'

'The fingerprints taken from Ackland's body match those we found on the personal items in his apartment. So he's definitely the murder victim. Others you took on the boat match those taken from Sir Bernard's body and from his house. There are some though from the boat that don't match either man.'

'They'd be Dr Bergmann's and the lifeboat man. Send down what you have by motorcyclist. We need them in time for the inquests tomorrow and we'll check the unknown prints with the doctor's and the lifeboat man's. The latter's we have. Anything else?'

'We're still waiting on the telegraph office. We've been a bit pushed, guv, so haven't chased them up. However, I reinterviewed Ackland's boss at the ministry and pressed him harder for information. It didn't take much to make him admit that Ackland was extremely unpopular. He's been shunted around more times than a steam train. Changing offices within the department, being promoted to move him on, given special projects — which, reading between and under the lines, were created to get him out of people's hair. But he could never be got rid of. Everyone breathed a sigh of relief when Ackland said he was considering early retirement, and they're not sorry to hear he's dead.'

'Not a very good obituary. But it matches with what I've been told. Did he say why he was thinking about retiring?'

'He was expecting to be knighted in the King's New Year Honours.'

Ryga whistled. 'I didn't think he was that senior a civil servant.'

'Oh, he was in rank, but rarely had departmental responsibility. As I said, everyone wanted shot of him. It was hinted that Ackland would be put on the list if he considered going. You know what they say about incompetence? Either promote or sack, and with Ackland it was promotion at every turn, with the ultimate, a knighthood — or would have been, if he'd lived.'

'It seems a rather dramatic and undeserved reward for someone universally hated and incompetent.'

'There is another thought. Perhaps he'd gathered information on those in power and with influence who didn't wish to have their dirty secrets — whatever they might be — exposed. He used that to get what he wanted.'

'A blackmailer. Yes, I can see that, given what I've learned of his character. Could that have happened in his relationship with Sir Bernard Crompton?' Ryga mused aloud. 'It would provide a motive for Sir Bernard having killed him. See if you can get anything more on Sir Bernard and Ackland. I might have to force the pace here, start making accusations and confronting my suspects, but I'm convinced that will serve no purpose. Everyone is united in their hatred for Ackland. And I don't know where Sir Bernard fits into this yet. Get someone to chase up the telegraph office tomorrow if you can. Put me through to the chief — oh, and Jacobs, hope you get chummy tonight.'

Street came on the line pretty quickly and Ryga brought him up to speed with all he had learned about Ackland, of Dr Plumley's findings and what he and Jacobs had discussed about a motive possibly being blackmail. Pascoe was listening in to Ryga's end of the conversation, his expression showing concern and astonishment in all the key places.

'I'll update the AC,' Street said. 'You'd better report in to Major Tweed.'

Ryga wasn't looking forward to that but it had to be done. He anticipated the response he would get and he was correct. During his relaying of what he had gleaned — albeit not in quite as much detail as he'd given Street — Tweed interjected with the occasional 'poppycock', 'rubbish', 'nonsense' and snorts.

Ryga replaced the receiver. 'Major Tweed believes a gang from London killed Ackland, brought his body down by boat, dumped him in the cove and then returned to the Smoke.'

Pascoe smiled. 'It's imaginative. I'll give him that.'

'Major Tweed also believes I'm an imbecile who couldn't direct traffic let alone solve a murder.'

'Then we'd better prove him wrong.'

'Nothing would delight me more. He'll be at my meeting with the coroner tomorrow morning. I shouldn't think I'll have anything new to tell him but let's have a look at those navigation charts.'

Pascoe spread them out on his desk after putting the typewriter on the floor. There were maps from Scotland down the west coast to Cornwall and Devon.

Ryga reached for his briefcase and removed the navigational instrumentation he'd taken off the *Patricia Bee*. Beginning to use them on the charts, he continued, 'We know he started from Rosneath, where he took possession of the *Patricia Bee* on Friday the thirteenth of April and that he put in at Troon. At eight knots per hour and with the right weather, that would have taken him about two to three hours. It's a little over twenty-one nautical miles. The Troon harbour master said the *Patricia Bee* stayed there overnight. From there he could have gone on to Stranraer. That would have taken him five to six hours, depending on the tides and weather. Then he could have sailed down to Whitehaven.' Ryga wondered what he would have done if he'd been skipper. He did some more measuring. 'I'd have then put in to Rhyl or Holyhead. Sir Bernard could have been joined by a valet at any of these ports. Then there's Aberystwyth, New Quay, Cardigan, Fishguard, Tenby, Swansea, Bude. But to reach the position where his boat was found means he didn't put into all of them.'

'He could have gone into Bristol after Tenby then down to Padstow, our Newquay, or St Ives.'

'I'd say that would have taken him too long. But we'll try a two-pronged approach tomorrow. I'll contact the harbour masters at Stranraer, Whitehaven, Rhyl and Holyhead. You see if you can pick him up at a Cornish port — Padstow, Newquay or St Ives.'

The desk sergeant put his head round the door. 'A Mr Chapman has just been in to say he's read the article in the newspaper and says he saw a man fitting Ackland's description on Saturday morning about 8.40 getting into a car along Wharf Road.'

'That sounds hopeful,' Pascoe said.

'Show him in,' Ryga said eagerly.

'I can't, sir, he was on his way to work and couldn't hang about. He drives for Melbury's and is on a long-distance route tonight so won't be back until tomorrow morning. That's his address.'

Pascoe took the piece of paper. 'I'll talk to him in the morning. Is there anything more you'd like me to do tonight?' he asked Ryga.

'No, you get off home.'

'Are you OK on the *Patricia Bee*? The offer of a bed still stands, as does joining us for a meal.'

'Thank you, but I'm fine,' Ryga lied. Maybe, though, he'd get a better night's sleep.

CHAPTER THIRTEEN

Friday 11 May

He didn't. Jory Logan's haunted, cadaverous face swam before him, along with the shouts of the guards and the smell of fear, the shivering in the freezing fog and snow, and the sweating fatigue in the sweltering heat of summer, and with it, the buzzing of those disgusting flies.

He shot up from the temporary bed in the saloon and vigorously doused his face in ice-cold water as though trying to cleanse himself of the nightmares. The tremors were back but, determined to ignore them, he made a pot of hot, strong tea and took a cup up on deck, where he watched the sun rise and the tide come in and some fishing boats sail out. Gradually, the sea and nature performed their healing miracles and, after shaving and changing, he walked briskly to Penzance. There he telephoned the harbour master at Stranraer but wasn't able to speak to him. He left a message regarding the possible putting in of the *Patricia Bee* and asked to be called back. He didn't have time to telephone Whitehaven, Rhyl and Holyhead. He'd do that later. Pascoe had left him a note to say he had gone to interview Mr Chapman and before doing so had called Newquay and

Padstow. Both harbour masters had said the *Patricia Bee* hadn't put in there. The St Ives harbour master had been out. Pascoe had asked for him to telephone Penzance police station when he was able to.

Ryga was early for his meeting with the coroner but, despite that, Major Tweed had beaten him to it, and as usual the chief constable was not in the best of tempers.

'I've told Mr Gregory that it's perfectly clear Sir Bernard died from shock and guilt, after falling out with Ackland and killing him.' Tweed sat stiff and glowering in a large leather seat opposite the coroner's desk.

That wasn't what he had said yesterday on the telephone. Obviously he'd thought the matter over and come up with a more realistic theory than a London gang.

'It's far from clear, Major,' Ryga contradicted, which caused Tweed to flush. 'If I might explain, sir,' he quickly continued, addressing the coroner, an amiable-looking man with intelligent eyes behind round tortoiseshell glasses.

'Please do, Inspector. Take a seat.'

'Thank you, sir.'

Tweed huffed and shifted.

Ryga set before them the facts of the investigation as he knew them. Exactly what he had told Tweed yesterday on the telephone. The coroner listened intently, while Tweed scoffed and sniffed his disapproval at intervals. Ryga ignored him. 'It is possible that Sir Bernard died from natural causes, and both Dr Bergmann and Dr Plumley will state that, but we haven't the results of the blood tests yet, which could indicate he was drugged. And we have no motive for why the two men would have argued, or why Sir Bernard would bludgeon Ackland to death and then shoot him in the face.'

Tweed looked about to say something, then snapped his mouth shut.

'I quite see that, Inspector, thank you,' Gregory calmly answered. 'And, in light of what you've said, I agree that you need more time to discover what really happened, if you can. I'll go through the formalities and adjourn.' He rose.

Tweed glowered at Ryga before stomping out ahead of Gregory, who raised his thin, grey eyebrows and gave Ryga a look as if to say, 'I know the Major of old, take no notice'.

Ryga made his way into the court, which was already beginning to fill. There were a few journalists, including two crime reporters he recognized from the national newspapers in Fleet Street. They nudged each other and gave him a thumbs up. He nodded a reply. Sitting beside them was a photographer. He wouldn't be able to take pictures in court but would slide away once he had noted all the major players and lie in wait outside to snap them as they came out. There were also several members of the public, mainly middle-aged women and elderly men, who had read about Ackland's and Sir Bernard's deaths and considered this a good morning's entertainment.

Ryga held back, waiting for PC Treharne. He wanted to know a little more about Pedrick, who he had glimpsed at the window of his house as he had walked past on his way to Penzance. Ryga had been tempted to call on him, especially when the man, obviously seeing him, had darted out of sight.

The court filled up further. There were now some young women carrying babies. PC Treharne entered and Ryga drew him aside.

'Do you know which hospital Mr Pedrick worked at when he was living in London?'

'No, sir, do you want me to ask him?'

'Leave it for now. Has he a boat?'

'No, sir. The stars and planets are more his thing.'

'Has he ever spoken about Sir Bernard Crompton? Possibly in connection with that rash on his face.'

'Eczema,' Treharne pronounced. 'My grandfather suffers dreadful from it, so I know it when I see it. Comes up worse when under stress.'

As Pedrick's was now.

Miss Enys entered with Dr Bergmann. Both looked his way before making to their seats. Behind them was Pascoe, looking pleased with himself.

'You have news?' Ryga asked as the sergeant joined him.
'Yes.'

But the court was called to order before Pascoe could continue.

Ryga was first on the stand to provide the name of the deceased, Sir Bernard Crompton, his occupation and address. He said that there was no next of kin to confirm identification and that Sir Bernard's previous housekeeper and secretary had been dismissed because of Sir Bernard's retirement, and, although the charlady, Mrs Marlow, could have confirmed the deceased's identity, Ryga had seen no need to bring her all the way to Cornwall to do so when they had formal identification from a photograph and from fingerprints.

Colin Blayde, the lifeboat man who had boarded the *Patricia Bee*, was next in respect of Crompton's death. His explanation of what had occurred didn't divert from what Ryga had read in his statement.

Next came PC Treharne, followed by Dr Bergmann. Ryga watched the latter carefully. He looked drawn but he gave his evidence calmly and professionally, which was what Ryga had expected. Bergmann reiterated that his original diagnosis remained unchanged — death due to natural causes, a seizure of some kind. This was confirmed by Dr Plumley, who followed Bergmann onto the stand. The coroner expressed the opinion that there were some questions yet to be answered surrounding the death, and blood tests to await, which drew a bristling frown from Plumley as though the coroner was doubting his medical competence. Tweed didn't look too happy about it either. Nor did Bergmann. Gregory adjourned the inquest for fourteen days. He immediately proceeded with the inquest on Ackland.

From where he was sitting, on a side bench, Ryga could see both Miss Enys's and Dr Bergmann's expressions — the first composed, the second strained. Bergmann shifted in his seat and pushed his hand through his hair, his body poised as though about to take flight, no doubt keen to return to his patients and his busy practice. Before the coroner could get underway, the door opened noisily and several people swung round in their seats. Jory Logan, with his hat in his hands, strode in. He paused, almost like an actor on stage, thought Ryga, then slid onto the bench on his right, causing those in it to shuffle along. His dark eyes seemed to have sunk deeper into his pinched face. His lips were drawn in a tight line.

Logan's timing was so perfect that Ryga wondered if he had been listening outside for the most effective time to make an entrance. He also wondered why he was here when he wasn't required to give evidence. Curiously, Miss Wargrove slipped quietly into the courtroom after him. Ryga's instinct told him they had prearranged a meeting outside. It confirmed his earlier thoughts that there might be more to their relationship than friendship and professional interest, certainly on her part. He wasn't sure on Logan's. Ryga had already surmised that Logan's wounds from the death of his wife and child hadn't healed, but perhaps he found some comfort in Miss Wargrove's kindness towards him. She took a seat in the row behind Logan. The reporters sat keenly forward. A hush descended on the court.

The first man to be called was the coastguard who had made the gruesome discovery through his binoculars and who had called Sergeant Marrack, who was first on the scene. Sergeant Marrack's testimony was followed by Dr Bergmann's. Then it was Ryga's turn. He could see the heightened interest in the crowd, knowing they were going to be disappointed. He gave the merest details, adding that the extent of the injuries to the face made it impossible for anyone to visually identify the victim, but this had been confirmed by fingerprints. Dr Plumley's testimony drew some gasps and mutterings though, as he stated that the deceased had been struck from behind and then bludgeoned before being shot at point-blank range when he was already dead. Time of death was sometime between late Sunday night and the early hours of Monday morning. The journalists' pencils flew across their pages. Ryga studied Miss Enys. She returned his gaze without emotion, her lean frame upright and stiff. Logan's too was impassive, while Miss Wargrove looked deeply troubled.

The coroner, having established the basic facts, again adjourned for fourteen days, as previously agreed with Ryga. Major Tweed rose, dashed Ryga a harsh glance and strode out.

There was a scuffle by the journalists to get out of the court and to a telephone to dictate the story, barging their way through the slow-moving people, who were keen to take their time and talk over the cases as they went, speculating, no doubt, on what had happened. Ryga deliberately hung back and watched as Logan, Miss Wargrove, Dr Bergmann and then Miss Enys left. At the door, the latter looked over her shoulder at him, but he couldn't read her expression. Quietly, he told Pascoe to slip out and observe them.

He spoke briefly to Plumley, who handed him a buff-coloured folder containing his reports, saying he was driving back to town. The inquests had taken just over an hour. Outside, Ryga saw Logan drive off. Pascoe's gaze followed the car before he turned to Miss Wargrove. Miss Enys approached Ryga. Her ankle was still bandaged, but it had healed enough for her to drive as her car was parked across the road.

'Do you think it will take you fourteen days to discover who killed Ralph?' she said.

'Possibly. Maybe even longer, unless you have something to tell me.'

She said nothing.

'Do you own a gun, Miss Enys?'

'Yes. It was my father's. I didn't shoot Ralph with it. Besides, it's not what killed him.'

The type of firearm used hadn't been revealed at the inquest. For now, Ryga would continue on the basis that Plumley's view that it was a Webley was correct.

'What kind is it?' he asked.

'A Webley Mark VI revolver.'

'And you have ammunition for it?'

'Of course. But I didn't fire it and you're welcome to check that. I only kept it in case the Nazis got here. I'd have taken the greatest pleasure in shooting a couple of them before they shot me.'

'Can you confirm where you were on Saturday morning?'

She looked at him askance. 'Ralph was alive then.'

He remained silent.

Her eyes narrowed. 'I see that you know. I was here in Penzance. That means nothing. I couldn't sleep. It was a clear night. I decided to take the boat out. I put in here not long after high water, about four o'clock.'

'Why?'

'Why not?'

'And you left when?'

'Just before high water in the afternoon. About three o'clock.'

'What did you do all day?'

'I walked back to Mousehole after putting in here and returned by bus in the afternoon.'

They would clarify that with the bus conductor. Ryga was certain he'd get confirmation because she wouldn't have lied about something so easy to check.

'Then I sailed the boat back to Mousehole.'

It was feasible. 'Did you see your late brother-in-law on Saturday morning?'

'You think I met him off the train? I didn't.'

'Thank you, Miss Enys.'

She looked puzzled at his abrupt end of questioning. 'Do you want to call in and see the gun?'

'Later.' *Let her wonder*, he thought, watching her hobble away. Who else would own such a weapon? The Bergmanns? Jory Logan? Captain Strout? He glanced over at Pascoe, who broke off his conversation with Miss Wargrove.

'It was certainly Ralph Ackland who got in the car Mr Chapman saw,' Pascoe reported. 'He gave a positive ID from the description, and the photograph that Miss Enys gave you confirms it. He's a reliable witness. Got his wits about him. It's a pity he didn't get the vehicle registration but he said it was a Rover with a dent in the rear bumper, a fender that was hanging slightly loose, and a crooked number plate. And I know whose car that is.'

So too did Ryga. Miss Wargrove had pulled up behind it at Tregarris House.

'I've just seen Mr Logan drive it away,' Pascoe said.

'Did Mr Chapman see who was driving it?'

'No. He just saw Ackland climb in. It drove off as he crossed the road behind it. I've asked the beat constable to make enquiries with the other residents and any passers-by for sightings. It being early Saturday morning though, it was quieter than on a weekday, so I'm not banking on getting anything more.'

'Logan left for London on Saturday evening,' Ryga reflected.

'But he wasn't here when Ackland was killed.'

'Not unless he got off that train and then drove up to London in the early hours of Monday morning, reaching there in time for the board meeting. Can you get Chief Inspector Jerram's car?'

'Yes.'

'Then let's collect it after some lunch and talk to Mr Logan.'

Ryga was in no hurry. He knew where Logan would be — if not at Tregarris House then at the mine. If Logan was the killer — and Ryga sincerely hoped he wasn't — then he wouldn't run away. Logan wasn't that type of man.

There was no Rover parked in front of the house and no answer to their knock when they reached there. Ryga told Pascoe to make for the mine, and a few minutes later, he pulled up behind the Rover with a battered rear bumper, a loose fender and a wonky number plate. They made for the office, where they heard upraised voices. Ryga indicated for Pascoe to stay back.

'You need to get away, Jory. For God's sake, forget this place and this bloody mine.' It was Strout.

'It will follow me wherever I go. How can I forget what he did?'

Ryga eased forward, but the telephone bell sounded, curtailing further eavesdropping. As he pushed open the door, the phone was still ringing. Both men jerked their heads towards him. Strout looked alarmed, Logan weary.

Strout snatched up the phone and bellowed into it. He listened for a moment as Logan waved them in, then snapped, 'I'll call you back.' He slammed down the receiver. 'What is it this time?'

'We'd like a word with Mr Logan, in private.'

'If you have—'

'It's all right, Ruan. I can deal with this.'

Strout hesitated, then picked up his hat and stomped out, slamming the door behind him with enough force to shake the grimy glass in the windows. Ryga could hear him calling to someone by the mine.

'Where were you on Saturday morning, Mr Logan?' Ryga demanded without preamble.

'I've already told you I was here at the mine.'

'What time?'

'I don't know. Early. I don't sleep well.'

'You drove your car here?'

'No, I walked. I often do.'

'So your car was left outside your house, unlocked?'

'Yes, of course. Why all the questions?'

'And what did you do in the afternoon?'

'I was here until two, walked home, had something to eat, dozed until it was time to catch the train to London.'

'Were you alone?'

'While at Tregarris, yes. The men and Captain Strout saw me here in the morning.'

'How did you get to Penzance?'

'I drove there.'

'And you left your car parked there?'

'Yes.'

'Where exactly?'

'I don't remember, some street by the railway station.' He sank heavily in Strout's battered leather swivel chair. It was as though he were afraid he might not have the strength to stay upright. He reached into the pocket of his jacket and withdrew a cigarette case. Extracting one, he tapped it against the case. 'You think I killed Ackland.'

'What time did you arrive in Penzance?'

'Five minutes before the train left. The ticket collector will confirm that.'

He already had, and that Logan had alighted from the return journey on Tuesday morning. But they hadn't asked if anyone had seen only Logan in that car on Saturday evening, and if it had been parked in Penzance until he had got back into it on Tuesday morning. An accomplice could have dropped Logan off not far from the station and driven onward to another station down the line, where Logan had alighted from the train and returned to Priest Cove to kill Ackland. But Ryga was still lacking a motive for him having done so. They would check for sightings of the parked car with the beat constable. Ryga could see Pascoe taking notes; he'd think of that himself.

'Did you loan your car to anyone on Saturday morning?'

'No.'

'Then how do you account for it being seen in Penzance shortly after eight thirty?'

'I can't because it wasn't there.' He put the cigarette in his mouth but didn't light it. Picking up a box of matches from the desk, his fingers played with it. 'Not unless someone took it from outside Tregarris, used it and then drove it back.' His eyes remained steadfastly on Ryga.

'We have a reliable witness who saw it.'

'Then either he or she is mistaken, needs spectacles or someone borrowed it without my knowledge, although I don't see why they should, or who it could be.'

But Ryga was certain Logan knew exactly who had taken it. Or he had driven it himself. Logan struck a match against the side of the box and lit his cigarette with a steady hand.

'What did you do on Sunday in London?'

'I had breakfast at the Great Western Royal Hotel, walked around, went to my club, slept, ate and slept again, or tried to.'

'We'll need the details of where you stayed.'

'The Overseas League. I went from there on Monday morning to the board meeting, which lasted until two o'clock. Then I had something to eat and drink at a nearby pub, and caught the night train back.'

'Do you own a gun?'

Logan drew on his cigarette before answering. Ryga was sure he saw amusement in those tired brown eyes. 'Yes.'

'What kind?'

'A Webley.'

'I'd like to examine it.'

'Please yourself.'

'I'd also like to look over Tregarris House.'

'What for?'

'Evidence that Ralph Ackland was there recently.'

Logan exhaled and laughed with bitterness. 'You think I picked him up from Penzance and drove him to Tregarris House. Well, I didn't, but go ahead.' He rose. 'The house is open. You won't find anything.'

'I'd like you to come with us.'

'You're arresting me?'

'No. I'd prefer you were with us while we search your house. And you can give us your gun.'

Logan crossed to the door and, throwing it open, called out to Strout, who was talking to a large man with a stoop.

'I'm to accompany Inspector Ryga and Sergeant Pascoe to Tregarris House, where they wish to conduct a search for evidence that I was entertaining Ackland before he was killed.'

Strout looked perturbed. He opened his mouth to speak but Logan continued. 'They will probably also wish to examine the interior of my car, as they think I picked up Ackland from the railway station on Saturday morning, instead of being here with you until early afternoon. And they suspect my gun might have been used to shoot him, and that I wasn't on the train to London but in Priest Cove.'

Ryga's senses were on full alert as he listened to this. He scrutinized Strout's face for any telltale signs because Ryga knew what Logan was doing. He should have separated them. Logan was telling Strout, *This is the story, so stick to it.*

Logan said, 'If they arrest me, don't bother to send for a solicitor.'

'I'll follow your car, sir,' Pascoe said.

'Yes, do that, why don't you,' Logan mocked. Ryga exchanged a glance with Strout. From his worried expression, Ryga could see that Strout, like him, knew that Logan was on the edge. It wouldn't take much to push him over. It wasn't a solicitor Logan needed, but a doctor.

CHAPTER FOURTEEN

Heading to Tregarris House, Pascoe said, 'It doesn't look good for him.'

'It does if the sleeping-berth attendant remembers him on the train the entire journey. But Logan could have an accomplice, and most probably has.' But who? Miss Enys? Would Logan go out of his way to help and protect her?

They pulled up outside the house. 'There's no one here,' Logan said, marching in, Ryga noticed, without needing to unlock the door. 'My cook, Mrs Masterman, has been and gone. The char comes in twice a week to do the downstairs rooms I use, and my bedroom and bathroom. This is not her day. And neither is Saturday or Sunday,' he added, waltzing through the hall. 'So you won't be able to check with her, or Mrs Masterman, who doesn't work Saturdays, and as I wasn't here on Sunday to have the roast dinner she usually plates up for me, you can't confirm that with her either, Inspector. No alibi for then. But I've got four board members in London who will tell you where I was on Monday.'

'I'd like Sergeant Pascoe to inspect the interior of your car.'

'The keys are in the ignition. And the stable block is unlocked if you want to poke your nose around it. But all you'll find is dust, cobwebs and rotting farm implements.'

Ryga handed Pascoe his murder case and the sergeant slipped out.

'Drink?' asked Logan, striding into the lounge.

'No, thank you.'

'Don't mind if I do.' He poured himself a stiff whisky. 'Where do you want to start? In here?' He waved the glass around the faded room.

'Upstairs. I'll work my way down.'

'Go ahead. You don't need me.'

'I'd prefer you to accompany me.'

Logan gave a twisted smile. 'In case I secrete some evidence while you're out of this room.'

Ryga smiled. 'Something like that.' Again he saw in Logan's eyes that connection between them. Their shared harrowing experience of the searches in the camps and the standing about outside for longer than necessary — in his case often in freezing cold, in Logan's in unbearable heat — and the punishments that followed whether warranted or not.

Logan tossed back the whisky. 'OK, let's get going.'

The stairs were dusty. The attic rooms more so, with cobwebs hanging from the ceiling, the windows grimy and the wallpaper peeling. The basic furniture — that of one-time servants, and latterly of evacuees or Bevin Boys — was broken, damp and dirty. There was no disturbance of dust to indicate anyone had set foot in them for months, years.

Descending to the first floor, Ryga said, 'Did you have help while your wife was alive?'

Logan tensed at the word 'alive', but his voice was even when he spoke. 'We did, but there are enough rooms on this floor to accommodate them. We had a daily help and a live-in maid, Mary. Shortly after Charlotte died, she married a mechanic and moved to Lynmouth in Devon. Her husband was offered a job there in a garage. We also had a cook-cum-housekeeper, Mrs Knowles, widowed. She died not long after Charlotte. Mrs Knowles was here during the war.'

Mrs Marrack had told Ryga that.

'Albert, her husband, was my father's gardener and May — Mrs Knowles — was a maid then. We used to have a few servants when times were good before the war, but the fortunes of the mines go up and down and the number of servants with them. There are six rooms on this floor, that's my bedroom and the bathroom next to it.' He indicated the rooms on his left. 'The gun is in my room.'

Ryga followed him in. Taking a swift look around the old furniture and the worn carpet, he again could see nothing that belied the fact Ackland had been in the room. Only Logan's clothes were in the wardrobe, but Logan wasn't stupid enough to have left Ackland's there, or his brown suitcase. 'Is there a boiler room?'

'In the basement.' He'd opened a drawer in the large chest. 'That's strange, the Webley's gone. I could have sworn I put it in here.' He looked genuinely puzzled.

Ryga stepped forward and began to move the clothes. There was gun oil where it had been and a box of ammunition. 'When did you last see the gun, Mr Logan?'

'Before I went to London. It was here on Friday. I shot some rabbits and rats with it.'

'Has anyone been in here since?'

'No.'

'But you leave your front door unlocked?'

'No point in locking it, is there? Nothing to steal and I don't care if they do.'

'There's your gun.'

'Well, yes.' He took his cigarette case from the pocket of his trousers.

'Is anything else missing?'

'Not that I can see.' He stared around. Ryga thought he looked confused but when he scrutinized the man more closely he saw anger. 'I don't know where it is, maybe I put it elsewhere.'

Ryga went through the drawers and wardrobe while Logan looked on. There was no sign of the gun. And no evidence to show that Ackland had been in here. Pascoe called up to Ryga. He stepped out onto the landing, followed by Logan. Ryga asked Pascoe to join him.

Logan said, 'That's Charlotte's room. Here's the key. I haven't been in it since she died and I'm not going in it now. You can finish your search on your own. I need a drink.'

He nodded at Pascoe as he pushed past him. Ryga turned to the sergeant. 'Did you find anything in the car?'

'Grey hairs, which could be Ackland's, and some prints. I've bagged up the hairs and taken photographs of the prints. There's no sign of anyone having been kept in the stable. It's got some old engines in it, gardening implements and other rubbish, all unused. Here's your case, guv.'

'Have a rummage around in the cellar. Poke inside the boiler. You know what to look for.'

Pascoe nodded.

'Logan says the gun is not where he left it. It appears to have vanished.'

'Convenient. In the sea?'

'Possibly. Only, he seems annoyed rather than relieved or guilty. When you finish in the cellar, look over the kitchen, scullery and boot room.'

Ryga unlocked the door to Charlotte's room. He had expected it to be pink but it was a sunny yellow despite the dull day. It was also thick with dust and cobwebs. Regardless, he could still smell a faint scent in the room. Charlotte Logan's. To him it reflected a gentle woman. The wallpaper was bright with big sunflowers, matching the counterpane on the bed, the curtains and the material around a kidney-shaped dressing table with a triple mirror.

He crossed to the windows and gazed out at the mighty, swollen sea. How many times had Jory Logan and his wife stood here together, happy, contemplating the future? A new and brighter start for them with a child on the way. But again, as early in their marriage, fate had dealt them a bitterly cruel hand and snatched the happiness from them. Sorrow settled on his shoulders and he struggled to shake it off.

He crossed to the silver-framed photograph on the bed-side table and, picking it up, dusted it over with his handker-chief. She was just how he had imagined her: fair with curly hair, delicate features, light-coloured eyes, a small mouth in an oval face. She wore a bright patterned summer dress that the wind was playing with and she was laughing into the camera. Pain stabbed at his heart. It was as if he had known her. But his pain wasn't solely for Charlotte but for all the wives and sweethearts of his fellow prisoners, including George Simmonds's wife. In the picture George had carried of Stella, taken before the war, she too had been laughing and looking forward to a future when the war wasn't even con-sidered a possibility. It had turned out different for so many. Now Stella Simmonds was a nervous, faded, tired woman worn out by the war and worry.

Ryga shook himself. These maudlin thoughts were getting him nowhere. Gently, he replaced the picture and steeled himself to open the wardrobes. Her clothes were of good quality, as were her shoes and hats. There was nothing here, or in her dressing table or chest of drawers, to tell him anything of relevance to the investigation. All that remained in this room was heartbreak, regret and waste.

He locked up and finished his perusal of the other rooms, which confirmed what Logan had said, that they were unused and no one had been in them. After searching the dining room and a study, also unused, he found Logan in the drawing room, smoking and drinking heavily. This room, the study, Logan's bedroom and bathroom, and the kitchen — all of which were used and cleaned regularly, wiping away any traces — were the only rooms where Ackland could have been kept. They'd need to question the charlady and Mrs Masterman to ask if they had noticed anything untoward, although Ryga thought someone else could have cleaned up — Miss Enys perhaps, or Miss Wargrove.

Ryga said, 'I'll take a look around the kitchen.'

Logan raised his glass at him.

Ryga's examination of that room was brief. He'd just finished when Pascoe joined him. 'Nothing but lumber in the basement, and the boiler hasn't been lit for some time. The boot room is full of junk, and old overcoats, raincoats and wellington boots that aren't Ackland's.'

'He might have got in that car but he didn't get out of it here.'

'Plenty of buildings at the mine and abandoned ones around the coast, including above Priest Cove.'

'Yes, but not where you'd expect him to wear a dinner suit.'

'He could have been undressed and then re-dressed in that.'

'It takes some doing but yes, it's possible, especially if more than one person was doing it. Dr Plumley says that Ackland's body showed no signs of being bound, so perhaps under threat he was made to undress and put on his dinner suit before being struck on the back of the head.'

'Maybe he was made to do so in that tunnel where he was held captive.'

Ryga considered this. 'When Logan had an alibi on the train?'

'Yes.'

'Send those hairs and the film up to the Yard by motor-cyclist, along with the bullet taken from the body, but before you do, take Logan's fingerprints.'

Logan obliged without a grumble. He gave them the addresses of the charlady and Mrs Masterman.

'Is that it?' he said, wiping his hands on his handkerchief.

'Yes, sir. We've finished for now.'

'A lot of things have finished, Inspector,' he said morosely.

His manner and words tugged at Ryga. 'Is there anything I can do for you?' he found himself asking.

'Like what? Turn back the clock? That would be nice, but you're only a detective, Ryga. You're not God, and even He can't do that.'

'I . . .' But Ryga didn't know what else to say.

'Don't mind me. I'll be fine. Fine.' He gave a short bitter laugh. 'You know your way out.'

Ryga told Pascoe to return to Penzance. The sergeant drove in silence. Ryga was grateful for that. He couldn't get that yellow room out of his head, or that picture of Charlotte Logan. Nor could he eradicate Jory Logan's mournful words and dejected manner, the sensations and memories they triggered of the men he'd lived with in the camp, and those who had died. As the years had passed, his nightmares had become more sporadic and his ghosts less frequent, but he'd been kidding himself if he believed they'd been banished for ever. Here, just as in Kent recently while working on a case, they had proved to be very much alive.

He dashed a glance at the sergeant's stoic expression as he negotiated the narrow roads. Pascoe had lost his wife in the bombing and he'd witnessed sorrow, carnage and despair. Ryga told himself how lucky he was to have a job he enjoyed and a career ahead of him. But neither of those things mattered if there wasn't someone to share it with. Pascoe had his sister and daughter. Ryga would dearly love to have someone.

His thoughts returned to Logan. He had lost everything he cherished. His future happiness had been brutally shattered three times: once with the war, once with the death of the longed-for child and then with his wife's tragic end. Logan's words to Strout at the mine before he and Pascoe interrupted them came to Ryga: *It will follow me wherever I go. How can I forget what he did?*

He must mean Ackland. What did Ackland do to Jory Logan? Whatever it was, it had to be after the war because Logan wasn't around during it. Maybe Miss Enys knew, but Ryga didn't wish to question her about it. Besides, he suspected she wouldn't tell him, leastways not the whole truth. Nor would the loyal Captain Strout. But someone else might: Mrs Marrack. He would talk to her in the morning.

At the station they found a message from the St Ives harbour master waiting for them. The *Patricia Bee* had put in there.

'The message says she arrived late Saturday afternoon,' Ryga read out to Pascoe. 'She stayed for two nights: Saturday and Sunday.' Ryga consulted his watch. It was late afternoon — too late, he thought, to head for St Ives and talk to the harbour master. Besides, Chief Inspector Jerram said he needed the car. Ryga could telephone but decided that he would postpone his chat with Mrs Marrack and instead spend the day at St Ives. He'd never been there and he thought it was an opportunity to combine work with leisure, and blow away some of those haunting memories. 'No need for you to come, Pascoe. You spend the weekend with your daughter.'

Pascoe looked hesitant.

'I insist. I don't think anything urgent will crop up, but if it does I'll telephone you.'

'How will you get there? Do you need the chief inspector's car? Only, it being the weekend . . .'

Ryga quickly interpreted Pascoe's meaning. 'I'll take the bus and I'll get in some walking. It'll do me good to stretch my legs, and it helps me to think. Only, don't tell Major Tweed or he'll think I've taken a two-day hiking holiday.'

'Well, I hope you have nice weather. And I hope the harbour master can tell us more about Sir Bernard and if there was someone on board with him.'

Ryga hoped so too.

CHAPTER FIFTEEN

Saturday 12 May

He arrived at St Ives just before half past eleven, having spent fifty minutes being jolted and shaken on the bus past fields and farms with imaginative names that he discovered weren't pronounced as they were written, much like Mousehole. Presumably this was designed to catch out foreigners.

The small harbour town was a delight with its splash of colour and warmth, its smell of the sea, mud and fish, its narrow, cobbled streets, crooked houses, alleyways, fishermen's cottages and granite harbour. Boats were laid out on the sand, with nets drying and other boating paraphernalia cluttering up the shore and quayside. The pier stretched out, boasting a white lighthouse on the end, and there were some larger fishing boats moored alongside it and some spaces where some were out at sea.

The harbour side and narrow streets were quiet with only a few strollers, some clearly visitors by their dress and idle manner. He'd read that the little town was growing in popularity as a tourist destination and was an attraction for artists because of the light. He passed two on the quay with easels, pallets and paintbrushes in action. The weather was also kind. The chilly May had decided to warm up to such an extent that he wished he didn't have his mackintosh on, although knowing the area and the British climate, it was bound to rain before his return to Penzance.

He wondered what Eva would make of the place. Perhaps she had photographed it in the past, although quaint scenes were not her style. She preferred the gritty towns, the working people, factories and potteries. He hoped she wouldn't take off for a war zone as she'd done after his first meeting with her, when she'd gone to Korea. Or be tempted overseas. She'd turned down America once, but perhaps she was having second thoughts. Would he miss her? His heavy heart said he would.

He made for the harbour office and was pleased to find the harbour master, Don Keeley, there. After introducing himself, Ryga learned that the *Patricia Bee* had radioed on the Thursday before last to request if she could moor up along the quayside on Saturday and Sunday. Keeley didn't know where he had radioed from, but it was Sir Bernard Crompton.

'He said he was on his way to Penzance and would like to stop over for two nights. Strictly speaking, his craft were a bit big for us, and the quay is for fishermen. I told him that but he was most insistent, and persuasive. He said it was important that he stay and he were happy to pay extra dues.'

Reading between the lines, and studying Keeley's expression, Ryga thought those extra dues might have found a way into someone's pocket. Not that it was any of his business, but the fact that Sir Bernard was very keen to stay at St Ives was.

'Did he say why it was important?'

'Not to me.'

But Ryga caught the sly glance. 'You suspected the reason.'

'Not until I saw her.'

'Her! You mean a lady and not the craft?'

'I do.'

This wasn't what Ryga had been expecting. Ackland's presence, yes, if whoever had picked him up from Penzance

154

in Logan's car had driven him here. That could have been a woman, but Keeley's undertone suggested a good-looking, younger one and that didn't match Miss Enys. Was it Miss Wargrove? 'Tell me what happened.'

'The *Patricia Bee* came in at about six and the lady showed up just afore seven. She were a beautiful boat and Sir Bernard were right put out that he'd taken longer to reach here than anticipated, afraid he might be too late for his lady friend.' Keeley winked. 'All dressed up he were when he greeted her, best bib and tucker, evening dress.'

Ryga's excitement increased, although he made sure not to show it.

'She climbed straight on board as though she'd been on it before.'

Interesting. First though, Ryga wanted to be certain it was Sir Bernard on board. 'Can you describe him?'

'Big man, white hair, ruddy face.'

It was. 'Did he sail her in alone?' He'd come to the woman in a moment.

'Ah, he did.'

'And how did he greet this lady? Did they shake hands or kiss?'

'Neither. She went below and he followed. I didn't see her leave, but I wasn't in my office all night.' He smirked. 'I came down here Sunday morning and the *Patricia Bee* were still here. I went home for my dinner and didn't come on watch again until 8 a.m. on Monday morning. She were gone by then.'

'On Sunday morning, did you walk down to her and hail the boat?'

'I did, but it were all closed up and no one answered. I thought Sir Bernard had gone for a walk or was asleep. He might have had a heavy night.' Again that knowing look.

'Do you have a deputy, or someone in the office when you're not here?'

'Ah, but he's laid up with influenza.'

'Can you describe this woman?'

'That I can. Attractive, late thirties, a bit anxious-looking, slender, black hair under a hat, olive skin like she was a foreigner perhaps. Held herself well, and had very dark eyes in a sharp face. She was wearing a black overcoat, and gloves.'

Ryga's brain whirled. Sarah Bergmann. It surely had to be her. This he hadn't anticipated. He asked if anyone had been around on Sunday evening who might have seen who had cast off.

'No one's mentioned it but I'll make enquiries.'

Ryga told him to telephone Penzance station if he had any further news to impart and set off to find somewhere to eat. So how had Sarah got here? Ryga was convinced it was her. By her own car? But if so where was her husband while she was being entertained by Sir Bernard? Did he know about this visit? Ryga couldn't help connecting this with the fact that Dr Bergmann had been on board that boat, and had deemed Sir Bernard's death to be from natural causes. Why hadn't Sarah told him she knew Sir Bernard? One obvious reason was because she had to keep that liaison from her husband. Into Ryga's mind came the idea that David Bergmann, having found out about his wife's association with Sir Bernard and her visit to his boat, had somehow managed to take his revenge on the skin specialist. But he quickly revised that because Dr Bergmann hadn't gone on board until after Sir Bernard was dead.

Ryga found a small café and ordered his lunch. Keeley could be mistaken about the description, and other women could and probably did fit it. Sir Bernard was some twenty plus years older than Sarah, but age didn't always enter into it when it came to attraction and infatuation. And Ryga had already seen from Mrs Bergmann's demeanour that something was troubling her.

He thanked the waitress for his pot of tea and was told his fish, chips and peas would be along soon. Sarah couldn't have turned up by chance. And by Keeley's evidence, Sir Bernard had dressed to receive her for dinner. A dinner he had cooked? Ryga thought that unlikely. Perhaps it had been a cold buffet or something he only had to heat up. Someone might have seen Sarah alight from the bus, or be dropped off, but not by her husband if she had been having an affair with Sir Bernard.

On finishing his meal he made for the police house, but before he reached it he bumped into the constable in one of the narrow roads. After introducing himself, he gave a description of Sarah and asked the officer to enquire with the bus drivers and conductors if she had been a passenger, and to ask around for any sightings of her coming or going. She'd got back to St Just somehow.

He set off for Penzance on foot. It was about nine miles. Sir Bernard must have got a message to Sarah to request a meeting, one he was very keen for her to keep. A telephone call, telegram or letter must have been sent, but from where? Certainly before Sir Bernard had arrived in St Ives. The Central Telegraph Office could provide information on that, and Jacobs was already investigating if a telegram had been sent to Ackland inviting him to Cornwall. Ryga would get Sergeant Marrack to check with the local telephone exchange to see if she'd received a call from one of Sir Bernard's port destinations, and to ask the postman if a letter had been delivered to her, although that would have risked her husband finding it. The same went for the telegram, although that could have been delivered while he was in surgery or out on a call.

Enjoying his walk despite a dousing from a couple of showers — he was glad he was wearing his mackintosh now — he turned his thoughts to Logan. He had been in London at the critical time of both deaths but there was still the fact both dead men's premises had been entered and ransacked. Logan would have had ample opportunity to enter and search them. How had he got hold of the keys though? Had someone passed Sir Bernard's keys to Logan after he'd sailed into St Ives, or before then, at another port perhaps? Ryga frowned. That wouldn't work, because Sir Bernard's keys were found on his body, and at that time Logan was in

London. It was impossible for him to have replaced those keys. There could have been a spare key. Yes, Logan could have been given that and Sir Bernard hadn't missed it.

All right, so how did Logan get Ackland's keys? Ryga's mind ran on as he turned down into the streets of Penzance. Logan could have picked up Ackland on Saturday morning, his walk to the mine being a lie. Alternatively, whoever had borrowed his car could have rendered Ackland unconscious and handed the man's keys to Logan. On his return from town, Logan had replaced them in Ackland's pocket knowing where he would find the body. Was that when he had shot him, or had someone else done that?

At the station Ryga called the Yard. Jacobs was in work, having completed a successful operation on Thursday night. The safecracker had been caught at the Astoria and Jacobs was finishing off typing up his reports from the interview with the felon and his accomplice, a female employee at the safe company who Jacobs said had denied everything for a while but finally admitted to it. Ryga congratulated him and requested that on Monday Jacobs enquire with the Central Telegraph Office regarding any communications sent to Sarah Bergmann. He also wanted more information on the Bergmanns.

'We've picked up more about Sir Bernard,' Jacobs said. 'Norwich Police have managed to track down his former secretary, Miss Angela Tamley. She worked for him from the end of the war until three months ago when he retired. He was a larger-than-life character. No gossip about him, but she says he changed his nurses rather more frequently than maybe he should have done. Either they left or he dismissed them. The detective who spoke to her says she hinted at a bit of hanky-panky going on there, although Sir Bernard never tried it on with her, maybe because she was older.'

'A ladies' man then.'

'Yes. Charismatic and intelligent. Handsome in his younger days, and distinguished looking as he got older. Ambitious with a reputation as a good surgeon. Does that help?'

'Might do. No joy with finding the housekeeper, Miss Pickford?'

'Not yet.'

Ryga typed up his interview with Keeley and then made his way to the railway station. He had ten minutes before the night train to Paddington departed at 8.45 p.m. Ryga hastened to the sleeping-berth attendant, hoping it was the same man who had been on the train last Saturday when Logan had caught it. He was in luck.

'Yes, I remember Mr Logan. He goes up on this train once a month and I'm usually on shift when he does,' was the encouraging answer.

'I want to know if you saw him on this train at any time last Saturday, throughout the journey.'

'I did, several times. I supplied him with tea and biscuits, although he interspersed that with whisky from a flask.' He winked.

'Can you tell me at what times you saw him?'

'Just before Plymouth around midnight, and again when we reached Exeter at 1.38 a.m., then just after Taunton; it must have been about 2.30 a.m.'

That seemed to clinch it. Logan was on the train. He couldn't have bludgeoned Ackland to death. But he still could have shot him.

'I asked him if he'd like an early morning call but he said it wasn't necessary as he slept badly and was bound to be awake long before we reached Paddington at 7.25 a.m. He alighted at 8 a.m. — passengers have to stay on board until then. He gave me a generous tip, always does. He said he was off to the Great Western Royal Hotel for breakfast.'

That confirmed what Logan had told him.

'I'd ask you why you want to know but I'm sure you won't tell me.'

'I just needed to confirm his movements with regard to an investigation.'

'That man found dead in Priest Cove. I read about it. My colleague was on the train that brought him down here. I can't see Mr Logan being involved. He's a nice gent. A troubled one though. Ill if you ask me, but then I'm no doctor. Is that all, as I must be getting on.'

Ryga said it was. He caught the bus to Mousehole and on Sir Bernard's boat made some tea, ate a few biscuits and spent some time going through his notes — too much time perhaps, recognizing that he was spinning it out. He was reluctant to sleep on that bunk for fear the nightmares would return. And because he was afraid he forced himself to do so. But his mind was too full of Sarah Bergmann and Jory Logan and, after tossing and turning and lying awake for what seemed hours, he rose and, again taking a blanket, went back to the saloon. He was angry for letting his emotions get the better of him. In the morning he'd take a long walk to St Just to talk to Mrs Marrack to find out more about the Logans.

CHAPTER SIXTEEN

Sunday 13 May

'Do come in, Mr Ryga.' Mrs Marrack again showed him into the neat, small living room, where a coal fire burned, and the dog snoozed in his usual position. Sergeant Marrack was hastily pulling up his braces and trying to do up his top trouser button at the same time, almost falling over in the process.

'Please, as you were, Sergeant,' Ryga said hastily. 'I'm sorry to disturb you both on a Sunday.'

'Think nothing of it, sir,' Marrack replied, braces in place and trousers fastened.

He'd probably been sleeping off his Sunday roast dinner, thought Ryga. He could smell it lingering in the cosy room. He'd taken his time walking the eight miles to St Just across country, stopping to eat his fish paste sandwiches, and had rested for a while in the bright morning, timing his arrival early afternoon.

Mrs Marrack said, 'Please sit down, Inspector, and I'll fetch us some tea.'

'I won't disturb you for long. It's mainly you I'd like to talk with, Mrs Marrack, about those war years. I'd like more background on some of the people involved in this investigation. And of course, if you can help, Sergeant, then more to the good.'

'Only too glad to oblige.' Marrack picked up his pipe and tobacco pouch from the table beside him. 'Do you mind, sir?'

'Not at all. It's your house.'

'Care for some yourself?'

'No, thank you. I don't smoke.'

Mrs Marrack took Ryga's mackintosh and, after hanging it up on the back of the door, bustled away to make the tea. Ryga took the seat she'd vacated. The dog opened one eye then resumed his nap.

'How are you getting on with your enquiries, Sergeant?'

'No one has seen hide nor hair of the *Patricia Bee* or Sir Bernard Crompton and I don't think anyone's lying to me.' Marrack began to pack the bowl of his pipe.

'Well, I've discovered that the *Patricia Bee* put in at St Ives just before six p.m. on Saturday.' Ryga told him about his interview with the harbour master. 'I want to keep that between ourselves for now, Sergeant. I'll talk to Mrs Bergmann presently.'

'Right you are, sir. It's a rum business, this. What I've learned of Mr Ackland doesn't put him in a good light. He wasn't popular and Mrs Marrack has told me about him. I saw him once or twice, but being overseas during the war our paths didn't cross.'

'I've been given to understand that Mr Logan is well respected.'

'Ah, he is. No one—' Marrack gave a quick test puff of his pipe — 'has a bad word to say about him.' Again another puff. 'Me included.' After another puff he seemed satisfied and struck a match to it, drawing on the pipe while moving the match in a circular movement over the tobacco. Ryga was well used to the ritual; he'd watched and waited while Street lit up, knowing there was no hurrying it.

'He's always been fair and a good employer,' Marrack continued. 'Knows the mines like the back of his hand.

Trained as an engineer. But he's a shadow of the man who went off to war, and his wife and child dying like that hit him hard.'

Ryga heard the rattle of cups from the kitchen. 'He's from Cornwall?'

'Yes. Over St Austell way. His father was also an engineer, invented some contraption to do with pumping water — don't ask me what, but it made him a fortune. He bought Tregarris House and the family settled there. Jory Logan went away to be educated, came back as an engineer like his father and took up the licence for the Catallack Mine.'

'His father didn't have it then?'

A car backfired outside and a piece of coal settled on the fire. The dog didn't budge.

'No. His father took to the land and horses. Breeding and riding them, I mean, not racing or betting. Tregarris House were once very grand and the house full of people and entertaining. Old Mr Logan died in thirty-four, his wife nine months after. By then Jory had already got the licence for the mine from Colonel Cavendish-Dorrian.'

'I've been to Tregarris House, it's very run down now.'

'It is.' Mrs Marrack entered with the tea tray, which she placed on the table. 'You'll have some cake, Mr Ryga.'

It wasn't a question. He made to rise when she waved him back in his seat. 'But who can blame him for letting the place go,' she said, pouring the tea. 'After everything he's been through, it's no wonder. Instead of time healing his wounds, he seems to be getting worse.' She placed the cup of tea and cake by Ryga's side on a small table, and poured one out for her husband, who rose and indicated that she take his seat. He pulled a hard-backed chair from the table towards them.

'Mrs Masterman, who cooks for Mr Logan, has told me he hardly eats a thing, and he looks as though he hasn't slept in days. He's also drinking too much.' She stirred her tea. 'He can't get over his wife's death or that of his little boy. To have such a double tragedy on top of all he endured in the war is enough to drive any man to drink and despair. He's a good man, Mr Ryga. He doesn't deserve all that's been thrown at him. Mrs Masterman says she's heard him say on the telephone that he wished to God the mine would go bust and then he can clear out.'

'Who was he talking to?'

'I don't know.'

'Do you know if he has any visitors?'

'Mrs Masterman says that she's seen Captain Strout and Miss Wargrove there, but that's all.'

'Tell me about Charlotte Logan. I've seen her photograph, she was very pretty.'

'She was. Delicate too, as I told you before, but not in a sickly way. By that I mean she was timid — no, that's not the right word.' She screwed up her face, cup poised in her hand, as she searched for one. 'She was gentle, yes, perhaps that's a better expression. She was always very anxious to please, perhaps a bit too much so. She hated it if she thought she had upset anyone, even if they were awful to her.'

'Was anyone awful to her?' Ryga thought of Ackland and the reputation he'd had. It sounded as though Charlotte Logan wouldn't have been able to stand up to him. Was that another reason for Logan hating him? Had Ackland made Charlotte's life a misery and now that she was gone he had sought revenge? He put his attention back to Mrs Marrack.

'The first billeting lady was a dreadful woman, as I mentioned before to you. A real gorgon who was useless at organizing but thought she was the cat's whiskers. She was a tyrant and often drove Mrs Logan to tears. Mrs Knowles, the then housekeeper, told me that, and I saw it for myself when I was at Tregarris House trying to help with the evacuees. We were all relieved when Miss Enys got rid of her and took over after her father died. Mrs Logan relaxed a little then, but she worried about Jory and the mine. Captain Strout was perfectly capable of handling it all and we told her not to fret herself, but she couldn't help it.' She swallowed some tea. Ryga did likewise and bit into the cake. 'Charlotte Logan always went out of her way to help people and saw the good in everyone. She couldn't believe some of the news that got through about the horrors of the war, and I think seeing Jory, and learning how he had suffered, was a mighty blow to her. I don't think she ever understood it and he probably shut it out, or tried to, so as not to inflict pain on her.'

'You mentioned before that Mrs Logan returned to London during the war. Did she have family there?'

'No. Her father killed himself when she was fourteen. He'd run a business of some sort — I don't recall what — but he'd gone bankrupt and couldn't face the shame. Charlotte's mother had a small allowance that was enough for her and her daughter to survive on. Then she died two years later of a heart attack — brought on by the stress, I expect. And that was the end of the allowance. Charlotte sold what she had and enrolled on a shorthand typing course. She became a secretary, and a very good one, I believe. She met Jory when she was asked by one of the directors to take notes at the board meeting. Jory fell head over heels in love with her and vice versa. We tried to tell her not to go back to London, what with all the bombing, and that she had friends here and could do her bit here just as well as in London, but she was so upset when she got the news Mr Logan was missing. She was convinced he was dead, and she couldn't bear to stay here. She left for London in May forty-two, after the fall of Singapore in the February of that year.'

'And she came back when?'

'January forty-five. The evacuees had gone by then and there were only a few Bevin Boys remaining. They left as soon as they could. Charlotte had heard that Jory was alive and would be returning. She had their room redecorated.'

'The yellow room.'

'Yes. The colour of sunshine, a new day of fresh beginnings and hope. It wasn't to be.' She shook her head sadly. The clock chimed and the dog changed position. Ryga could hear Marrack supping his tea. The smell of his pipe filled the air. He swallowed some of his tea and ate more cake.

'Do you know where she lived in London?'

'No. Mrs Knowles said Mrs Logan didn't write to tell her, or to ask how things were going. It was as though she'd cut herself off from her life here. At one time we thought she might have got hurt, or worse, in the bombing, because we'd had no news of her. But Captain Strout said she was fine because the income from the mine, Mr Logan's share, was being paid into her bank account in London and the account hadn't been closed.'

Ryga wondered which bank. He'd have to get that from Strout, who he suspected wouldn't tell him. Logan might, but he'd want to know why. Perhaps he could get Jacobs to send out a circular to all the banks asking them if they had had an account in Charlotte Logan's name. Would it make any difference to his enquiries though? Probably not.

'Why wasn't Charlotte conscripted? Being of the right age and without any children, I'd have thought she would have been called up.'

'She had a medical certificate. Weak heart. And living in London didn't do it much good neither. When she arrived back here she'd aged. Her face was pinched and faded. She'd lost weight and she was even more anxious than before, and quieter. I thought she might have been ill but she never said, and I didn't like to ask. Mrs Knowles said the same. Charlotte picked at her food and had several bouts of taking to her room for days on end. She never went out. We thought she'd improve when Jory came home but, well . . . he was in a pitiful state, and had health problems.'

Sergeant Marrack's pipe bubbled and the dog yawned. Ryga finished his tea and refused another cup. 'Was she pleased when she heard she was expecting?'

Mrs Marrack looked wistful. 'Over the moon. A new life meant a new one for them both. She lost two babies early on though, which put a strain on her health and nerves. Mr Logan's too. But the third time she managed to carry. Her pregnancy wasn't easy, but they looked forward to the baby being born.' A shadow crossed her plump, kindly face. 'She had a difficult birth, and then the poor little mite wasn't right. I don't know exactly what was wrong with it but it wasn't normal,' she added in hushed tones, then sighed heavily. 'It's not fair that one family can suffer so much sadness, is it?'

'No,' Ryga said reflectively, having witnessed this before.

'Jory worshipped Charlotte, but she wasn't the woman he had left behind and he wasn't the man she'd waved off. I think they both hoped the baby would help heal their relationship. I don't know if he blamed her for the child not being right, or he blamed himself because of something medical on his part, brought on perhaps by his suffering at the hands of those Japanese.' She shook her head, her expression solemn. 'Charlotte took to her room and wouldn't leave it. Jory threw himself into his work, and when he wasn't at the mine he'd take long walks along the cliff edge all times of the day and night. That's where he found her body — at the foot of the cliff below the house. Dreadful.'

Ryga hadn't realized that was how she had died. He had thought her health had failed after the birth and death of the baby.

Marrack spoke up. 'The inquest found death by misadventure.'

'Was there an autopsy?'

'Dr Bergmann did it.'

Ryga silently mulled this over.

Mrs Marrack picked up her story. 'Everyone thought it was suicide and the coroner was being kind to Jory by saying it was an accident. It's the belief around here that, unable to live with the awful tragedy, she threw herself off the cliff in despair. She knew Jory would be out and wouldn't be able to stop her. He took it very badly, and he's got worse over the last year.'

It was a tragic story and Ryga's sympathies with Jory Logan deepened. He was mightily glad Logan had an alibi for the time of Ackland's death. 'Did Dr Bergmann attend Mrs Logan's confinement?'

'Yes, and he was there when the baby died. He and Mrs Bergmann were deeply upset. We all were.'

Sergeant Marrack nodded and puffed on his pipe.

'How long have the Bergmanns lived here?' Ryga finished his cake. 'That was delicious.'

She beamed. 'Thank you. Dr Bergmann came from London as a partner to Dr Warner in 1943. Dr Warner retired soon after that. His health and eyesight were failing. He moved to the Isle of Wight to live with his sister. I'm not sure if he's still alive. Mrs Bergmann came down here shortly after her husband. He's a very good doctor. Mrs Bergmann helps him out in the practice.'

Ryga didn't wish to probe too deeply into the Bergmanns; he wanted to speak to them first, but he asked Sergeant Marrack to make discreet enquiries about them. Mrs Marrack might also pick up some information. 'It's not that I suspect them of anything, but there are certain aspects of the case that need clearing up. I need to know from the postmistress and postman if Mrs Bergmann received any letters from London between the thirteenth of April and the fourth of May or any telephone calls between the twenty-seventh of April and the fourth of May. Don't worry too much about the dates, that's just for your background. Any correspondence or communication with London should be noted.'

'You can rely on us, sir,' Marrack said.

'I know I can, Sergeant.'

Ryga took his leave, wondering if while he was here in St Just he should tackle Sarah Bergmann about her visit to the *Patricia Bee*, but he decided to leave it until the following day. He'd like Sergeant Pascoe with him, who didn't yet know the news he'd got from St Ives. And he wondered if it would be best to interview Mrs Bergmann when her husband was out on his calls. She might be more forthcoming.

Mrs Marrack had said they had come from London, where both dead men had lived and worked. All right, so the city was a big place. Bergmann had already admitted he had recognized Sir Bernard but had said it was from medical articles, not personal contact. That could have been a lie. Perhaps Bergmann had worked in the same hospital as Sir Bernard. But if so, why lie about it? Bergmann had also known Ackland, although he'd said fleetingly.

He headed back across the countryside to Mousehole. He made some tea and sat drinking it, listening the rain on the deck. Jacobs might have some information from the Central Telegraph Office the following morning, and the Marracks from the postmistress or postman. Meanwhile, he'd tackle Sarah Bergmann.

CHAPTER SEVENTEEN

Monday 14 May

'You're mistaken. I was not at St Ives that night or any other. Why should I visit Sir Bernard Crompton? I didn't even know he was in Cornwall let alone in St Ives,' Sarah Bergmann vehemently declared. They were in the small office opposite the patient waiting room. Her husband was in his surgery, and there were two patients waiting to be seen. Ryga had thought Dr Bergmann would be out on his calls but he'd obviously had a heavy surgery and was running behind time. No matter. The sound of a baby crying reached them down the hall.

'But you did know him,' Ryga stated.

'I—' The buzzer sounded in her room and she rose. Her relief was evident. 'That's my husband, if you'll excuse me.'

Pascoe whispered, 'The description from Keeley *is* vague.'

'I know, but it must have been her. She's definitely ill at ease and she looks far more troubled than when we first interviewed her.' Ryga kept his voice low, although the baby's cries would drown out anything they said.

'She could have gone with her husband's permission.'

Ryga walked around the desk and flicked over the pages in the diary. 'She could but he couldn't have driven her there, or been with her, because according to this—' he stabbed at the diary entry — 'he was attending a patient at Morvah. The call is logged as 6.25 p.m.'

'That's just off the coast road to St Ives. It would have taken him about thirty to forty minutes to reach St Ives. He could have taken her there, dropped her off, driven back to attend to the patient, then returned to St Ives to pick her up.'

Ryga relayed the name of the patient to Pascoe, who jotted it down. 'I'll get Sergeant Marrack to check it out.'

'Also ask Sergeant Marrack to instruct the constable at St Ives to cast around for any sightings of the doctor's car there at the critical time.' Ryga had already briefed Pascoe regarding Marrack's enquiries at the post office. 'And ask the bus drivers and conductors when you return to Penzance to see if she was a fare, unless she changes her story and admits it.'

A door opened. Ryga quickly returned to the other side of the desk as Bergmann entered, followed by his wife. He seemed agitated and looked incredibly tired. The baby's crying grew louder, accompanied by a hacking cough from another patient.

'Inspector, my wife has told me why you're here and I can assure you she did not go to Sir Bernard's boat on Saturday night or any other night.'

'But you weren't with Mrs Bergmann all the time, Doctor,' Ryga evenly replied.

'Are you accusing us of lying?'

'No, just stating a fact, sir.'

Bergmann's lips tightened and his brow drew in a deep frown. He looked about to erupt, then Ryga saw him make an effort to get a grip on his emotions. 'This description of a woman visiting Sir Bernard's boat could fit any number of women in the neighbourhood.'

'You're right, sir. But as it fitted Mrs Bergmann, and due to the possibility she might have known Sir Bernard through you, she was our first port of call.'

'Well, you're mistaken. Now, if you'll excuse us, I have two more patients to see. I'm running very late because of having to attend the two inquests on Friday, and there are calls to make.'

'Of course. I'm sorry to trouble you.' Ryga's apology seemed to take the Bergmanns by surprise. 'We'll just take Mrs Bergmann's fingerprints to eliminate them from our enquiries.' A look of horror crossed her face.

'But Sir Bernard's death was due to natural causes!' Bergmann burst out.

'The inquest hasn't found that, as you know, Doctor. I'm sure Mrs Bergmann won't object.' Ryga smiled at her. She didn't return it but bit her lip anxiously. 'We can do that while you see to your patients, sir. Oh, and we'll wait until your surgery is finished to take yours. That will save us returning and you the trouble of calling into Sergeant Marrack to give them.'

Bergmann hesitated. He threw a concerned glance at his wife. 'If you must,' he said with ill grace. 'Sarah, send the next patient in.'

She left the room. Quietly Bergmann said, 'My wife wasn't anywhere near that boat and has nothing whatsoever to do with Sir Bernard Crompton. After this I trust you will leave us alone.'

Ryga said nothing. The baby's wails came from the corridor and faded slightly as Sarah showed mother and child into the surgery. She returned and exchanged a glance with her husband before he marched out.

Pascoe opened the murder case and began to take her prints.

'How long have you lived here, Mrs Bergmann?' Ryga asked politely. She studied him as though looking for a trap.

'Since 1943, when my husband took over Dr Warner's practice.'

As Mrs Marrack had told him the previous day. 'You were both in London before then?'

'Yes. We arrived in Britain in March thirty-eight, just before the *Anschluss*.'

'You're Austrian?'

Pascoe pressed her forefinger on the card and rolled it slightly.

'No, German, but Jewish.'

'Ah.'

'We'd already left Germany when we saw how things were developing there. We thought we might be safe in Austria but that wasn't to be. We had to get out.'

'That must have been terrible for you.'

'Not as bad as if we had stayed.' She was still searching his face, looking for some trick.

'I was a prisoner of war in Germany for four years.'

'Oh, I . . . yes,' she said haltingly and her expression eased a little. Ryga also saw Pascoe's shocked look.

'How did you end up here in Cornwall?' Ryga took the seat opposite her desk.

She shifted. Pascoe said, 'Just the other hand to do, Mrs Bergmann. Be finished in a jiffy.' Ryga knew he was spinning it out so that he could get more information from her. The baby was still wailing and the waiting patient coughing.

'We arrived well before the declaration of war, so David was able to get a work permit from the Home Office. He worked at Guy's Hospital in a junior position.' Her eyes dropped. Ryga recalled that Sir Bernard had been a consultant there. 'David heard from a colleague, or he might have seen an article in his medical journal — I forget which — that Dr Warner wished to retire and his practice was up for sale. We thought it would be good to get out of London, and being a mining practice, it would still be helping the war effort. David was at first taken on as a partner and then we sold some jewellery that we'd managed to bring out of Austria to buy the practice.'

The crying baby became louder as the door opened. The buzzer sounded. Ryga rose. 'Your fingers are black, Mrs

Bergmann. I'll ask the next patient to go in and Sergeant Pascoe will give you his handkerchief to clean them.'

'No!' She sprang up. 'I'll wash them in a moment after showing the patient in.' They let her go as Pascoe set aside his fingerprint paraphernalia. The coughing man was shown into the surgery. Mrs Bergmann didn't return; Ryga assumed she was in the scullery washing her hands.

'She's taking her time,' Pascoe said, *sotto voce*. 'To avoid further questions.'

Ryga agreed. The coughing man ceased for a few moments. Ryga could hear a tap running. The telephone rang but there must have been an extension in another room as it abruptly ceased and they could hear Sarah's voice. Ryga again flicked through the pages in the doctor's diary while Pascoe stood at the door. There was an entry for the Monday morning when Miss Enys had sprained her ankle. The call was logged at 6.10 a.m., and after that another at seven o'clock and by the side of it '*Patricia Bee*', when Dr Bergmann had been summoned to the boat. After that there were a handful of calls and names listed, showing that Dr Bergmann had indeed had a busy day after his surgery hours.

Bergmann's door opened. Footsteps sounded in the hall. Sarah opened the front door and they heard her say she hoped the medicine would ease the coughing. She arrived in the room at the same time as her husband. He submitted to having his fingerprints taken, silently and sternly. Ryga didn't attempt any further questioning. Sensing this, Pascoe became a great deal more efficient.

Once completed, Ryga apologized for keeping them. Climbing in the car, he said, 'There's a great deal she's not telling. I'm convinced she visited that boat. Jacobs said there were other prints on board — let's see if any of them match hers.'

Back in the office they examined them and the photographs Jacobs had returned. They found Dr Bergmann's and Blayde the lifeboat man's. There were none that matched Mrs Bergmann's.

'She must have kept her gloves on,' Pascoe said.

'Or cleaned that boat thoroughly.' Ryga telephoned Street, told him what he had to date and asked him to set in motion enquiries about the Bergmanns. Being refugees, they'd be able to follow their trail.

One of the beat constables returned to say that Logan's car had been parked in a side street on Saturday night until Tuesday morning.

Ryga hadn't forgotten those pieces of rock, or the fact that Logan's car had been seen picking up Ackland. He thought it was time to explore the unsavoury idea that had occurred to him after the inquest. 'There's the possibility that Miss Wargrove picked up Ackland from Wharf Road.'

'But why would she when she disliked him so much?' Pascoe said, bewildered. 'And Ackland wasn't down here on official business. If she did meet him, why wouldn't she have used her own car?'

All this Ryga had already mulled over. There was one reason. 'Because she's protecting Jory Logan. There's something between them, certainly on her part, that is more than loyalty and respect. I saw that at the inquest. They came in together after it had begun; perhaps they'd been making sure their stories tied up.'

'But she couldn't have bludgeoned Ackland to death!' Pascoe looked appalled at the idea.

'You know her?'

'No, but I saw her at the inquest and she doesn't look capable of it.'

'Many murderers don't look capable of killing, but they do. She has access to the right kind of weapon — in fact, she showed it to me in her office: a geologist's hammer. And she knows about those rock pieces.'

Pascoe looked pained. 'Well, I hope you're wrong.'

Ryga did too. He wondered if Pascoe was attracted to Miss Wargrove.

They called at the council offices to be told that she was out on a site. Establishing where that was, they headed for it in Jerram's car. It was on the northern outskirts of the town. Pascoe pulled in behind two cars parked at an open gate leading into a field, in the middle of which was a large copse of elms and oaks. Miss Wargrove was standing close to the trees with a stout middle-aged man wearing a dark overcoat, trilby and wellington boots, and a slimmer, younger man in sturdy brogues and a tailored dark grey raincoat that matched the colour of his trousers. Miss Wargrove, seeing them, said something to the two men before making her way towards them, her expression one of concern.

'What brings you out here? It's not Jory, is it? Has something happened to him?'

Ryga answered. 'Not as far as we know. We won't keep you long from your meeting. Can you tell us where you were at the weekend, Miss Wargrove? We need to check the movements of those who knew Mr Ackland.'

She thrust her hands in the pocket of her reefer jacket. Her eyes flicked between them. 'I can't see why you need mine. I had nothing to do with Mr Ackland coming here. You can't surely suspect me of being involved in his murder, that's too awful.'

Pascoe shifted a little uncomfortably. 'Of course we don't.'

'Then why ask?' she snapped.

Ryga replied. 'Because I believe that you and Mr Logan are close, and that you could be helping him to cover up something connected with the murder.'

A flush spread up her neck and face. Pascoe studied his shoes.

'I would never condone murder, or get myself involved in such a terrible crime,' she emphatically stated. 'I'm appalled you could even think that.' Then the fury subsided. Perhaps it was Pascoe's shameful look that softened her. 'I suppose it's your job to think the worst. Yes, I am close to Jory, but not in the way you think.' Her eyes darted between them. 'I'm deeply concerned about his health. Charlotte's death has broken him. The last thing he needed was Ackland showing up here, alive or dead.'

'Why do you say that?'

'It's obvious, isn't it?'

'Not to us,' Ryga insisted, wondering if he was at last going to get to the truth behind this.

She glanced over her shoulder. The middle-aged man was waving a hand around the field while the other nodded.

'Jory has enough to do to keep the mine running,' she said, somewhat evasively to Ryga's mind. 'Even though he's lost interest he'll continue with it for the men's sake. Ackland, as I told you, Inspector, was a mean, hateful man, with a superiority complex. He had no understanding of what Jory had suffered at the hands of the Japanese, or of his difficult rehabilitation. All Ackland could do was harry Jory about productivity targets and threaten to put in bad reports, to stop or curtail any grants. He belittled Jory, said he wasn't fit to be a mine owner. Jory wanted to tell him to go to the devil, which is where I hope Ackland now is. I'm not sorry if that sounds heartless.' She withdrew her hands from her pockets and twisted them. 'Jory had to think of Charlotte and his child. The mine was his livelihood and supported him and his family. Then his little boy died and Charlotte fell to her death not long afterwards. Jory wanted to tell the board, the committees and Ackland to do their worst, but he didn't.'

She took a deep breath and again glanced behind her. Distractedly she said, 'They want to build houses on this field. Those trees are hundreds of years old and there's a ruined fort beneath the ground just the other side of them. But then people need homes. I just wish they didn't need them here.' She looked distraught, but her sorrow, thought Ryga, wasn't for a lost field and fort that she couldn't save, but for a man she loved who she couldn't rescue from destruction. After a moment she continued. 'Captain Strout stopped Jory. He's like a father to him. Jory felt he couldn't let Captain Strout or the men down. Can anyone blame him for showing no compassion when he heard that Ackland was dead? The man who had emotionally blackmailed him and . . .' She broke off. Her eyes fearful and yet pleading. Ryga could see that she couldn't bring herself to speak the truth even though she wanted to. She'd been skirting around it. It was time to help her out.

'Who also blackmailed Charlotte Logan — is that what you were going to say? Mr Logan was away at war. She was unhappy and vulnerable. He took advantage of that.'

She pulled off her scarf. Her auburn hair framed her anguished face. 'You think I've just given you a motive for Jory killing Ackland, but he didn't.'

'We know that,' Ryga answered steadily.

'You know? But how?'

'He was in London at the critical time. We've checked, Miss Wargrove. It's why we have to ask people for their movements. Did Ackland make things difficult for Charlotte Logan in a personal way?'

'You mean did he force himself on her? I don't know. She moved back to London.'

Yes, thought Ryga, *where Ackland worked and lived*. And he was certain that Miss Wargrove did know. 'Did Mr Logan tell you his suspicions about Charlotte? Is that how you know?'

'Of course he didn't.'

'Captain Strout then?'

She said nothing.

'Did Charlotte know Sir Bernard Crompton?'

'I don't know. I can't see how she would have, unless she met him in London. I told you what Ackland was like.' Her face flushed. 'Because I would have nothing to do with him, in that way, he never spoke to me unless it was imperative. He tried to make things difficult for me at work by criticizing my professionalism, opinions and qualifications. He belittled me at every opportunity, ignored me at meetings, and he even put in a report saying I was incompetent.'

Ryga saw Pascoe's stern expression.

'Thankfully those above Ackland didn't agree with him, although I was told to cooperate with him more. They didn't know what that meant.' Her eyes blazed. 'I was *never* going to do that.'

Miss Wargrove was a strong-minded, intelligent woman; Charlotte hadn't been, according to what he had learned from Mrs Marrack. He could see how Ackland could have manipulated her. It left a sour taste in his mouth. He was heartily glad Logan's alibi was rock solid.

Pascoe cleared his throat. 'So, what did you do over the weekend, Miss Wargrove?'

She pulled herself up and took a breath. Her voice was more even when she answered. 'On Saturday I took a packed lunch and walked along the coast. I arrived back in Penzance about four o'clock and didn't go out again. My landlady will confirm that.'

'Did you see Mr Logan?'

'No.'

'Or Captain Strout?'

'No. Only some tourists, a few walkers and amateur geologists.'

'And on Sunday?'

'I went to church in the morning, then visited a friend in Newlyn. I can give you her details, Sergeant. I arrived home at about seven thirty and I didn't go out again. There is one thing though that has occurred to me. Those pieces of rock that you showed me, Inspector. This might seem strange, and have nothing whatever to do with the murder . . .'

'We'd like to hear anything that might help.'

'I said there was apatite in them, the mineral that gives those green streaks in the granite. Well, it struck me that "apatite" is derived from the Greek word for "deceit".'

Five pieces of rock in each man's pocket, five people deceived. 'Do you believe the two men were dishonest?'

She ran a hand through her hair. 'Ackland was. I don't know about Sir Bernard.'

They watched her walk back to the two men. 'You'll need to verify her alibi, Pascoe. And I need to ascertain she's correct about "apatite" meaning "deceit". That might not have any bearing on the case, but it's strange nonetheless given what we've learned about Ackland, who appears to have been highly deceptive in manner. She didn't need to tell us the meaning.' Ryga opened the car door. 'She wanted to draw our attention to it. Especially now she knows Logan is off the hook for a murder change.'

Pascoe started the car. 'Then she is involved in all this.'

'In a way, yes, but how deeply, I'm not sure.' Ryga gave Pascoe instructions to make for the mine. 'I think Ackland persuaded Charlotte to leave Tregarris, where she had Miss Enys and Captain Strout to look out for her. He didn't want that. He didn't want her to have any friends. He isolated Charlotte just as he did his wife, Phyllis. In London he could control her. He had an affair with her. She was lonely and anxious. She thought her husband was dead. Then she learned Jory was a prisoner of war in the Far East and she was probably convinced by Ackland that he would never return. According to what Miss Enys told me about Ackland's ways, he must have reiterated this again and again and deceived her into thinking she'd be left alone with only the mine for an income, and that was dependent on him continuing to recommend it for support. He ruthlessly exploited that. He made her believe he could help keep it going, that he had influence if she showed her gratitude.'

'The bastard!' Pascoe recovered himself. 'Sorry, guv.'

'It's all right, I agree. I'd like to know where she lived. I didn't find her identity card or ration book in her room. Logan could very well have destroyed them. I'll get the Yard to enquire at the councils for her registration details.'

Pascoe stopped to allow some sheep to saunter across the road. 'Why would anyone use Logan's car to pick up Ackland and therefore implicate him in his murder?'

'Because they knew Logan would have a cast-iron alibi. Whether or not it was done with Logan's permission and knowledge is another matter. Several people knew what Ackland had done to Charlotte Logan — Captain Strout, Miss Wargrove, David and Sarah Bergmann, and Miss Enys. Maybe one of them killed Ackland to prevent Logan from doing so.'

'And incur a capital charge! No, I don't see that,' Pascoe said, moving off. 'And where does Crompton fit into all this?'

'I don't know. Yet.' But he would. And how would he feel when he found Ackland's killer? Usually when he brought a criminal to justice he experienced a degree of satisfaction. This would be very different.

CHAPTER EIGHTEEN

A man went to fetch Strout. They waited in the small office for some minutes before he appeared — dirty, tired and irritated. Ryga got straight to the point and told him that they believed Ackland had exploited Charlotte Logan. The mine captain tried to bluff it out but Ryga cut him short.

'It's no use Strout, we know. No, Jory Logan didn't tell us, and I haven't said anything to him.'

Ryga could see the thoughts chasing across Strout's lined face. Then his body slumped and he sank heavily onto the broken, dirty chair. 'Ackland was a vile man. He insinuated himself at Tregarris House. I tried to look out for Charlotte. I warned her what kind of man he was. I could see through him the moment I first set eyes on him. He was one of those sly creatures who thought he was more than he was. I saw him looking at women, not lecherously but coldly, and that's what put me on the alert. It were as though he hated them.' Strout's words were weighed down with sadness and fatigue.

'All women?'

'All the ones round here, leastways. Ackland persuaded Charlotte to go back to London where I couldn't keep an eye on her. I don't know what he did, and I don't like to think of it, but when she came home she was a shadow of herself, jumping at every word someone said and terrified of Jory. I put it down to Jory's condition. He was broken, physically and mentally. He thought Charlotte's manner was because she was disgusted by him. He went to one of those rehabilitation places. My wife and I, and Miss Enys, tried to bring Charlotte out of her shell but it was difficult. Dr Bergmann was good to her too, giving her medication and advice, especially when she was expecting. But she rarely ventured out. She seemed so afraid.'

Ryga could sense Pascoe's tension beside him and understood it. He was experiencing it himself.

Strout continued. 'Jory knew nothing about Ackland pestering Charlotte when he was away at war. We had no proof, and even if we had we'd never have told him. After the war, when Ackland came down from London on mine business, he expected to be put up at Tregarris House, as he used to before he took Charlotte off to London. I tried to persuade Jory that the man should go to an inn but the first time Jory wouldn't hear of it. He soon changed his mind.'

'Why?'

'Because he'd seen evil in all its forms in the camp and he recognized it in Ackland. Charlotte refused to leave her room. She said she was ill, and the poor creature probably was at the thought of sitting across the dinner table from that . . . that filth.' Strout spat on the grimy floor.

'Was it then that Mr Logan discovered or suspected what had happened?' Ryga asked.

Strout shook his head. 'No. He had no idea.'

'Are you sure?'

Strout ran a hand over his face. 'Jory came to despise him more as time went on, as everyone did.'

'He asked you about Ackland.'

'Yes, and I told him what I thought, but I never breathed a word about what I suspected he'd done to Charlotte. I couldn't hurt them by doing that.'

'Perhaps someone else did.'

'Not Miss Enys, she'd never tell.'

'She knew what Ackland was like because of her sister.'

Strout nodded.

'And Miss Wargrove knew because Ackland tried to intimidate her,' Ryga continued.

'Ah. He tried to lose her her job because she were too good and clever for him, but she'd never say anything to Jory about Charlotte.'

'And what about Dr Bergmann, or his wife — would they have told Mr Logan?'

'No,' Strout asserted with vigour.

Ryga left a short pause. The wind whistled around the building and through the cracks in the door and windows. It brought with it the rumbling and clanking of the mine. 'Did Mr Logan confront Ackland?'

'Not that I know of.'

'Did he shoot him in the face?'

'No.'

'Do you know who bludgeoned Ackland to death?'

'No, and what's more, I don't care, and that's a terrible thing for a Christian man to say. But I pray to God you never get who did it.'

'Where were you on the Saturday morning before last, Captain?'

'Here, as I always am, with Jory, and half a dozen men can swear to that.'

'And on Sunday night and the early hours of Monday morning?'

'At chapel Sunday evening until eight o'clock; the minister and several parishioners can verify that.'

'And after chapel?'

'At home with my wife until I came here at seven o'clock Monday morning.'

'And your wife will confirm that.'

'If she has to.'

The door opened and a man halted on the threshold. 'You should come, Captain, there's a problem.'

'Nothing serious, I hope,' Ryga said.

Strout hauled himself up. 'Soon find out. But if it were, Fragdan here wouldn't be asking politely and the siren would have sounded.'

Ryga watched the two men set off for the mine. In the car, he addressed Pascoe. 'Strout could easily have slipped out of his home on Sunday night with or without his wife's knowledge and killed Ackland.'

'How would he have got there?'

'Walked, with a flashlight. He could probably do it blindfolded, being so familiar with this countryside and with his miner's instinct.'

'His motive?'

'To stop Logan doing it.'

'Would he risk his life for that?' Pascoe asked dubiously.

Ryga stared in the distance. Quietly he said, 'Yes, I believe he would.'

A silence fell between them as they headed back to Penzance. What they had learned about Ackland preying on Charlotte had left a bitter taste in Ryga's mouth and he knew it was the same for the sergeant. Captain Strout had access to any mining tool he wished to use as a murder weapon to bludgeon Ackland to death. There was also Miss Wargrove, whom he'd considered earlier, with access to a geologist's implement. Either of them could have put the rocks in Ackland's pocket, but not in Sir Bernard's. At the moment the most likely people to have done that were the Bergmanns. But why would they? Why had Ackland been wearing evening attire? Did he believe he was going to dine with Sir Bernard? Had the two men in fact dined together? Could Ackland also have been on board the *Patricia Bee* when Sarah Bergmann boarded her? Keeley hadn't seen him but he might have been below decks and his arrival by car gone unnoticed.

Arriving at the station, Ryga was cornered into giving another press statement by a local journalist who had been lying in wait for him. Thankfully the Fleet Street reporters had returned to London, where no doubt they were digging around for more on both of the deceased. Ryga said little more than he had before, that enquiries were progressing.

He called the Yard but Jacobs had gone home. He could ask one of the other detectives to check on the meaning of the word 'apatite', but Jacobs had a Greek contact and might get more from him. It could wait until the next day. He also had Miss Enys's Webley to inspect.

Pascoe called Sergeant Marrack and gave him their earlier agreed instructions, to check out the patient Bergmann had visited early Saturday evening. After typing up his reports, Ryga decided he needed exercise. He found a fish-and-chip shop open in Penzance and, eating pensively, he made his way on foot to Mousehole, hoping the sea air would blow away the taste of Ackland. It was a pleasant evening. Jacobs's words about Sir Bernard reverberated in his head — *charismatic, intelligent, handsome*. Could Sarah have had an affair with him in London? Was she still in love with him? Or perhaps Sir Bernard was infatuated with her and had arranged to meet her because this was where he had decided to retire?

Ryga looked up as a particular noisy herring gull dived and wheeled overhead. Another, perching on the roof of one of the houses on his right, answered the call. They'd have his chips if he wasn't careful. He finished them and threw the newspaper in a litter bin. What had happened on board the *Patricia Bee* on Saturday night? Why hadn't anyone seen Sir Bernard Crompton on that Sunday?

He trekked on, along the cliff road, as his mind ran through these thoughts. Before he realized it, the small outcrop that was St Clement's Isle came into view and he was drawing close to the narrow, twisting lanes of Mousehole. Steps gave off to his left and he headed down them to the shore. It was high water but there was still room for him to walk. Above him was the coastguard station. The coastguards had been questioned by PC Treharne and the man on duty hadn't seen any boat close to the *Patricia Bee* when it had been reported drifting.

He stopped and stared at the small island as Pascoe's tales about it returned to him: *local boys often swim out to it.*

Was it possible someone had been on the *Patricia Bee* and had swum from the boat to the island and then to where he was now standing, especially on the high tide? Could a swimmer have had a car already parked up on the road? Or had someone been waiting for him in a car? It had been very early morning with no one about to witness it. But that didn't mean whoever it was was a killer. On the contrary, he or she wasn't, not if Sir Bernard's death had been due to natural causes.

Had Sarah Bergmann and Sir Bernard gone out on the boat early Monday morning? And, after Sir Bernard had been taken ill, had she panicked and swam ashore, not wishing to be found on board with another man? No, he couldn't see Sarah swimming to the shore from the boat, although there was nothing to base that assumption on. For all he knew she could be a highly accomplished swimmer.

He frowned as his mind ran round those thoughts. What if she *was* an excellent swimmer? What if she had stayed on that boat all Saturday night and Sunday? But surely she would have been seen. She could have stayed below decks. And she could have gone out on the *Patricia Bee* with Sir Bernard, having decided to leave her husband. But from what he'd seen of the couple it didn't appear their marriage was on the rocks, although she was disturbed by something and she looked unwell. Could she have repelled his advances and he'd had a heart attack as a result? But no, that wouldn't work either because she wouldn't have stayed on board all of Sunday and into the early hours of Monday. Could she have killed him and left no trace of it? Could she then have piloted the *Patricia Bee* until she thought it safe to leave and then swam ashore?

He removed his hat. There was no reason why a woman who knew about the sea couldn't have sailed the *Patricia Bee* alone. Only, he didn't know if Sarah had that knowledge. Miss Enys did. Perhaps she had coached her. Sarah could have drugged Sir Bernard on Saturday night — there were still the results of the blood tests to come through — then wiped the boat clean of her fingerprints and, when they drew close to St Clement's Isle, lowered herself from the boat and swam to the island.

'Oranges and lemons,' came a voice from behind, making Ryga start. He turned to find the bent, frail figure of Silas with his dog on a rope lead. 'The old nursery rhyme. *Oranges and lemons say the bells of St Clement's.* That's in London, aren't it, mister?'

'It is. In fact, there are two St Clement's churches and they both claim to be that featured in the nursery rhyme — the St Clement's in Eastcheap and St Clement Danes in the City of Westminster. It was badly damaged in the Blitz.'

Silas looked thoughtful. 'The rhyme ends with the execution of prisoners: *Here comes the chopper to chop off your head.* They hang people now.'

'Only the guilty ones.'

'I doubt that, mister. And some don't deserve to be hanged.'

'Even if they're guilty of taking another person's life?'

'They might see it as justice.'

'You mean taking the law into their own hands?' Ryga thought of Ackland's killing and of Miss Enys, Strout, Miss Wargrove and Logan, all of whom had expressed the view that they hoped he would never find Ackland's murderer.

He studied Silas keenly, an old man with sharp eyes, who most people took for granted. He'd become so much a part of the landscape that no one really noticed him, or took much heed of what he said. He was always around the harbour or on the piers. 'You overheard someone talking about justice,' he said.

Silas shrugged.

'They were here?'

'I'd better be going; Jed will get restless.' He indicated his dog, who had lain down beside the old man, looking anything but restless.

Ryga wracked his brains wondering how to get Silas to share what he knew. He was certain he knew something.

Threatening and browbeating would only serve to silence him for ever. Besides, it wasn't Ryga's way. Bribing him would get the same result as it would offend the old man. Silas was no fool. He was observant and astute, and, as Ryga peered across at the island, he knew that Silas had mentioned the nursery rhyme for a reason.

'I'll walk with you a while, if you don't mind,' Ryga said. They fell into step together towards the harbour. 'Are you on the quayside every day, Mr Able?'

'Silas. Ah, come rain or shine, hot or cold, gale or calm. There's always something to see and hear.'

'On the day the *Patricia Bee* was found by the lifeboat crew, were you on the quayside in your usual spot?'

'No, but as it happens, I was up early that morning, looking for Jed. He'd got out of the house and fancied a walk along the shore. I found him not far from where I met you a moment ago.'

'Despite it being dark?'

'It was just after dawn. A dull day but there were some light.'

'Not many boats out that time of the morning.'

'Not many, no.'

'Apart from the *Patricia Bee*.'

'Ah. But she were some way off.'

'Before the lifeboat got to her?'

Silas nodded, holding Ryga's gaze.

'And not many people out and about, except the milkman,' said Ryga.

'And the doctor.'

'Dr Bergmann?' Ryga asked casually, with a quickening heartbeat, while trying to disguise his keen interest, although he doubted he was fooling old Silas. He suspected this was where Silas was leading him.

'He were tending to Miss Enys.'

Not that early in the morning — sunrise had been at 5.40 a.m. — and her accident had been up at her house, not here on the quayside. The time of the call to attend to

Miss Enys had been logged in the doctor's diary at 6.10 a.m., which meant Bergmann couldn't have reached Mousehole until about 6.35 a.m., possibly later.

'Was he in his car?'

'I'd best be off,' Silas murmured. But he'd only gone a couple of paces when he turned. 'Did you know that Clement became the patron saint of sailing? He was tied to an anchor and thrown into the sea.'

'Yes, I did. I'm a former merchant seaman.'

Silas nodded. The dog whimpered. 'She's often up before the lark, Miss Enys. That's when she must have done it. Twisted her ankle.'

Ryga watched Silas roll his way around the harbour with Jed padding beside him. Walking on, he considered what he'd learned. Silas had seen Dr Bergmann early on the morning the *Patricia Bee* had been cast adrift, but he hadn't been in his car. Silas hadn't said as much but he'd avoided answering the question. Bergmann had been in someone else's car. A person who got up before the lark and had sprained her ankle, only it hadn't been sprained then. It also hadn't been Sarah Bergmann who had swum ashore and been met by her husband, it had been David Bergmann, who had done so and been met by Miss Enys. The sprained ankle was a phoney. Bergmann had conveniently been at Gulls Nest when PC Treharne had telephoned Sarah in St Just for the doctor.

Why had the Bergmanns lied? Why would they wish to cover up Sir Bernard's death or cause it? Had David gone on board after his wife had confessed to him that she'd murdered Crompton, most probably by poison? David had devised the plan of taking out the boat and casting it adrift to make it appear like a natural death. He'd arranged to be called out so that he could assert that, and had hoped there wouldn't be a post-mortem. Ryga was fully expecting the blood tests to show up some noxious substance. He needed to discover Sarah's motive for murder. And how did they and Sir Bernard Crompton fit in with Ackland? Then an idea struck him. He stood stock-still. Of course. Why hadn't he thought of it before? It was so obvious. His mind had been far too sluggish and weighed down with memories and emotions. Phyllis Ackland's death certificate. Who had signed it? He wagered he knew. His first thought was to ask Miss Enys to confirm his suspicion but he changed his mind; he didn't wish to alert her as to his way of thinking. Instead, he'd get someone at the Yard to look it up at Somerset House. He also decided not to question her about her sprained ankle. He was certain she would deny being above the harbour early that morning, waiting for Bergmann. But there was still that Webley to inspect. He struck out up Raginnis Hill towards Gulls Nest.

CHAPTER NINETEEN

He had reached the driveway when he was met by Mr Fallows.

'A quick constitutional down to the harbour and back before it rains,' Fallows announced. Ryga didn't think the man looked up to it, and certainly not at any speed, but he didn't say. He hadn't gone two paces when Edna called out and came hurrying towards them.

'You forgot your cap, Mr Fallows.'

He stretched a shaky hand to his thinning hair. 'So I did. Thank you, Edna. How careless of me. I was in a hurry to get away before Mr and Mrs Varley buttonholed me.' He plonked the cap on his head and nodded a farewell at Ryga.

Edna shook her head after him. 'Forget his head if it weren't screwed on. Nice man. I wondered if he and Miss Enys would, well, you know.' She almost winked as Ryga walked with her back up to the house. 'But I guess she's been a spinster for so long that it might not suit her having a man about the place, and one who I don't think is that well. He looks right peaky and has the shakes. My Ted says he's seen that before in some customers. Nervous disease, bit like Mr Pedrick has.'

'I didn't know that.'

'Oh yes, sometimes he twitches like mad. I've seen it myself, but then his nerves were shot to pieces in the Great

War and I think Mr Fallows's must have been in this last one. Not that he talks about it. Well, he's not here for that, is he? But to get some good, fresh sea air. Mind you, the Varleys talk about nothing but the war and what they and their two boys did. Bloomin' heroes, the lot of them if you had a mind to listen to it. A wonder Hitler wasn't quaking in his shoes long before it was over.' She laughed.

'How is Miss Enys's ankle?'

'Mending nicely, sir. You'd hardly think she sprained it.'

Quite. He glanced up at the window, where Miss Enys was looking at them. She disappeared from view.

Ryga said, 'It was a good thing Dr Bergmann could attend to it so quickly and so early in the morning.'

'Yes, he was here in a jiffy.'

'And in all that awful rain that morning.'

'Rain? What rain?' She looked puzzled then her expression cleared. 'But you're right. I was forgetting. His hair was wet and he had no hat. They must have had a shower at St Just.'

'That must be it. I expect Dr Bergmann telephoned Miss Enys on Tuesday morning to make sure her ankle was healing.'

'He did but it was after lunch.'

'Of course, he'd have been busy in surgery and with calls before then.' Ryga smiled. And tending to Ackland's body with him, Pascoe and Marrack. 'Do you serve breakfast on Sundays?'

'If we have guests. After that I wash up and have the rest of the day off. And last week I had Saturday night off too. Ted and I went to the pictures in Penzance. Miss Enys said she'd see to the dinners, which was right good of her.'

'The day she sailed to Penzance and back.'

'She did. Mad, if you ask me. She was in and out like a yo-yo. Couldn't settle.'

'Did she have breakfast on that Sunday?'

'Yes, she took it in her private sitting room, as usual.'

'And the Varleys and Mr Fallows on Sunday?' Edna seemed untroubled by his questions and not even curious as to why he was asking them.

'Only the Varleys. Mr Fallows don't eat breakfast. He's usually up and out. And he was up very early that morning. I heard the door go.'

'But you didn't see him leave.'

'What, get out of bed before seven? Not likely.' She laughed.

Was it Mr Fallows though, thought Ryga.

'Edna, when you've quite finished gossiping, Mr and Mrs Varley are waiting for their dinner.' Miss Enys stood in the doorway.

Edna pulled a face at Ryga before disappearing.

'You've come to examine the Webley,' Miss Enys grumbled.

'If convenient.' He removed his hat.

'Go through to the guest sitting room.'

Ryga could hear the Varleys talking in the dining room. He noted that Miss Enys was leaning on her walking stick and hobbling a little.

He gazed around. The room was comfortably furnished with an array of armchairs and a sofa, two bookcases, a smattering of ornaments, tables with magazines on them and a radio. There was also a nice view of the harbour. The *Patricia Bee* would easily have been seen from here and from the dining room, as well as from Miss Enys's upstairs sitting room and the guest rooms, although Edna had said none of them had been awake at that time.

'Here it is.' She thrust the weapon at him.

It didn't take much to see that it hadn't been fired in years, probably not since the end of the Great War.

'Satisfied?' she snapped.

'That your gun wasn't used to shoot Mr Ackland, yes.' He handed it back. 'How is your ankle?'

'Getting better.'

He nodded. 'I'll be on my way.'

His abrupt departure momentarily stunned her. She made to speak then shrugged.

Outside, instead of turning left down to the harbour, he strode up the hill, knowing that she was watching him from one of those windows, and that she'd ask Edna what they had discussed. Then, he suspected, she would telephone the Bergmanns, warning them to be on their guard. And they would tell her that he and Pascoe had already been around asking questions, unless Miss Enys already knew that. David Bergmann could already have telephoned that intelligence through to her.

He turned into the rough lay-by where he had parked Miss Enys's Ford on Wednesday in order to consult the AA road map. This time his study was of the ground beneath his feet. It had rained since the Monday of the arrival of the *Patricia Bee*. The tyre tracks in the mud could be from when he had parked here, or from any other car that had pulled in here since then. He could gain nothing from them.

He turned his attention to the view. He didn't need any telescope or binoculars to see where the *Patricia Bee* had been sailing. From here he could see right down into the harbour as well as the road that led to Newlyn, and where he had been hailed by Silas. He could also see Fallows passing the Ship Inn heading towards Newlyn, and Pedrick on the quayside staring across the harbour. Something nagged at him. There was something not quite right about what he was seeing and yet he couldn't put his finger on it. Maybe it would come to him later.

He strolled down the hill and made his way to the Ship, where he was greeted like a regular. There were only two elderly gents in the corner at their customary positions.

'It's quiet being Monday, and with it being so unseasonably cold,' the landlord said, pulling him half a bitter. 'The holiday season hasn't properly started yet, which is why the missus has the night off. Otherwise I'd offer you some food.'

'I've already eaten. This will do fine. I think I'll have a warm-up.' He took his drink to a table at the fire. His thoughts turned to another pub in September on Portland, where he had enjoyed a few drinks in the bar with the quarrymen, and with Eva. She had inherited her aunt's cottage there. It had been his first murder case outside of London. He recalled the room he'd taken in the Quarryman's Arms and the soft sound of Sonia crying in the night. It stabbed at his heart. The eagerness of her son to become a detective made him smile though, but it vanished when he recalled their rapid and silent departure. That had to be because of Sam Shepherd's reappearance. He drained his glass.

It wouldn't be long before he had the reasons for all of Pascoe's 'odd things' and a few more of his own. Yet, instead of filling him with excitement and satisfaction, as it usually did, it had the opposite effect. He experienced that same sense of allegiance to Logan as Strout, even though he hardly knew the man. He also felt a loyalty to Charlotte and her memory. If all he had learned was true then she was a victim of a spiteful, scheming man. And Logan had suffered enough. Ryga was disturbed by the fact that he wasn't doing his job by remaining impartial. It wasn't the first time he had experienced this. He told himself that it was better to be sensitive than heartless. But not at the expense of justice. And, as he again tossed and turned that night, he came to the same conclusion as others had in this disturbing case, and had been at pains to point out to him: maybe this was one instance when it was better not to apprehend a murderer.

CHAPTER TWENTY

Tuesday 15 May

Ryga was at the police station long before Pascoe, having caught an early morning bus after his restless night. Before that though, he'd called in at the coastguard station and asked if they'd seen Miss Enys's boat in the harbour on Saturday late afternoon, or had seen it come in. They had. It tied in with her testimony, as he had fully expected. He hadn't heard back from the constable enquiring with the bus conductors if she had been on the bus from Penzance to Mousehole on Saturday afternoon as she said, but he was sure that hadn't been a lie.

At his desk he telephoned to the Yard and asked them to instigate several enquiries, then he typed up his notes from his conversation with Silas and his interview with Miss Enys. After that he settled down to read the reports, to get all the facts clear in his mind and see what, if anything, he had missed. As he read, he steeled himself to be impartial but couldn't quite succeed in feeling anything but distaste for Ackland. He'd met men like him before, quietly ruthless, totally self-centred, egocentric, without any compassion and empathy — clinical, cold and calculating. It was entirely possible that he had had a powerful hold over Sir Bernard, a secret he could use to manipulate and blackmail him. Had he used that for years and Sir Bernard had finally broken? Had his retirement and his purchase of the boat given him the opportunity to wreak revenge? Ackland could have dined on board the *Patricia Bee* on Saturday night after Sarah had left the boat. No one had seen her leave, so perhaps no one had seen Ackland arrive. He had been driven there in Logan's car but not by Logan. And that meant someone was in league with Sir Bernard to dispose of Ackland.

His brain felt fuggy with going round in circles and he was pleased when the telephone rang. He was even happier and felt renewed vigour when he came off the line a few minutes later, after questioning the caller and jotting down some notes, just as Pascoe entered.

'You've got something,' Pascoe said, seeing Ryga's expression.

'Confirmation that a man was on that boat with Sir Bernard Crompton. Our valet.'

'Where? When? Who?' Pascoe asked eagerly, hanging up his hat and coat.

'I can say where and when but I don't know who. That was the Stranraer harbour master. One of his men has reported seeing a man boarding the *Patricia Bee* around six Monday evening on the sixteenth of April. He was carrying a suitcase. Wiry, smartly dressed, dark overcoat and wearing a hat, which means we have no idea of the colour of his hair or if he had any. The man who saw him says he was probably in his early fifties.'

'And he conveniently got off before Sir Bernard's assignation with Sarah Bergmann at St Ives. Why hasn't he come forward?'

'Perhaps he hasn't heard the news of Sir Bernard's death. Or perhaps he has and doesn't want to get mixed up in it. He might have stocked up on provisions at Stranraer. I asked the harbour master if anyone had seen him doing so, or going out and about, or if anyone had delivered victuals to them, but he didn't know. He said he'd ask around. If the valet went ashore to buy provisions, he might have used his own ration book. Someone might remember his name from that. Yes, I know that's a long shot,' Ryga added to Pascoe's dubious look, 'and he probably used Sir Bernard's ration book when he needed to, but we might get a lucky break. I'll telephone the Stranraer police and ask them to make enquiries. Right, so where did this valet travel from in order to reach Stranraer?'

'He might be a Scotsman. Or perhaps he came from the north of England. He might even have come across on the ferry from Larne in Northern Ireland.'

'Sir Bernard's former housekeeper has retired there. She could have recommended someone she knew, or a relative, for the position. What was her surname?' Ryga flicked back through his notebook. 'Miss Joyce Pickford. Check if any of the sailings from Larne to Stranraer coincide with the time the valet arrived, and if there was anyone booked on the ferry by the surname of Pickford, or who fits the somewhat vague description of our valet.'

Pascoe jotted this down. 'The valet could have got back on the *Patricia Bee* at St Ives after the lady left and then left the boat to drift off St Clement's Isle.'

'He could but that doesn't fit with David Bergmann's hair being wet, and him being so conveniently on hand for Miss Enys's phoney accident.'

'Phoney!'

Ryga swiftly brought him up to speed with his talk with Silas and Edna's information. 'I think Sir Bernard dismissed this valet, or perhaps gave him some time off so that he could be alone with Sarah Bergmann. He was expecting the valet to rejoin the boat at Penzance. When the valet arrived in Penzance he heard the news of the death and thought he'd be wiser taking off than getting involved.' But Ryga sat back, frowning. 'That doesn't add up though, because where were the valet's clothes? He wouldn't have taken all of them with him if he intended on rejoining the boat, which means he was dismissed, and Sir Bernard intended to make the remainder of the journey alone.'

'Or with Ackland,' Pascoe suggested.

'No. He was expected back at work on Tuesday.'

'Perhaps Sir Bernard thought he could get another valet at Penzance to take the first man's place.'

'Perhaps he did. We don't know where he went from Stranraer to St Ives, aside from those destinations we've already discussed. We know he didn't put in at Newquay and Padstow. I was detailed to phone Whitehaven, Rhyl and Holyhead, which I haven't done. I got sidetracked with other aspects of the investigation. I'll do it now. First I'll call the Stranraer police and get them to make enquiries at the railway station and local grocer and butcher; you try the ferries. Then you call Swansea, Bude and Fishguard.'

They settled down to it but didn't get answers immediately. Ryga didn't expect to. It might take some days before they had the information, which was frustrating but inevitable. The Stranraer police would make enquiries and the ferry company would check their passenger lists for anyone called Pickford. But they had one fairly quick result: the harbour master at Whitehaven said the *Patricia Bee* had put in there late on the eighteenth of April and had left early on Sunday the twenty-second. He hadn't taken particular notice of the men on board but, yes, there had been two and, yes, he would ask around for a description of them.

While Pascoe attended to some outstanding paperwork and two reports of housebreaking overnight that needed investigating, Ryga took a walk around Penzance mulling over the investigation. He took some lunch in a café by the harbour and returned to find there was a message for him to telephone Major Tweed. This he did, reluctantly. Tweed wanted an update. Ryga fudged it, saying they were making little headway but a number of enquiries were in place, including some at the London end into both Sir Bernard and Ralph Ackland. Tweed reminded him that the clock was ticking and if he failed to come up with a result by the date of the reconvened inquests, then the case their end was closed. Replacing the receiver, Ryga considered for a moment or two whether that might be the best option.

The ferry company telephoned to say that no passenger by the name of Pickford had been on their sailings at the appropriate time. And the harbour masters at Swansea and Bude said the *Patricia Bee* hadn't put in there. Sergeant Marrack also telephoned to say the St Ives harbour master had reported that no one had seen the woman on the boat Saturday night and Sunday. And the bus drivers hadn't taken her as a fare, either there or back. He'd also been able to establish that Dr Bergmann had been on that medical call at Morvah. He had arrived about an hour after the call had been made. That fitted in with him having taken Sarah to St Ives beforehand. But so far neither the sergeant nor Mrs Marrack could establish Mrs Bergmann having received postal or telephonic communication from London during the dates Ryga had specified.

It was late afternoon when Jacobs rang with the next piece of news that moved the case forward and it was as Ryga had suspected. Phyllis Ackland's death certificate had been signed by Sir Bernard Crompton. It had to be either Crompton or David Bergmann. Miss Enys would have known this and might even have obtained a copy of the death certificate, yet she had claimed not to know Crompton. That was true in its strictest sense but she had known the name and Crompton's relationship with Ackland.

'Was there a post-mortem?'

'No.'

'Which means Sir Bernard attended her in her sickness, which is stated as what?'

'Pneumonia and heart failure. And you're right, guv, Sir Bernard must have been their doctor because we can't find Ackland, or his late wife, registered with one in their neighbourhood. Nor is there a medical record for them with the doctor who took over Sir Bernard's patient list. We've finally tracked him down and checked.'

'Which means that either no records were kept, or they were destroyed or given to Ackland before Sir Bernard retired.'

'They're not in his safe deposit box, which we've finally had opened. There was some jewellery that looked to be his late wife's, some gold sovereigns, his passport, university and medical qualifications, and that was about it. No correspondence or photographs. The intruder could have taken the Acklands' medical records. Perhaps Sir Bernard kept them back intending to give them to Ackland later.'

'If so, that means there was something secretive and suspicious in Sir Bernard's treatment of Phyllis Ackland.' Ryga thought of those pieces of rock — deception. What had Phyllis Ackland really died of?

'We've got more on the Bergmanns,' Jacobs continued. 'They arrived in Britain, as you said, in 1938 — David Bergmann a qualified doctor and Sarah a nurse. But German nursing qualifications weren't recognized by the General Nursing Council so Sarah Bergmann came in on a Domestic Service Permit, it being an acknowledged shortage. You'd have thought that a qualified doctor and nurse would have been welcomed with open arms, but not so. I've been reliably informed that the medical profession was dead set against them, scared of losing their jobs and their lucrative practices. They made it very difficult for medically qualified refugees. Each refugee required a guarantor, who undertook it so that they would not become a burden on public funds.'

Ryga quickly caught on. 'Sir Bernard Crompton was Dr Bergmann's guarantor.'

'He was. Although he wasn't knighted at that time.'

'Why didn't Bergmann tell me this when I asked if he knew Sir Bernard? He said he knew of his specialism and that was it.'

'Maybe because they had falling out. In early 1940 Dr Bergmann was interned for being an alien.'

'His guarantor went back on his word?'

'Seems that way. Bergmann was released in September the same year to work at Guy's Hospital, and we all know why.'

It was the first wave of intensive German bombing — the Blitz. Every medical person was needed. 'Was Sarah Bergmann interned?'

'No, that's the strange thing about it. Although perhaps a domestic servant was classed as being more valuable than a doctor,' Jacobs said cynically.

'That wouldn't surprise me. And Miss Enys ran a domestic staffing agency,' Ryga said keenly. 'I need to know where Sarah Bergmann worked and what happened with Dr Bergmann after he started working at Guy's.'

'There's more,' Jacobs said.

'Saving the best for last?' Ryga joked.

'Maybe. We've struck lucky with the telegram. The porter at Abercorn Mansions, Melton, remembers Ackland receiving one Friday the twenty-seventh of April. I've been in touch with the Central Telegraph Office, who were much more on the ball this time. They took the telegraph message by phone because the post office where it was sent didn't have a tele-printer. I'll read it out: *'From the* Patricia Bee, *Bernard Crompton. Due to arrive in Penzance Friday 4 May evening. Catch night train. Will meet you at harbour, Saturday morning. Stay as long as you wish.'*'

'That's interesting because Crompton arrived at St Ives on Saturday the fifth of May, not Penzance. It fits, how-ever, with Ackland walking down to the harbour on Saturday morning, where he was met by someone. We have a witness who saw him get in a car. Ackland thought Sir Bernard's craft would be there or he would be taken to it.' And perhaps he was. 'Where was it sent from?'

'It was telephoned to the post office in Holyhead.'

Then the *Patricia Bee* had put in there. But Ryga said, 'Telephoned? Not communicated in person?'

'Yes.'

'Which means it could have come from anywhere.'

'It could, but Ackland sent a reply to the Holyhead post office saying he would catch the 9.45 p.m. night train and arrive in Penzance at 8.20 a.m. Saturday morning.'

'So the telegraph boy must have delivered that reply to the *Patricia Bee*. With a bit of luck he might be able to give us a better description of the valet than we have. Yes, we've got a sighting of a man who went on board the *Patricia Bee* at Stranraer. I think the valet must have intercepted the telegraph boy because it sounds a ruse to get Ackland here with the purpose of murder.'

'Is this valet your killer?'

'Maybe, or he's an accomplice. Enquire with the Central Telegraph Office again, Jacobs. Ask if a telegram was phoned through to St Just between the ninth of April when Sir Bernard left London and the fifth of May when he arrived at St Ives. Or if any other telegram was sent to the *Patricia Bee* during that period. Oh, and Jacobs, can you find out the Greek translation for "apatite"?'

'Mine's a moussaka.'

'Spelled A-P-A-T-I-T-E.'

'Mine's still a moussaka. OK, guv. I'll pop round to Dimitris now. He'll know.'

'He might even serve you that moussaka if you ask nicely.' Dimitris was proprietor of a very popular Greek restaurant not far from the Yard.

'Nah, the wife's got lamb stew tonight. Want to speak to the chief?'

'Yes.'

'I'll put you through and I'll be back in two shakes of a lamb's tail.'

Ryga laughed. He briefed Street, who said he'd put more men at Ryga's disposal at his end if he needed them. Street added, 'The press seem to have got bored with the story. Long may that last.'

Ryga rang off and again telephoned the Holyhead harbour master. This time he was in luck. 'I was about to call you, Inspector,' the harbour master said. 'You were making enquiries about the *Patricia Bee*. She put in here late on Sunday the twenty-second of April and stayed until Saturday the twenty-eighth, left early morning. The weather was bad that week, forcing them to stay put. No, they didn't say where they were heading. One of the men on board paid the harbour dues — light brown hair, narrow features.'

It sounded like their valet. Next Ryga called the Holyhead police and asked them to make enquiries at the post office and shops for any sighting of this man and if he had sent any telegrams, made any telephone calls or bought provisions. He was particularly keen to know if a telegram had been received addressed to the *Patricia Bee*, and if so, who had received it.

He'd only just come off the line when Jacobs rang back. 'Dimitris says "apatite" sounds like "to deceive" in Greek.'

Miss Wargrove had been right. 'We've got two dead men who, it appears, practised a fair amount of deception, which finally caught up with them. Thank you, Jacobs. You can go home to your lamb stew now.'

Coming off the line, Ryga discussed the developments with Pascoe, who had returned from his burglary investigations.

Pascoe said, 'My money's on them making for Fishguard after Holyhead.'

'I'd say you're right, given the distance and linking that in with the date the *Patricia Bee* arrived at St Ives.'

There was a knock at the door and a constable entered with a message, which he handed to Pascoe. 'And she didn't put into Swansea.' Pascoe indicated the piece of paper. 'We're still waiting for replies from Rhyl, Fishguard and Tenby. But we can discount Rhyl because, according to these dates, it's clear that the *Patricia Bee* went straight from Whitehaven to Holyhead.'

'Yes, and it's the onward journey we're concerned with and where the valet disembarked. Hopefully we'll get replies tomorrow from Fishguard and Tenby.'

Ryga took his leave of Pascoe and walked to Mousehole, his mind churning things over: the missing logbook, sea charts, ration book and valet. Then there was a doctor with wet hair; a sprained ankle that wasn't sprained; Ackland's personality, his deception and manipulation; five pieces of rock in the dead men's pockets, five pieces of deception. Things were beginning to fall into place. There were still some gaps, but perhaps the following day he'd be able to plug them.

CHAPTER TWENTY-ONE

Arriving at the station, Ryga asked the telephone exchange to put a call through to Abercorn Mansions in London, giving the number.

While he waited to be connected, he recalled his early morning call on Pedrick, who had taken some time to answer Ryga's persistent knocking. Eventually he'd emerged, dishevelled and nervous, refused to let Ryga in and had denied knowing Crompton or Ackland. But Ryga had eventually wheedled out of him that he had consulted Sir Bernard Crompton at the St John's Hospital for Diseases of the Skin before the war for the eczema on his face. He'd left London when the bombing had started and hadn't seen Crompton since, and he'd never heard of Ackland.

Ryga believed him and said so, but he challenged him about the *Patricia Bee*. Ryga had tried reassurance, but when that had failed he'd become serious and told Pedrick that withholding information was a criminal offence. Pedrick had capitulated. Yes, he'd seen the boat through his telescope, and yes, he'd seen someone dive overboard. But he wouldn't say who that was, save that it was a man. Pedrick continued

206

to deny having seen this man swim ashore and meet someone. It was a lie — Pedrick knew full well who both were — but he wouldn't shift. Maybe he'd cough up later if Ryga needed him to.

The porter came through on a surprisingly clear line, and Ryga introduced himself, saying he had some questions to ask about the Acklands. 'I've been given to understand that Mrs Ackland was ill for some time before her death.'

'That she was, sir, although I didn't see her to ask how she was. Being an invalid, she never went out.'

'Who was the doctor who attended her?'

'Can't tell you, sir. In fact, I don't know if one ever did, until it was too late.'

'Too late? You mean by then she was seriously ill?' Ryga understood what Melton meant but he wanted confirmation of it.

'No, sir, the poor woman was dead.'

'Who was the doctor?'

'I don't know his name, or if he told me I've forgotten it. Big man, distinguished, imposing manner.'

Crompton. He'd arrived to verify death and sign the certificate. 'Did Mrs Ackland ever get taken to hospital?'

'Not that I know of. Her maid, Annie, never said she had, but she was very worried about her mistress. She told me she wanted to call in the doctor but Mr and Mrs Ackland wouldn't hear of it.'

Mr Ackland, more like. Miss Enys had mentioned there had been a maid.

'What was wrong with Mrs Ackland?'

'I don't know. Annie said it was her nerves making her ill.'

Ryga guessed they could well have contributed to her illness but he also suspected it was more than that, and maybe Marjorie Enys knew this. He wondered where Annie was now; she might be able to tell him more. He asked if Melton knew.

'Mr Ackland said she left to marry a Canadian serviceman.'

'Annie didn't tell you this herself?' Ryga asked puzzled, his mind swimming with racing suspicions.

'I didn't even know she was courting and I never saw her with a man. She left sudden like, without even a goodbye. I thought it odd at the time.'

Ryga thought it odd now. All his instincts about what might have happened to Annie were now on full alert, along with a wave of horror.

'And if she had been in love, then why did she look so down in the mouth?' Melton continued. 'She was a quiet girl, about eighteen, and if I'm any judge of young women she'd have been happy, full of romance. If you ask me, Inspector, she got depressed looking after Mrs Ackland and doing all the housework and cooking. I think she asked for more money, and Mr Ackland refused and sacked her.'

Ryga thought not. 'Wouldn't she have told you that? She'd have been very indignant.'

'She was probably afraid of him. He could have watched over her while she packed her bags and seen her off the premises. I wouldn't have put it past him. I didn't see her leave. He was a difficult man to work for, close-mouthed and mean.'

'When did you last see Annie?'

'It was a night when we took a terrible pasting from the enemy, May forty-one. Most of the residents went down to the shelter, but of course poor Mrs Ackland couldn't. I knew Annie was out because I saw her leave before the siren sounded, although it wasn't her night off and she didn't say where she was going. I assumed on some errand for Mrs Ackland. I hadn't seen her return, so I went up and rang Mrs Ackland's bell. There was no answer. I didn't know what to do. She might have been asleep — some people managed to sleep through all the bombing, though how they did is a mystery to me. I was minded to use the pass key, but I knew she was a recluse and an invalid, and Mr Ackland would probably get me sacked if I did. I crossed my fingers and went to the basement. Hold on a moment . . .'

Ryga could hear him talking to someone.

'Postman.' Melton came back on the line. 'I tell you, Inspector, I was mightily glad when I came up from the shelter that the house and street were still standing. I rang Mr Ackland's doorbell and he answered. He was in a right mess, all dirty and dishevelled. He said he'd got caught up in the raid but that they were fine. I thought he meant Annie was there too, that she'd returned after the raid. I didn't think nothing of it until two days later when I happened to mention I hadn't seen her and he told me she'd left to get married. He said he would be looking after Mrs Ackland until he could get help. I didn't see how he could, what with working, but he said he'd manage. As it turned out he didn't need to for long because poor Mrs Ackland passed away two weeks after that. He availed himself of the apartment's charlady and his meals were cooked by the resident chef and taken up to his room. That is, when he was here. He was out at night quite a lot. Working, he said, or away on war work, and since the war he dines a lot at his club, and said what business was it of mine when I asked polite like.' Melton dropped his voice. 'I did wonder if he'd found himself another woman.'

Maybe he had. She'd not come forward though. But then she might be the type of woman who wouldn't. And there might not be just one. Captain Strout's words flashed through Ryga's mind: *I saw him looking at women, not lecherously but coldly . . . It were as though he hated them.*

Ryga registered what Melton had also said about Ackland being away from the apartment often after Phyllis Ackland had died. Charlotte Logan had been living in London.

'Did Annie have any relatives?'

'I thought not. She never spoke of any but then we didn't have much time to chat and couldn't when Ackland was on the prowl. But a man came here, oh, a couple of years ago, asking if Mr Ackland had had a maid called Annie and I said yes. He said he was her father. Nice man. Recently discharged from the army. He'd lost touch with his daughter during the war. I told him what Mr Ackland had said and he said he'd return when Mr Ackland came home from work.'

'And did he?'

A bell sounded in the background. 'Excuse me, Mr Ryga, I have to answer this.' Ryga heard him say he'd be along in a jiffy. When he came back on the line he said, 'I'm sorry, Mr Ryga, but I'll have to go. Woman in number four has a large spider in her bathroom. When I get there I'll probably find it's no more than a tiddler.'

'That's OK, you've been most helpful, Mr Melton. Did Annie's father speak to Mr Ackland?'

'I don't know, sir. I never saw him again to ask him.'

'Just a couple of other things before you go. What was Annie's surname?'

'Baxter.'

'Did Mr Ackland have the locks changed after his wife's death?'

'No.'

'Thank you. If anything else occurs to you, could you please telephone Sergeant Jacobs at the Yard? No matter how trivial it might seem.'

'Okey-dokey.'

Next Ryga telephoned the Yard and asked an officer in CID to circulate Ackland's details to the Soho station for any information or sightings of him in and around that area, in the clubs or with the girls on the streets. 'The beat constables might have seen him, or the local ne'er-do-wells might recognize the description. Also, enquire with the Canadian Embassy to see if a visa was issued to Annie Baxter, or if there's a marriage certificate for her at Somerset House in 1941 — or at any time, come to that. I don't have her exact date of birth, but she was probably born in twenty-two or -three.' Ryga knew they wouldn't find one. 'And check her birth certificate for her father's full name and date of birth.'

He took himself off to the public library, after leaving a message of where he was for Pascoe. There he spent four quiet hours, with a break for something to eat. Methodically, he studied the reference books of poisons and their medicinal qualities and usage. There seemed to be so many, but gradually he began to make a note of those he thought most appropriate from the lists of medicinal poisons. They would have been easily accessible for Sir Bernard, being a medical man. He would have been able to get them from the hospital, whereas Ackland would have needed to visit a chemist and sign the poisons book.

Cantharidin was one such drug. It had at one time a reputation as an aphrodisiac used to stimulate women sexually, usually with fatal consequences. Ryga's thoughts turned to his instructions to the Yard. Could Sir Bernard have acquired the drug for Ackland to use on his wife, and on Charlotte Logan and others — the women he might have associated with from the clubs and the streets? The thought caused his stomach to clench.

It was also used to counteract severe pain, such as that of sciatica, or it could be diluted to stimulate the scalp. Crompton had been a skin specialist, so he'd have been able to get hold of cantharidin for scalp diseases. An overdose would cause blistering of the mouth, nausea, vomiting and diarrhoea. If they located Annie Baxter, she could tell them of Mrs Ackland's symptoms, but that was why she had been dispensed with and in all likelihood disposed of.

Chloroform was also a possibility and easily obtainable. Ryga already knew without reading that it was used to ease the pain of childbirth and as an anaesthetic. However, from what he had learned from Miss Enys and the porter, he thought that the effect of administering this drug would have been too quick. Phyllis Ackland had been ill for a considerable time, or so they'd been told. Maybe that wasn't true.

Then there was insulin. Ryga jotted it down, then crossed it through, but morphine and codeine were possibilities. Both could have been given to Mrs Ackland to ease pain initially from some ailment and then steadily increased. But what pain had she suffered? Without medical notes it was impossible to discover. She probably had no idea she was being given either of these drugs. It wouldn't have been a sudden massive overdose because, he read, that would have meant a much quicker death. But then Ryga rapidly reconsidered. A fortnight after Annie Baxter had left, Phyllis Ackland had died. So perhaps she'd been gradually fed morphine, depressing the central nervous system and making her less able to move, communicate and do anything for herself, then Ackland had helped her on her way with a large dose. Crompton would certainly have had access to these drugs and would have prescribed morphine to alleviate pain in some of his patients' severe conditions.

Ryga ploughed on. Arsenic. In its elemental state it was hardly absorbed by the body and therefore not poisonous, but arsenic compounds were lethal if given as an overdose or used cumulatively. Small doses over time, he read, were stored in the heart, lungs, liver and kidneys. And, Ryga recalled from a previous investigation when he was a constable, it could be detected in a post-mortem from the hair, nails and teeth. But as there had been no post-mortem on Phyllis Ackland, the possibility of her being poisoned with arsenic, or any other substance, was never going to be discovered, not unless the body was exhumed. Street would have to apply to the Home Office for that and he'd need hard evidence for it to be authorized. And now, ten years after her death, it might not show up anyway. And with both culprits dead it might be thought unnecessary.

He read that strychnine in low concentrations was used as a nerve stimulant and a tonic to help improve the appetite of convalescing patients. Another drug Crompton could have had access to. The list seemed endless. But he turned back to arsenic and read more deeply. Arsenic compounds were used for the treatment of such diseases as diabetes, psoriasis, syphilis, skin ulcers and joint diseases. Sir Bernard would certainly have used it as a treatment for some of his patients.

Closing his notebook, he wondered if the doctors who had taken over Sir Bernard's cases at the hospitals would be able to confirm if arsenic compounds or strychnine, chloroform, cantharidin, codeine or morphine had been used by Crompton. It went against their oath of confidentiality, and at this stage of the investigation, Ryga couldn't justify a warrant.

On his return, he had a message to say that Sergeant Jacobs had telephoned and could Inspector Ryga return the call as soon as possible. This he did.

'There was some trouble over one of Bergmann's patients,' Jacobs reported. 'A possible case of negligence in January forty-two. Sir Bernard spoke up for him and the charges were dismissed.'

'Crompton seems to have blown hot and cold where Bergmann is concerned.'

'And Sarah Bergmann worked for him as a domestic.'

'Ah. It sounds as though Crompton was as manipulative as Ackland as far as women were concerned.'

'Perhaps Sarah Bergmann was a willing partner in a relationship with Crompton. And he asked her to join him on his boat.'

'Not from what I've seen of her,' Ryga vehemently declared. 'I believe she was a victim of his deception and represents one of those pieces of rock found in his pocket, as does her husband.'

This was a dirty case with the smell of wickedness about it. If what he suspected was true, that these two men had abused their positions and manipulated and blackmailed their way to the top, then they'd got what they had deserved. But that was not his judgement to make.

CHAPTER TWENTY-TWO

Thursday 17 May

Ryga was tempted to take Pascoe into his confidence about his research and Jacobs's latest information, but didn't. Not only was there more he wanted to discover first, but Pascoe was involved in his own investigation into yet another burglary overnight and both Chief Inspector Jerram and Major Tweed were badgering him for a quick result. 'I'd like one too,' was Pascoe's sarcastic remark to Ryga. 'But I can't pluck burglars out of thin air. And we're two men short in CID.'

'And no doubt Major Tweed thinks you're spending too much time with the Scotland Yard man on an investigation that should be centred on London.' Ryga smiled. 'No, I didn't listen in and I'm not psychic. I think I have the measure of Major Tweed.'

'What will you do next, guv? On the case, I mean.'

'I'm waiting for some more information from the Yard. Once I get that I won't be far off solving it. Meanwhile, I'll take a walk.'

Pascoe looked regretful as he left to interview the distressed householders who had been robbed. Ryga took his walk directly to the library, where he again consulted the medicinal use of arsenic in its treatment of various diseases. Two hours later he tried to clear his head of disturbing thoughts by walking around the harbour, but they kept returning to those two men — Crompton and Ackland. He stopped for some lunch, although he didn't feel hungry. It was shortly after his return to the station that Jacobs rang. Pascoe was still out pursuing his enquiries.

'There is no marriage certificate for Annie Baxter, who fits the profile of the maid in terms of location, age and the time of her disappearance,' Jacobs announced.

Ryga wasn't surprised.

'And the Canadian Embassy haven't issued a visa for her.'

'That confirms my worst thoughts.'

'You believe she was murdered?'

'Yes, by Ackland.'

'Nasty.'

'Did you get her father's details?'

'Yes. Victor Baxter. Date of birth, eighth of July 1900.'

'Melton says Baxter had recently been discharged from the army when he made enquiries about his daughter a couple of years ago. See what details you can get from them and if they have a forwarding address.'

'Righty-ho. The enquiries in Soho are ongoing. We might get word of Ackland there. The Central Telegraph Office have again come up trumps though. They took a telegram from a public telephone box on Monday 13 April, paid for in the usual way by putting the required number of coins into the slots. It said, "*Will meet you on board. St Ives harbour. Saturday 5 May, seven p.m.*" It was relayed to the post office at Fishguard Harbour for delivery to the *Patricia Bee*. It wasn't signed.'

Fishguard. The *Patricia Bee* had left Holyhead on Saturday 28 April, the day after the telegram to Ackland had been sent. It would have taken about ten hours to reach Fishguard. They'd gone straight there.

Jacobs said, 'Although the telegram wasn't signed, the CTO confirm it was sent by Sarah Bergmann, or someone purporting to be her.'

'I think it was her. And for Crompton to know that he must have corresponded with her previously by telephone or letter, although Sergeant Marrack has checked with the exchange and the post office and that doesn't seem to tally.'

'The rendezvous could tentatively have been arranged before Crompton left London. Or from Scotland before his valet joined the boat.'

And that had been outside the time frame of Marrack's enquiries. Ryga said, 'If Crompton had previously telephoned her, why didn't she say yes or no over the phone when he insisted on seeing her?'

'Maybe she had to think it over. She didn't know if she could get away without her husband's knowledge.'

'Oh, he knew. But she could have used that as an excuse to stall Crompton in order to buy time for what they had arranged.'

'Which was?'

'Bergmann boarding that boat, killing Sir Bernard and then abandoning it. Only, I hope I'm wrong. Any joy in finding Sir Bernard's housekeeper?'

'Not so far. The solicitor is back on Monday and we should be able to get her address then from Sir Bernard's will.'

Ryga rang off and immediately asked to be connected to the harbour master at Fishguard. While he waited, hoping that he'd be able to speak to him, he considered the facts, but he hadn't got far before the harbour master was on the line.

'I'm sorry I've not got back to you before, Inspector, but it's been that busy. Yes, the *Patricia Bee* put in here,' the harbour master answered with a musical Welsh lilt. 'Came in late on Saturday the twenty-eighth of April. Paid her dues on the Sunday, said they'd be staying until Tuesday and then going on to Tenby if the weather held.'

'And did they?'

'I don't know, but they left here on the Tuesday. Nice craft, it was. Big man at the helm, white hair. Sir Bernard Crompton, his man said, is it?'

'His man?'

216

'Manservant, crew or some such. Pleasant, wiry, no airs and graces with him.'

'Did he give a name?' Ryga asked keenly.

'Don't remember one. I didn't see him cast off when I watched her leave.'

'Thank you, sir, you've been most helpful.'

Ryga asked the operator to get him Tenby Harbour. It took some time getting through, only to find the harbour master was out performing his duty. The man who answered couldn't help him but said he'd leave a message for the harbour master to call him back. Ryga stressed it was urgent and that he would expect a call within the hour. He used the time to go through his notes and all the reports. He drank his second cup of tea, ate two biscuits and listened to the blustery wind and rain bashing against the window, punctuated by the ringing of the desk sergeant's telephone, the low rumble of voices from the public area and a lorry's gears grinding down. Ryga twirled his pen, considering where next he should go with the investigation. He needed to work out his strategy. However, in order to do that he needed the answer from Tenby. It finally came through.

Triumphantly, he learned that there had only been one man on the *Patricia Bee* on arrival at Tenby and that had been Sir Bernard Crompton. He'd entered the harbour on Wednesday 2 May. He'd left very early Saturday 5 May and had been grouchy at having to stay over on Friday night because of the weather.

Armed with this knowledge, Ryga once again set out for the library, where he asked for a copy of *Bradshaw's*. For some time he poured over the railway timetables, making a note of the trains from Fishguard. Finally, putting away his notebook, he made for the railway station and asked the ticket inspector for details of those who had alighted from the train arriving there at 7.45 p.m. on Saturday 5 May. Only three passengers had done so: a couple in their early sixties and a wiry man, early fifties. Ryga also asked if that same man had boarded a train since then. The answer was no. Next he asked where the train had stopped while consulting his notes made from *Bradshaw's*. He nodded in satisfaction.

Outside the railway station, he enquired of the taxi drivers whether they had picked up any fares at that time. None had. He wasn't disappointed; he'd expected that. He stopped at a small café for some tea and cake. The afternoon was drawing on. Replenished, he set out for the bus terminus, spoke to the depot manager and interviewed a couple of bus conductors. The answer to his enquiries was again as he had expected: the male passenger from the train hadn't caught a bus.

He returned to the police station and requested Jerram's car. Pascoe had already come back and gone out again with a uniformed officer to interview a likely suspect.

It was just after 5.20 p.m. when he arrived in Mousehole. Marjorie Enys's harrowed expression when she opened the door to him showed the strain she was under. She stepped back to allow him entry, turned and led the way into the dining room in silence. Only then did she speak. 'It's all right, we won't be disturbed. Edna is out with her fiancé, the Varleys and Mr Fallows left today. You've come to arrest me for the murder of Ralph Ackland.'

'Did you also kill Sir Bernard Crompton?'

'He died of heart failure,' she said flatly.

'Just as your sister did.'

Her eyes flashed fury. 'That's what Crompton put on the death certificate, as you well know by now. I'm sure you will have checked. But the real cause of her death was poisoning. Of course, there being no post-mortem, that was never discovered.'

'What makes you think it was poison?' Ryga wasn't going to say that he'd already come to the same conclusion.

'Please sit down, Inspector, unless you feel it inappropriate and wish to take me in for questioning.'

'I'd like to hear it all, but I need to caution you that what you say could be used in evidence against you.'

'I couldn't care less about that. Sit and take your notes. I won't go back on my word.' She sat heavily in one of the chairs by the table in the window. Ryga followed suit. He made no attempt to retrieve his notebook.

'I had my suspicions of poisoning when my sister first became ill,' she began, 'although I didn't know that until she became more incapacitated. She didn't take my telephone calls, and when I called round, Ackland told me she was too weak, or was sleeping, and couldn't see me. However, I persisted and when I saw the maid leaving the house one day when I happened to be there, I managed to get my sister to answer the door. I was horrified by her appearance. I wanted to call the doctor but she told me she was already seeing a very good doctor, a specialist, who was helping her. I said he didn't seem to be doing her much good and I insisted on calling one myself. She was absolutely terrified. I told her that I wouldn't take no for an answer and that she could pack her things and come and stay with me. She wouldn't budge. Then Ackland came home from work. He more or less threw me out.'

'Why didn't you go to the police?'

She eyed him incredulously. 'With the bombs reigning down, and an invasion imminent? Who would have been interested in me saying I thought my sister was being mistreated by her husband? And with Ackland high up in the civil service, no one would have taken any notice of me. I'd be told I was being neurotic and what went on between a husband and wife was none of the police's business.'

Ryga could well imagine the scenario.

'Over the years I've reproached myself for not at least attempting to report it. I've been consumed with guilt for leaving her there.' She brushed back a strand of her greying hair, her eyes full of anguish. 'After my visit to my sister I decided to approach the maid.'

'Annie Baxter,' Ryga prompted, when she seemed to dry up.

She visibly started. 'You know about her?'

'The porter mentioned her.'

'Yes, a nice girl — quiet, biddable but bright. Ackland had replaced the previous maid and got this new one at the beginning of the war. She came from the orphanage where she'd been raised. The children were being evacuated and the orphanage was closing, and it suited Ackland to have someone who couldn't go blabbing to their family, and Annie didn't have any friends.'

But she'd had a father, living, according to Melton. Perhaps Annie hadn't known that. Ryga said nothing. Miss Enys continued.

'I managed to talk to her outside the apartments. I waited until she came out to do some shopping. She was very worried about my sister but couldn't talk freely as she was afraid her employer would see her. I arranged to meet her in a Lyons' Corner House on her next day off, which was the following week. I was still living in London then. She never showed up. I was concerned. I spoke to the porter, Melton, who told me that Annie had left to marry a Canadian serviceman. I didn't believe it. I thought that she'd had enough and upped and left or joined up. She was too young to be conscripted. Then I received a telegram from a neighbour to say my father was getting more feeble-minded and would I come, as she was worried about him. I shut down the agency and hurried here. As I told you before, I found him in the hands of an incompetent housekeeper who was stealing from him and neglecting him. I dismissed her and took charge.'

She took a breath. Her expression was a mixture of sorrow and irritation. 'I wrote to my sister to tell her but received no answer. I telephoned. Again, I received no answer. I tried when Ackland was at home but he rang off abruptly, after telling me my sister didn't wish to have anything to do with me. My father took worse. He died. I sent Phyllis a telegram informing her but got no reply. I was tied up with his affairs, the funeral and all the turmoil that goes with death. I subsequently telephoned Phyllis during the daytime when I knew Ackland would be at work but she wasn't answering the phone. The porter offered to take a message up to my sister but I declined. There didn't seem much point.' She stared out of the window for some moments. 'The next thing was a telegram from Ackland to say that Phyllis had died. Her death certificate had been signed, there was no post-mortem and I could attend the funeral if I wished. I went, as I told you, although I was amazed he'd even invited me, but then he was expecting to benefit from our father's will.' A twisted smile played at the corner of her lips. 'If there was one small crumb of satisfaction it was the look on that evil face when I told him that Phyllis's share of our father's estate all came to me. He said he would consult a lawyer. I told him to go ahead. He got nothing. And that's what he deserved: nothing. Except the death that came to him.'

A seagull squealed noisily overhead and several answered it. Ryga watched a cat pause as it sauntered across the front lawn of the house. He silently agreed with Miss Enys. Ackland had been a wicked man. Worse than many violent criminals he'd come across.

'What do you think happened to Annie?' he asked.

'The same as you,' she answered sharply. 'But not until recently. Back then I suspected he'd paid her off, or scared her away.'

'You said "recently". What made you change your mind?'

She looked taken aback for a moment but quickly recovered. 'He told me, before I killed him. So now you can arrest me.'

Ryga had no intention of doing that, yet. There were still some miles in this journey to undertake before he came to the end of his investigation. Marjorie Enys wouldn't run away.

'How did Annie die?'

'He met her, as arranged, at a wharf down by the river. He struck her and ditched her body in the Thames. There was so much death, what with all the bombing, that one more unidentified body washing up — if it ever did — wasn't going to make much difference. And no one was going to investigate it, if she was found. She was never reported missing because she'd supposedly left to marry this mythical Canadian.'

'And Charlotte Logan? Did you warn her about Ackland?'

'Of course I did. Strout too. He could see through that devil, but Charlotte wouldn't listen.' She sat forward. 'You have to understand, Inspector, that Ackland, while no oil painting, not even handsome, had an air about him that made some women feel sorry for him. Women that are kindly, gullible and naturally submissive like Phyllis and Charlotte, and he played on it to the full. Ackland could see that wouldn't work with Miss Wargrove. She bore his silent treatment towards her bravely, but Charlotte didn't have that strength of character and she was terrified of being left alone to fend for herself, and fearful of poverty.'

'Because of her background. Ackland played on the fact that her father had gone bankrupt and had left her and her mother in a precarious position. I imagine he told her it could happen again with the mine.'

'I can see you've done your homework.'

'Ackland convinced Mrs Logan that the future of the mine and her financial security depended on him.'

'Emotional blackmail, and as despicable as the financial kind. Charlotte was highly susceptible.'

'He told her the house would be sold to pay off the debts, leaving her with nothing.'

'Yes, and he convinced her that Jory was dead. Strout and I tried to reassure her that she was safe, and would be well provided for. She had the mine, which the government would eventually hand back after the war, but she said they might not — Ackland's doing. She also thought the Germans would invade and take the mine and the house away from her — another of Ackland's despicable lies. We tried to tell her that we would look after her and there was a chance that Jory was alive, a prisoner perhaps. Of course, we didn't know then how those evil Japanese treated prisoners.' Her hands clenched on the walking stick. 'But she firmly believed he was dead. Ackland played the grieving widower with Charlotte, saying he understood how she must feel. He said how a change of air and scenery would do her good. I said, how can the ruined buildings, the bombs, the carnage, do anyone any good, but she said she could work for the Red Cross or the Women's Volunteer Reserve. She did neither of those things, as I discovered.'

'No, and she wasn't conscripted because of a medical condition — a weak heart.'

Miss Enys's mouth hardened. 'And you know who signed the certificate.'

'Sir Bernard Crompton.'

'Another vile hypocrite. He knew full well what was going on with Ackland, first with my sister and then Charlotte, and he said and did nothing. He was as guilty of murder as much as Ackland was. Ackland kept Charlotte a virtual prisoner, just as he had with Phyllis. Kept her all to himself.'

Ryga fully understood her feelings of rage at the wickedness of Ackland and Crompton. But that, as he'd told himself so many times, only ate you up and eventually destroyed you. And he had a job to do.

Miss Enys continued. 'Then towards the end of the war Charlotte had word from the War Office that Jory was alive. They wrote to her in London, where she'd obviously had to register her change of address for her ID card and ration book.'

Ryga hadn't traced that. 'She must have been shocked.'

'And horrified that she'd given herself to that creature when she was still married,' Marjorie Enys hissed. 'Ackland had told her time and time again that there was no hope. He'd said he had it on good authority from the Ministry of War, him being a civil servant. He told her there was no record of him being captured. Jory would never return.'

'How do you know that?'

Again there was that flicker of annoyance. Then, jubilantly, she said, 'I made him tell me that before I killed him.'

Ryga thought of the apatite in Ackland's pocket, and of all the people he'd deceived.

'Charlotte came back a nervous shell of a woman, thin, pale and afraid.' Miss Enys's voice was filled with bitterness and sorrow. 'And still Ackland had the gall to come down here when he could have asked for a transfer to another area or department. Even when he saw what they had done to Jory, he didn't change. He had not one ounce of empathy and kindness in his soul. The world is a better place without him.'

'What do you think your sister was being poisoned with?'

'I don't know.'

But she did. 'Was it arsenic?'

She shrugged. 'I've told you I killed Ralph Ackland. I'm prepared to take my punishment. I took him to Priest Cove to confess his dirty sins and then bludgeoned him to death. I don't care that I'll hang for it.'

'Ackland would never have gone with you. Why should he when he had cut off all ties with you?'

'I threatened him. I told him that unless he agreed I would tell everyone his filthy secrets. I would go to the police and tell them he murdered my sister.'

'That wouldn't have brought him to Cornwall.'

'Oh yes it would. I was a loose cannon. He couldn't risk it. He had to protect his reputation. He was hoping for a knighthood in the next honours list. He thought he could shut me up, just as he had done the others, except Charlotte who . . . slipped and fell off the cliff. Although he good as killed her. I said I would meet him on my boat on Saturday morning at Penzance Harbour. That suited him fine because he didn't think anyone would see him get on board. He could kill me and then go on to see his partner in crime, Sir Bernard Crompton.' She hissed the name with disgust.

Ryga registered that she knew Sir Bernard had been in the area. But she was lying. There was Mr Chapman's evidence that Ackland had got into Logan's car for a start. 'When did you kill Ackland?'

'Not immediately. When he got on board on Saturday morning, I struck him and rendered him unconscious. He was in the cuddy and I covered him with a sailcloth. I walked briskly back to Mousehole, as I told you. I had to take a chance on his possibly regaining consciousness, but he hadn't when I returned by bus early afternoon. I took the boat out and motored her to Priest Cove.'

'How did you manage to get him out of the boat?'

'He'd regained consciousness by then. I had my Webley. I forced him to go ashore and made him undress and change into his dinner suit. Then I made him confess. I had one bullet in the chamber. I played Russian roulette with him. He couldn't talk fast enough.'

'And the pieces of rock in his pocket?'

'I put those there after I killed him. You know what they mean?' she asked cautiously.

'I do. They represent the people Ackland deceived: Annie Baxter, Phyllis Ackland, Charlotte and Jory Logan, and yourself. "Apatite" being derived from the Greek word for "deceit".'

'Clever, Inspector. But then I saw from the beginning you were no bumbling local officer.'

Her eyes held his defiantly. Her confession was good but it wasn't the truth. Not only was there Chapman's testimony, but there was also the fact that the Mousehole coastguard had seen her boat come into the harbour on Saturday late afternoon and the coastguards above Priest Cove hadn't seen any boat there on Saturday, Sunday or Monday morning. He rose. She struggled up. But he held up his hand. 'No need for you to come with me.'

'You're not arresting me?' she asked, puzzled.

'No.'

'But I'm making a confession. Where are you going?' She was now deeply worried. She hurried after him. There was no limp and no dependence on the walking stick. He didn't answer her.

CHAPTER TWENTY-THREE

He drove along the deserted moorland clifftop towards St Just. He could have fetched Sergeant Marrack but he didn't. He had to deal with this alone. He still wasn't sure how it would work out. Something had sparked this recent interest in Ackland that had led to his death. The fact that Sir Bernard had retired and had been piloting his new boat around the Cornish coast was a factor that had been seized upon to meticulously plan and carry out this crime. These were revenge killings. And having completed the quest — the death of two deceiving, corrupt men — there would be no more.

He knew as soon as he had left her that Miss Enys would telephone the Bergmanns. He didn't mind that. In fact, he was counting on it. They could clam up, they could lie, but Ryga didn't think they would when faced with what he had discovered.

It was surgery time and there was no escape for them. Ryga had to wait until seven o'clock for the surgery doors to close. He drove to Priest Cove, parked above it and walked along the cliff path for a mile to the coastguard house and then back and down to the cove, feeling weighed down with sadness but also with a knot of anger churning inside him, not against the killer but against the dead men. He knew it wasn't professional but he couldn't help how he felt. He'd control it though, and do his duty. But would he?

It was 6.35 p.m. when he pulled up outside the doctor's surgery. He was too restless to wait any longer. Bergmann's car was there. Sarah wasn't in her little office. Had she already left the house on Miss Enys's warning?

Ryga took a seat in the waiting room and waited patiently. He wondered if Bergmann knew he was there. When the last of the patients had left, Ryga rose. He flicked the catch on the outer door. The last patient must have told Bergmann there was another man in the waiting room, a stranger. No buzzer came to summon him. Bergmann emerged from his surgery before Ryga reached it. He looked exhausted. His dark eyes were ringed with fatigue. His face was pale and drawn. There was still no sign of Sarah.

'We'll go through to my consulting room. Please sit.'

Ryga did because he thought if he remained standing, so too would Bergmann, and the man looked to be on the verge of collapse.

Bergmann took his chair behind the desk. 'What can I do for you, Inspector?' he began politely, but it was uttered like an automaton, as though Ryga were a patient and not a policeman.

Ryga felt like saying, *You can tell me the truth for a start*, but that would have been trite and wouldn't get him the result he required anyway.

'You were in Mousehole the day Sir Bernard's boat was found drifting, but you weren't tending to Miss Enys's ankle sprain, you were swimming from the *Patricia Bee* to the shore.'

Bergmann remained silent and watchful.

Ryga continued. 'Miss Enys met you in her car along the shore with some of your dry clothes. She drove just past her house to where your car was already parked in a rough lay-by higher up the hill.' Bergmann's expression remained impassive. 'After Miss Enys dropped you off, you changed your clothes in your own car while she returned to her house.

It was just after five forty and high water. It was sunrise and overcast, you counted on no one being abroad. You took a chance on the milkman, but even if he spotted Miss Enys's car down by the harbour, he probably wouldn't have thought much of it. But he didn't see you.'

'Then how—'

'Do I know? That doesn't matter. You waited in your car. There is a good view of the harbour from that lay-by. You saw the lifeboat go out to the *Patricia Bee*. You watched as they secured a line to the craft and the lifeboat man boarded her. You saw him come on deck and talk worriedly to his fellow crew members. They brought the craft into the harbour, where you saw the lifeboat man run to the coastguard to report what they had discovered on the *Patricia Bee*. Miss Enys was also watching from her room. After the lifeboat man had left the coastguard, she went into her garden, pretended to slip and sprain her ankle, and cried out to Edna to help her, which she did. Edna telephoned here and your wife, taking the call, said you would come straight away.'

Bergmann still said nothing but Ryga could see a deep anxiety in those dark eyes. The clock seemed to tick even louder and a floorboard squeaked close by.

'You left a short lapse of time then drove from the lay-by to Gulls Nest, where you bandaged Miss Enys's phoney sprained ankle. Edna noticed that your hair was wet when she let you in, thinking you must have got caught in a shower over at St Just, because there had been no rain in Mousehole that morning.'

Bergmann's eyes stayed riveted on Ryga.

'PC Treharne telephoned your surgery and was told by your wife you were tending a patient in Mousehole. Mrs Bergmann said she would telephone the patient, Miss Enys, and tell you to go down to the *Patricia Bee*. Which you did, where you declared Sir Bernard Crompton had died of natural causes.'

Bergmann shifted and picked up his pen. His eyes now held fear and desperation. Ryga heard a soft shuffling behind the doctor's surgery door.

'You need to prove all this, Inspector. My wife and I know nothing about any of this.'

'Of course you do. It's because of your wife that you killed Sir Bernard Crompton,' Ryga said calmly.

Bergmann sprang up and ran a hand through his strong black hair. The door flew open and Sarah marched in.

'We didn't kill him,' she declared, but her voice had no force, only desolation. Her face was ashen, her hands constantly twirling and moving. She swayed as if to faint. Ryga rose and offered her his chair as her husband crossed to the sink and poured her a glass of water. She wasn't faking her distress. This ordeal had affected her deeply. Bergmann handed his wife the glass and pressed a hand on her shoulder. She sipped nervously.

Ryga addressed her in a gentle voice. 'You came into Britain on a Domestic Service Permit because the General Nursing Council wouldn't accept German nursing qualifications and there was an acute shortage of domestic servants. You worked for Sir Bernard Crompton.'

She dashed a glance at her husband. He nodded. His lips tight. His eyes haunted.

Shakily she said, 'I applied for jobs advertised in the *Daily Telegraph* while David got a medical position at the hospital. I wasn't suitable for any of them, not because I wasn't willing to work but because I was German, a Jew and a refugee. There was a lot of prejudice. I enrolled with Miss Enys's agency and she got me a living-out position with Crompton. When he knew I was a qualified nurse I assisted with patients from time to time, but my main role was kitchen maid and cleaner.' She took a gulp of water.

'He wanted more than that,' Ryga said quietly.

Her hand flew up to her husband's, still resting on her shoulder.

Softly Ryga said, 'I'm sorry to distress you, Mrs Bergmann, that is not my intention. I don't need to know any more. Suffice to say that he emotionally blackmailed you. When you refused to submit, he had your husband interned even though he had acted as Dr Bergmann's guarantor to enter the country and practise medicine.'

Bergmann answered. 'I was released, but not because Crompton spoke up for me — he didn't — but because the country desperately needed doctors with the bombing and the huge numbers of casualties. I didn't find this out until later.'

Ryga could see Crompton's kind of deception. It sickened him. 'Crompton boasted to Mrs Bergmann that your release and reinstatement at the hospital was down to him, and that she should be grateful.' And Ryga knew what that meant: more emotional blackmail.

With a trembling voice, Sarah muttered, 'He said, "Now do you see how influential I am?" He told me if I left his employment he would see that David lost his job at the hospital and that he would create enough speculation to make influential people believe he was spying for the Germans. I didn't believe he could go that far. I was desperate to get away from him. I told him to do his worst, not thinking he would attempt to wreck David's career.'

'But he tried. The negligence case.'

She nodded and closed her eyes as though trying to obliterate the past.

Bergmann moved around his desk. 'One of my patients at the hospital died under my care. I was accused of negligence and hauled up before the hospital board and the medical council. Sir Bernard spoke up for me and the charges were dismissed. I was grateful to him. Yes, Inspector, I actually thought he was genuine. I didn't know how malicious he was then and how he was abusing and blackmailing Sarah, although I could see that something was desperately wrong with her.' His voice shook with emotion.

Ryga wondered if Crompton's secretary, Angela Tamley, and his housekeeper, Joyce Pickford, had been aware of his actions. They might have had suspicions and kept quiet. Or perhaps Crompton had chosen his occasions to seduce Sarah very carefully. The secretary wouldn't have lived in. Ryga didn't know if the housekeeper had done so, but even if she had she would have needed to leave the house to shop and conduct other errands.

'Sarah became very ill,' Bergmann was saying. 'Crompton dismissed her. He had no choice; she was too sick to work. I thought the cause was the bombing, and the stress of the war. I needed to get her away from London, to somewhere safe. Miss Enys had kept in touch with Sarah, so I knew she was living in Cornwall, and that seemed to be relatively safe from bombing and a very long way from London. There was a hospital in Penzance. I was sure I could get taken on there.' He ran a hand over his face and sat. 'I telephoned Miss Enys and told her we'd like to move to Cornwall, that Sarah was unwell and I'd applied to the hospital there. I asked if she would take us in temporarily until we could find somewhere to live. She told me that Dr Warner was looking for a partner. His eyesight was failing. She'd talk to him. And this is where we came.'

'And you were happy,' Ryga said grimly, 'until recently. Until Charlotte Logan's tragic death.'

Bergmann started. Sarah's skin paled so much that it was almost transparent.

'I don't know what you mean,' Bergmann stammered. But he did. 'What has Mrs Logan got to do with this?'

'A great deal, Doctor,' Ryga said quietly. 'You conducted a post-mortem on Charlotte Logan because it was suggested that she could have been pushed over that cliff, or fallen under the influence of drugs, or committed suicide. What you discovered from a blood test shocked you. Charlotte Logan had venereal disease — syphilis, to be precise.'

Bergmann held Ryga's stare for what seemed an age. His eyes were tormented. Sarah gripped the glass so tight that her knuckles were white and Ryga feared she'd shatter it. The clock ticked sonorously on, and a dog barked somewhere in the distance.

Finally, Bergmann nodded. 'I thought Jory must have passed it on to her. I knew he'd had no contact with women throughout the war, but he could have had afterwards. He could have returned impotent, not having had sexual intercourse for so long, it's not uncommon. So I thought he might have gone to a prostitute to help him rekindle his sexual urges. I wondered if he might have latent syphilis. I don't know how much you know about the disease.'

'I've read it up.' The library had enlightened him. 'But please tell me so that I can fully understand what happened.'

'As you know, syphilis is contracted through sexual intercourse. The infected person might not even be aware they have caught it, especially if they are asymptomatic, as I thought Jory might be.' His brow knitted. 'One or more open sores, called chancres, develop, usually on the genitals, or inside the mouth, and, because these sores are often painless, many may never even notice them.' Bergmann took a breath and continued wearily. 'The latent stage of syphilis — the hidden stage — begins after the sores, rashes and other signs and symptoms have cleared. They can do so on their own without any treatment in three to six weeks, but the person still has syphilis. That person could stay in the latent stage for the rest of his or her life. Some people relapse and go through the secondary stage, meaning they'll again develop the signs and symptoms. This can happen more than once. Each time the secondary stage ends, the patient returns to the latent stage. That means it can still be given to another person. The syphilis bacteria can stay in the blood for many years, and there is a very high rate of relapse. Penicillin, the new treatment, will help overcome this, but it's early days yet where that is concerned, and many of the older doctors don't trust it. I wondered if Jory Logan thought he'd been cured, or was unaware he had it, and had passed it on to his wife. I thought he should know because . . .' He faltered, then continued. 'Because although he was distraught over Charlotte's death, in time he might meet someone else and could give it to her.'

'You spoke to him about it, with dire consequences.'

'I could see from the moment I broached the matter that I'd made a dreadful mistake. He didn't have venereal disease.

He'd never had it, and he realized that his wife had had sexual relations while he was away. If only I could take back those words,' he cried in anguish. Sarah eyed her husband with a pained expression.

Bergmann took a breath and continued. 'He wasn't cross about it, just sad. He said he couldn't blame her. She hadn't known if he would return, and they had been married only a short time before he'd left and had been captured. That is the measure of the man, Inspector,' he added defiantly. 'I told him that Mrs Logan had never consulted me, or Dr Warner, and it was highly probable she had no idea she was infected — not everyone shows or notices signs of it, as I've said. But Logan was desperate to know who had given the disease to his wife. He thought it must be someone local. I told him it could have been some years ago — four, five, six years. She was obviously asymptomatic and unaware she had the disease, as was I. Logan considered that it might be a serviceman, someone stationed in Penzance, or a Bevin Boy.'

Ryga knew exactly where Charlotte Logan had contracted the dreadful disease and from whom, as did Bergmann: Ackland. He'd been infected during one of his sexual forays into Soho and given it to his wife. Crompton knew of this. It explained why there were no medical records and no visits to any local doctor. No one had been able to see Phyllis Ackland, save a maid who had grown more concerned about her mistress's illness and who had been silenced when trying to raise the matter. Phyllis Ackland's treatment had been with arsenic and mercury-based drugs acquired by Sir Bernard Crompton — a skin specialist who hadn't tried the new treatments of penicillin on her because that might have alerted a chemist or another doctor to her condition. But Crompton would have had access to penicillin via the hospital, he didn't have to say who it was for. Perhaps he wasn't entirely convinced of its effectiveness in curing syphilis, as Ryga had read some doctors weren't, particularly the old-school type, which Bergmann had also mentioned. Or perhaps Ackland didn't want his wife cured, which was what

Marjorie Enys believed. She knew what her sister had died of, as did all those involved in the murder of Ackland and Crompton.

Ryga said, 'Logan questioned Captain Strout, Miss Enys and others and he learned of the attention and influence Ackland had over Charlotte. He put that with the fact she had moved to London, Miss Enys's sister's illness and death, and Charlotte's terrified behaviour when Ackland showed up at Tregarris House. Also his reading of the man. Did Logan approach you, Doctor, and ask if it was Ackland who had infected his wife?'

Bergmann made no reply.

'Did the baby's death come as a result of Mrs Logan being infected?'

'I didn't know it at the time, but yes, and the miscarriages before it.' Bergmann looked thoroughly wretched. 'Asymptomatic pregnant women can transmit the infection to their infants in utero five years or more after infection. When first born the little boy seemed normal, but it soon became clear to me that his growth reflexes weren't. I couldn't diagnose what was causing it. There was a general, steady decline until the child died six months after his birth. Mrs Logan was understandably distraught. I treated her for depression but to no effect.' Bergmann looked desolate.

Ryga left a short pause before turning to Sarah. 'Why did you send a telegram to Sir Bernard on the *Patricia Bee* to say you would meet him on board on Saturday the fifth of May?'

'I didn't.'

'How did you know that was where he would be?'

'I didn't know.'

'Why did you put Sir Bernard's prints on that whisky bottle and glass?'

Her eyes darted to her husband.

'Or did you do that, Dr Bergmann, as you piloted the craft from St Ives early Monday morning? Or perhaps you impressed his prints on the glass and bottle after he was dead and then replaced his hands across his chest, with his fingers splayed rather than clenched, before wiping away your prints and any of those made by Mrs Bergmann?'

'I thought I was supposed to be parking my car in the lay-by that morning?' He spoke airily but it was false bravado.

'No, that was Mrs Bergmann.' Ryga addressed her. 'You left the *Patricia Bee* late Sunday evening after drugging Sir Bernard on Saturday, making sure to keep out of sight until your husband took over from where you'd left off.'

The telephone rang. Sarah gave a startled cry. Bergmann looked at the phone as it persistently shrilled. 'It might be an emergency.'

'Then you'd better answer it.' Ryga knew even before Bergmann lifted the receiver who it was. Someone else Miss Enys had telephoned.

'I can't . . . It's not . . . It's for you, Inspector.'

Ryga took the receiver and listened. His eyes flicked to the Bergmanns. Into the receiver he said, 'I'll be there in ten minutes.' Replacing the phone, he said, 'I'm sorry for what has happened but there is no justification for murder and, being a doctor, you of all people should understand that.'

'Which is why neither of us has murdered anyone.'

'Not even Crompton.'

'He was already dead when I arrived on his boat,' Bergmann insisted.

Yes, and had Sarah killed him, or had her husband? Time for him to broach that later. Now he had an urgent summons to attend and one that could not wait.

CHAPTER TWENTY-FOUR

Logan's car was in the driveway but there was no sign of him. The front door was open and, despite Ryga knowing Logan wouldn't be inside, he called out. Receiving no answer, he hastened to the clifftop above the bay where Charlotte had died.

The wind was barrelling off the Atlantic. It was half an hour off sunset. The heavy sky made the day darker and in the dim light stood the gaunt frame of Jory Logan, gazing out to sea. Some instinct must have warned Logan that Ryga was approaching, even though he'd made no sound. Spinning round, his ravaged face softened.

'I'm sorry to drag you out here, Inspector, but I thought it might be a fitting end to this affair. You can hear my confession. I have no interest in what happens to me.'

'You have no confession to make,' Ryga answered evenly, though his heart was racing. 'You didn't kill Crompton or Ackland. Yes, you shot Ackland in the face, but that was after finding him already dead, which deeply annoyed you. You had wanted to kill him. You had wanted to kill both men. You had planned to do so, and the others had let you believe that you would have that chance. Instead you were on a train with a cast-iron alibi and they committed the murders in your absence.'

'They're all good people, worth a hundred — no, a thousand more than the two cowardly, cruel devils who wrecked so many lives.'

'I wouldn't have thought you would judge a man's worth.'

'Because of my experience.' He gave a harsh laugh. 'I learned that we count for nothing. I also learned that evil exists in all sorts of forms. But this isn't about me.'

'You need help. I can make sure you get it.'

'Oh, I'm far beyond that, Inspector. There is no help for people like me. Ackland destroyed so many lives and he just didn't care. Neither did Crompton. They believed only they mattered. They protected themselves with bullying, blackmail and threats. They should have been exposed while alive but that would have damaged too many people.' He turned away and looked out to sea. 'Poor Charlotte. It wasn't her fault. She was deceived by that despicable creature. He preyed on her nerves, her anguish and her fear of being left alone and in poverty until he could manipulate her as he wished. Then I spoiled things by being alive and returning home. Sometimes I wish I had died in that cesspit of torture. Then I'd console myself with the fact that I would rid this country of two of its evil souls.'

The sea crashed onto the rocks below in a great crescendo and roar. Ryga had to prevent Logan from looking down. 'You discovered where Charlotte lived in London from her identity card, which you destroyed when she died. You went there.'

'Yes. I found the building still standing, although some around it had been flattened in the bombing. That must have terrified Charlotte. I located the agents after speaking to a tenant who had lived there at the same time as Charlotte. The tenant remembered Charlotte; she was very pretty.' Logan's expression softened and he looked wistful for a moment before the tautness returned. 'The tenant said he'd only spoken to her once, when they had gone down to the shelter together. He had seen a man, her husband, who was in civvies but away a lot. I discovered the flat had been rented in Charlotte's maiden name even though the agents must have seen her ID card and wondered about that, but money obviously spoke. Ackland had probably convinced Charlotte that way was best; he needed to remain anonymous, for some reason he concocted and which she believed. I couldn't get this man's name from the agents; I didn't know then it was Ackland. I wondered if I would ever find out. Then I found some papers in her belongings exempting her from being called up because she had a weak heart.'

'Signed by Crompton, and untrue.'

Logan nodded. 'It was only when I mentioned the name to Marjorie Enys that she said the same doctor had signed her sister's death certificate and we began to put things together. To think that I had been sitting in the same room as the man who had killed my wife and son. I had listened to his moans, his carping, his odious voice commanding this and that. If I'd have known about Ackland before Charlotte's death, my God, how I would have taken pleasure in killing him.' He ran a hand over his tortured face. His foot shifted and some scree fell down the cliff to the shore.

'Your wife said nothing about him?'

'No. It only dawned on me afterwards that she always took to her room and stayed there when Ackland was down. She'd feign some illness and wouldn't join us for dinner. I could barely tolerate eating with the man myself but I put up with him because of the mine.'

'Didn't Miss Enys or Captain Strout tell you anything of Ackland's attentions towards your wife?'

'Strout told me Ackland was the devil himself, but no one wanted to harm Charlotte or hurt me, so they remained silent. Charlotte told me nothing of the affair. I wish to God she had. I would never have punished her. I would have helped her. But Ackland had instilled in her the need for her silence. He probably told her that if I discovered what had happened I would throw her out of the house and divorce her, and he could never be associated with a divorced woman. He had a position to consider. She'd be left alone and impoverished.'

From what Ryga had learned of Ackland, he considered that Logan had to be right.

'She didn't deserve the agony she went through, and the illness that was inflicted on her. Ackland was vile, taking advantage of a lonely, frightened woman.' His jaw went rigid and his fists clenched, then in a second the fury ebbed and Ryga was afraid despair had taken its place.

'You searched Crompton's Harley Street house on the Sunday before the board meeting. How did you get his keys?'

Logan stared into the darkening night as though elsewhere. Someone had given Logan those keys beforehand and it couldn't have been Sarah. When she went on board Crompton's boat, Logan was on the train. And Crompton's keys had been found in his pocket. Someone had taken those keys beforehand and had one copied. Ryga knew it must have been the valet who had left the boat at Fishguard.

'Who gave you the keys to Ackland's flat?' Again Logan remained silent. Ryga pressed on. 'You returned from London on the overnight train on Monday. You went straight to the cove early Tuesday morning and discovered Ackland dead. Furious, you dragged him from the tunnel and shot him in the face. You put the keys back in his pocket. Your search of his apartment was to see if there was anything that linked him to Charlotte so that you could remove it. You wanted to protect Charlotte's memory.' And Logan had chosen the moment to enter Ackland's apartment when Melton, the porter, wasn't there. Probably before he'd come on duty on the Sunday morning, or during his lunch break. The search of both Ackland's and Crompton's premises had been conducted in a fury. Logan had vented his anger and frustration in those properties. 'You should have left Ackland in that tunnel.'

'It was a mistake. By the time I thought about rectifying that, you had already found him. I was livid at being cheated of killing him and of never hearing his confession.' He took a step forward.

'Logan, stand back. Don't be a fool,' Ryga said, alarmed.

'It's over for me, Ryga. It was the moment I came home. I tried hard. But there was nothing for me then and there's nothing now. The mine will soon be finished. I'm glad David told me about Charlotte, because hunting down and killing those two men gave me a purpose. I'm tired now, Ryga. I'm not going to spend time in prison for being involved in killing Ackland, I've already served all the time in prison any man can stand. I don't know what's out there.' He waved his arm at the turbulent sea. 'And there's only one way to find out. I take full responsibility and the blame for killing Ackland, despite your alibis. I bludgeoned him to death, then shot him. Crompton died a natural death; he was dead when David went on board his boat. You'll find my confession at the house.'

Ryga reached out but he was too late. Tentatively approaching the edge, he stared down at the mangled body of a man whose mind had been broken by events way beyond his choosing and control. It had been too much for him to take. There had been no peace for Logan, and many others like him. Ryga hoped he had found it now.

CHAPTER TWENTY-FIVE

Logan's false confession was on the mantelpiece in the room where Ryga had first met him, and where their shared haunting memories of captivity had, unspoken, shot through them in that handshake. After pocketing it, Ryga drove to the police house in St Just. His heart was heavy with a deep sorrow. The 'if onlys' ran through his mind along with the 'should haves'. If only he hadn't come here. If only he had accepted Crompton's death as natural causes and returned to London. He should have played this differently. He should have prevented Logan's tragic death. And yet he knew that Logan had become resigned to death long ago, so resigned that it held no fear for him. It was life he couldn't face. Such a tragedy after everything he had lived through in Japan during the war. Ryga wanted to shout in frustration at Miss Enys and the Bergmanns for starting this, but they hadn't. Ackland had.

Marrack was stunned and saddened by Logan's death. Ryga instructed him to request the lifeboat to recover the body and to transport it to Penzance, and also to call the desk sergeant at the station there to arrange for it to be taken to the mortuary. Then Ryga telephoned Sergeant Pascoe at his home and said that he would pick him up. 'I'll explain everything when I see you.'

Pascoe was waiting impatiently when Ryga drew up outside some thirty minutes later. In the car to Mousehole, Ryga told him all that had happened.

'Miss Enys killed Ackland with an accomplice,' was Pascoe's sad reply.

'Yes.'

'Who? Strout?'

'No. Annie Baxter's father.'

Pascoe did a double take. 'But who? How—'

'You'll soon know.'

A light burned in the downstairs dining room and the hall. The door opened and Marjorie Enys stood framed by it. She had been expecting him. David or Sarah had telephoned her.

Bluntly, Ryga said, 'Jory Logan is dead.'

She blinked hard, searched his face and then that of Pascoe's, as though looking for a trick. Seeing there was none, she stepped aside and they entered. Removing their hats, they followed her into the dining room.

'How did Jory die?' she asked.

'He fell to his death in the same place as Charlotte.'

'Fell!' Marjorie Enys said sharply.

'Yes, fell, like Charlotte. His foot must have slipped. I was with him. I couldn't do anything to save him.'

Marjorie Enys's hand grappled for the chair and she sank into it. 'Thank you,' she said sincerely. Ryga knew what she meant.

'Before he died he told me about Charlotte's ailment.'

'But I thought Doctor—'

'How her nerves were affected by the baby's death, so much that she couldn't cope.'

She searched his face. 'You're a good man, Ryga.'

Pascoe looked puzzled.

'Can we sit down?' Ryga asked.

She nodded. 'You'll know that Strout will be distraught over Jory's death.'

'Yes, along with all the men. He was very well respected.'

'He was, and I'll do everything in my power to protect his reputation and that of Charlotte's. So too will others.'

Holding her gaze, Ryga said, 'We know Mr Logan played no part in the murder.'

Her eyebrows knitted and she scrutinized him, her mind racing. He knew that among her thoughts was the gun that Logan had shot Ackland with. The one that was missing. Ryga suspected Strout had taken that when he'd heard about the shooting and had probably ditched it in the sea. Ryga was risking his job by covering up for Logan, but he had to. He, and others, owed Logan so much more than could ever be repaid. And Logan wasn't the killer, nor could he be taken to court now as an accessory. He said, 'We know he was on the train to London at the time of Ackland's death and in London when Crompton died.'

'I don't know what you expect me to say.'

'The truth. But if you won't speak it then perhaps Mr Fallows will tell it. I think he should join us now, Miss Enys.'

Fallows walked in, his face haggard, his eyes haunted. Major Tweed had been right, Ackland's killer had come from London, but he hadn't returned there the day before, as Miss Enys had said. Ryga had known she'd lied because he'd asked the ticket collector if any man of Fallows's description had boarded the train, and they hadn't.

Pascoe was looking baffled as he removed his notebook and pencil from his coat pocket.

'I'd do it again,' Fallows said. 'He killed my daughter.'

Gently, Ryga said, 'Please sit down, Mr Fallows. Sergeant Pascoe will take notes and I have to warn you both—'

'We know all that,' Miss Enys dismissed. She was looking older than her years, but not as old as Fallows, who crumpled onto the seat. There was a jug of water on the table and two glasses. Miss Enys poured a drink and passed it to him. He took a gulp.

'I've come to the end. It's the hangman for me.' He shrugged. 'But what do I care? I might cheat him yet. Oh, I won't escape, I couldn't, and I don't wish to. I'll plead guilty, but God, if you believe in Him, and I don't, might see me off before then. I have an incurable nervous disease.'

Looking at his sunken features, shaking hands and weary eyes, Ryga thought he might not have long and this ordeal would probably hasten his demise. It struck him how much Fallows had declined since he'd first set eyes on him leaving this house eight days ago, the morning after Crompton had been found dead on his boat. When he had seen him at Sennen Cove, shuffling along in the heavy rain, and had set him down in the harbour to climb the hill, dejection and resignation had already settled on him. There had been just that glimpse of army bearing he'd witnessed from the lay-by at the end of the road that had nudged at him and triggered an idea.

Fallows could have returned to London immediately after he had killed Ackland, and might even have escaped discovery and arrest, but it wasn't his way. He wouldn't let others take the blame for something he had done, and Ryga believed he had wanted to be caught. Although Ryga didn't have Fallows's army record from Jacobs, when they did get it, Ryga's instinct and knowledge of men convinced him it would be exemplary. Fallows, like Logan, was courageous, but was also a man eaten up with despair and bitterness, and consumed with guilt and regrets.

Fallows said, 'Ackland confessed to killing my daughter.'

'Annie Baxter. That's your real surname, not Fallows.' Ryga saw Pascoe's raised eyebrows.

'Yes.'

'Ackland confessed after you had beaten him, before you bludgeoned him to death.'

'It only took a couple of punches to loosen his tongue, and I know how to punch.'

'The army taught you.'

'They trained us to kill men. I've also done a bit of boxing, both in my youth and in the army.' He took a long draught of water with a shaking hand. Miss Enys looked about to speak, then closed her mouth. Her lips tightened but her eyes held deep concern for Fallows as he continued.

'You need to understand the background, Mr Ryga, unless you already know it.'

'Some.' Ryga threw a glance at Marjorie Enys. 'Annie went to work for Ackland on the outbreak of war when the orphanage she was working at, and where she had been raised, was closing. The children were being evacuated. She didn't know that you were alive.'

He nodded. 'Annie's mother died when she was four. I was working as a chauffeur and my wife as lady's maid to a well-to-do family in Kent. For a while I managed to get various women to look after Annie, but it didn't suit the family and my services were dispensed with. The tied cottage was needed for a new couple. I had no family and therefore no choice but to place Annie with an orphanage in London while I tried to find work. It was tough. The recession was beginning to bite. Eventually I got a good job as valet and chauffeur to Sir Gerald Dowd. They couldn't take a child in the house but at least I was earning, and I sent money to the orphanage with instructions that Annie should have what she wanted and a good education. I received letters of thanks from them but never from Annie. I thought that perhaps she wasn't a letter writer.'

When in reality, Ryga thought, the matron of the home had been pocketing the money. He could see that Fallows had eventually drawn that conclusion. 'Didn't you ever visit her?'

'I was told it would be too distressing for her. It would be disruptive as she had settled in well. I thought they knew best. Yes, I was that much of a fool.' His voice was harsh. 'I worked hard and sent every penny I could to the orphanage. Then Sir Gerald died and I was looking for a new post and times were even harder. Annie left school and the orphanage wrote to say she had got a domestic job. They didn't say where, even though I asked them. The matron said they would forward my letter on to her, leaving it up to her to tell me. I didn't hear from her. I thought she was punishing me by cutting me off, as she believed I had done with her when she was a child. I was upset but I didn't do anything about it.'

'And you learned from Miss Enys that Annie never left the orphanage, but was working unpaid for them until Ackland showed up and wanted someone who had no one to write home to about her employer.'

He swallowed hard and took another drink of water. 'I believe the orphanage never told her about me. And I did nothing. I'll go to my grave with that guilt on my shoulders and I deserve it. If I had acted all those years ago, I would have saved her from her terrible fate. I'm as guilty as that foul man who killed her. The hangman will be my retribution. And don't tell me I should have gone to the police when I learned what he had done, and that I shouldn't have taken the law into my own hands, because that wouldn't have given me half the satisfaction. I couldn't have stomached seeing Ackland talk and scheme his way out of a murder charge. He was wealthy, with powerful connections. Annie was just a maid and there was no proof.'

Ryga could see how this had eaten away at him until he had lost all reason.

Fallows pulled himself together with an effort. 'I was fighting for the country the other side of this godforsaken world, in South Africa. I hardly had time to think; staying alive and defeating the Nazis were my priorities. That's what I told myself. After the war I began to wonder more and more how she was. Had she survived? Had she married? Did I have any grandchildren? But still I did nothing.'

He paused and took another long gulp of water. Marjorie Enys watched him.

'I stayed on in the army in West Germany. I was batman to Colonel Harrison, a good man who, when he died, left me a small legacy. It was totally unexpected. He knew I had a daughter and the last thing he did was urge me to try and find her. When I was discharged in forty-nine on account of ill health, and with money enough not to need to look for another job, I immediately set about trying to find Annie.'

He lifted the glass with trembling hands.

'I went to Somerset House to see if I could find a marriage certificate for her but there wasn't one. Next I looked for a death certificate — nothing. That didn't mean she hadn't been killed in the bombing; her body might have been unidentified. I contacted the War Office to see if she had been conscripted but they had no record of her. It was as though she had never existed. I considered putting an advertisement in one of the national newspapers but decided to look for the matron of the orphanage. I went to Rochester, where the orphanage had been. It was no longer operating but a neighbour told me where I could find a cook who had worked there, and who was living in the town. She told me about Annie having worked at the orphanage until she'd got a job in London on the outbreak of war for a Mr Ackland, a civil servant, and that was all she knew. I returned to town and went through the telephone directory. It didn't take long to find where he lived. I went there and talked to the porter, who said they'd had a young lady called Annie working for Mr and Mrs Ackland during the early years of the war.'

'And you called on Ackland.'

He wiped a shaky hand across his eyes as though trying to shut out the image of that interview.

'I didn't take to him from the start. He said he had no idea where she was, she'd just walked out to get married. I knew something was wrong. I smelled a rat, and believe me I can smell them. There were many of the nasty scheming creatures in Vienna and West Berlin after the war, exploiting poor innocents. I chatted to the porter.'

As Melton had told Ryga.

'He said that he'd never heard Annie speak of a boyfriend and that she'd been worried about Mrs Ackland's declining health. Mrs Ackland died a fortnight after Annie had left. I went away thinking this over. I didn't have the name of this supposed Canadian serviceman, and there had been no marriage certificate, but that didn't mean they weren't married.

They could have wed in Canada. I asked if she'd applied for a visa to travel there.'

Fallows had done what Jacobs had. Ryga said, 'And, like us, you found there was no record of that.'

Fallows nodded. 'I mulled it over and then I recalled that the porter had said Mrs Ackland had a sister, Miss Enys, living in Penzance in Cornwall, who had been very worried about her sister. I thought at least Miss Enys would be able to tell me more about Annie. I came here a year ago. I stayed in Penzance and found Gulls Nest and Marjorie.'

Marjorie Enys studied Fallows, concerned, as he continued.

'We talked. Marjorie told me of her suspicions about Ackland and her sister. We suspected that Annie had discovered that Ackland was poisoning his wife and he killed Annie because of that. We couldn't go to the police because we had no evidence of it. He'd only have denied it, and it was too late to do a post-mortem, so they wouldn't exhume the body. The police wouldn't take my word, or Marjorie's, against those two — Crompton and Ackland.'

He took a deep breath, his sunken eyes tormented with sorrow.

Ryga exchanged a glance with Pascoe. They were both thinking along the same lines — that Fallows looked in danger of collapsing. Ryga said, 'You and Miss Enys planned what to do.'

'And we took pleasure in it,' Marjorie Enys declared defiantly. 'But we had to wait for the right opportunity. We learned that Crompton was planning to retire and had commissioned a new motor yacht to be built.'

'How?' Ryga asked, although he suspected Dr Bergmann had told Miss Enys that. He had read about it in the medical press, as he had told him earlier, and possibly made enquires with his former colleagues in London, which he'd passed on to Miss Enys.

But Miss Enys had another source of information. 'I'd kept in touch with Crompton's housekeeper who I had placed with him, Joyce Pickford. We often corresponded by letter and she telephoned me to tell me she was returning to Northern Ireland because Crompton was retiring and was going to sail his new boat back to London when it was ready in April. I asked if he was going alone. She said that he was hoping to engage a valet. She'd be no good because she didn't like boats and it wasn't her type of job, and besides she was too old for that malarkey.'

'And you recommended Mr Fallows and said where Crompton could get in touch with him.'

Fallows said, 'It gave us the perfect opportunity, because Ackland would jump at having a free weekend on a luxury yacht. Crompton contacted me. I said I would be very interested and gave him references. I'd piloted a motor yacht for a Commander Fitzvillier before the war and had a great deal of experience.'

He paused and Pascoe looked grateful because it enabled him to catch up on his shorthand notes. A sudden squall of rain beat against the windows. Fallows looked at it automatically yet he didn't register it. It was as though he were elsewhere. And, Ryga thought, he was.

'You joined him at Stranraer.'

'I caught the night train from Euston and reached Stranraer Harbour in the morning, a week after Crompton had travelled up. He took over the boat on Friday the thirteenth of April, and sailed it alone to Troon and then on to Stranraer. I got supplies in, familiarized myself with the craft, and we left there for Whitehaven on the eighteenth of April.'

It was as Ryga had discovered. 'From there you sailed to Holyhead, where you telephoned a telegram to be delivered to Ackland, ostensibly from Crompton, to ask him to join the *Patricia Bee* at Penzance.'

'Yes. Crompton knew nothing of it. Ackland replied in the affirmative, as I knew he would. I was able to intercept the answering telegram, before the boy could give it to Crompton. The weather forecast for the week was bad. I knew we would have to stay at Holyhead for some days. So far, everything was going to plan.' A smile briefly played at his lips before the shutters once again came down. He continued like a soldier giving a report to his officer. 'On Saturday the twenty-eighth of April we were able to leave Holyhead and made for Fishguard, where I departed from the boat. I told Crompton that while ashore I had telephoned to my daughter who was ill and I had to return to London. He didn't like it.'

'But you sweetened the pill by handing him a telegram, supposedly from Sarah Bergmann.' Ryga's eyes flicked to Marjorie Enys. So did Fallows's. 'It said that she would meet him on board his yacht at St Ives.' And Crompton had rubbed his hands with glee and thought he could continue his exploitation of the distressed woman. 'Instead of catching the train to London from Fishguard you caught the train to Bristol Temple Meads and from there to Penzance, arriving on Tuesday the first of May.' Ryga had evidence of this from his enquiries at the railway station after his studies of *Bradshaw's*.

Fallows nodded. 'I had to kick my heels for a couple of days before Ackland was due to arrive. I used the time to walk the coast and think over how I was going to confront the man who had killed his wife, and my daughter.'

Ryga picked up the tale. 'Early Saturday morning, before Ackland arrived, you walked to Tregarris House and took Logan's car from outside. He often left it there unlocked.' Ryga believed that it had been arranged that way and that Fallows had then given Logan the key to Crompton's Harley Street house, which he'd taken from him before leaving the *Patricia Bee* or had had a copy of it made. Miss Enys had given Logan the key she had to Ackland's place, her sister's one, which Ackland was unaware of. Fallows had been designated to meet Ackland because Marjorie Enys had known that if Logan had done so he would have killed him before setting off for London.

Ryga studied her stoical expression. As he'd heard from Logan, she had persuaded him that they would wait until the early hours of Tuesday morning to kill Ackland, when

Logan returned. In reality, they had no intention of doing so. It would have been simpler if Marjorie Enys had let Fallows take her car, but Logan needed those keys before setting off for London. Her sailing to Penzance on the same morning had been perhaps a whim, or to assuage her restlessness. Or perhaps to watch from a short distance as her despised brother-in-law got in that car to be taken to his death.

They hadn't counted on a sharp-eyed workman returning home from his night shift remembering seeing the dented bumper and loose fender. And neither had they anticipated that Logan, furious at being cheated out of having a hand in Ackland's death, would drag his body from the tunnel and shoot him.

Ryga looked at Pascoe, who gave a slight nod to indicate he had all this down in his notebook. 'Tell us what happened, Mr Fallows.'

'I told Ackland that I had been asked to pick him up by Sir Bernard and that I had been loaned the car by Mr Logan in order to do so. He never queried it. I was beneath talking to anyway, as far as he was concerned, being a mere manservant. On the way across the moor, I played my foot on the accelerator so that the car jolted as if it had a petrol blockage. I said I needed to take a look under the bonnet, and why didn't he get out and stretch his legs. He did and that's when I struck him on the back of the head with my walking stick, which I'd taken from the floor beneath my seat. I manhandled him into the car and drove to the cove. I managed to get him out, and dragged him down onto the shore and into the tunnel. It took some doing. I was exhausted, but my hatred and fury gave me strength.'

Pascoe's shorthand flowed. The clock struck ten. No one spoke until it had finished, then Fallows continued.

'I wanted Ackland to become conscious so that I could tell him who I was, and why I was going to kill him. I must have hit him too hard because he wouldn't come round. He was alive though. I waited.' He took a breath. 'I daren't leave him in case he came to and staggered away. I could have finished him off then but I wanted to tell him of the lives he'd ruined. I wanted to see and smell his fear. I wanted him to beg me to spare his life, which I would never have done.'

Pascoe cleared his throat.

'I dozed off. When I came to, Ackland was still unconscious. But he had a pulse. I prayed he wouldn't die, not until I could confront him.'

Ryga interjected. 'Then you showed up in the cove, Miss Enys, early on Sunday morning, because Mr Fallows hadn't returned.' Edna had heard the front door.

She glanced at Fallows. 'I told Victor to leave Ackland. But he wouldn't. I fetched some food.'

'From the Bergmanns, where you told David what had happened, but not Sarah because she was still on board Crompton's boat, where she had been since Saturday night, keeping below decks, not answering when the harbour master hailed her. Making it seem as though the craft was locked up and deserted. She had to make sure that Crompton stayed in a deep, drug-induced sleep until her husband could arrive and take the boat out.'

He caught Pascoe's troubled glance. Marjorie Enys was tight-lipped and Fallows looked as though he was in a trance.

'What happened with Ackland, Mr Fallows?'

With an effort, Fallows brought his concentration back. 'When he eventually regained consciousness, I forced him change into his evening attire to make it look as though he had dined on board the *Patricia Bee* if anyone discovered his body and enquiries were made, as they were, although we didn't expect his body to be found — not for some time, at least. We anticipated that he would be reported missing by his employer. The porter at Abercorn Mansions might also report he hadn't seen Ackland, not since he left to catch a train. The police would investigate and would discover the telegram.'

'Why didn't you take Ackland's suitcase to the *Patricia Bee*, Miss Enys?'

'I forgot. By the time I remembered, it was too late. PC Treharne had already been on board. I wondered if he might not have searched the boat and I could still get Ackland's things on board, but not only did Silas take up watch but Sergeant Pascoe also went on her. Then you and he together. I didn't then know who you were, but I surmised you must be another detective, and Sergeant Pascoe would certainly have noticed if the clothes had suddenly miraculously appeared.'

'You didn't need to come down to the pier the first night I was there to find out who I was because Dr Bergmann telephoned to tell you that on Tuesday afternoon. You wanted to know what was happening, and what I thought about Ackland's death, so decided to invite me to breakfast.'

'Yes. You'll find his belongings in my room.'

'Along with the missing items from Crompton's boat, including his ration book and chequebook?'

She nodded with tight lips. Ryga could see she was determined not to tell him who had taken the sea charts and those other items from the *Patricia Bee*. It could only have been one of two people: Sarah or David. Unless Miss Enys had driven to St Ives Saturday night when Edna was at the pictures with her fiancé and taken them. Ryga was convinced that was what she would say when pressed.

Pascoe looked up. 'You intended that Sir Bernard should die, otherwise he would have denied all knowledge of sending the telegram and Ackland's arrival.'

She glanced at Ryga. 'We just wanted to keep him out of the way until after Ackland was dead. Sarah had worked for him. We knew he would jump at the chance of seeing her again. We didn't realize he would suffer a fatal seizure.'

So that was the way it was going to be, thought Ryga. But then he'd known that. Perhaps Crompton had died a natural death on board the *Patricia Bee* after all. Or perhaps Sarah or David Bergmann had killed him. The blood tests might show he was drugged, but not sufficiently to have killed him. There were other non-detectable ways of killing someone, as he'd read in the medical dictionary in the library — a shot of insulin or air, for example.

Pascoe's voice broke through Ryga's thoughts. 'Did Ackland confess to killing his wife?'

'He said he didn't intend to, that he was trying to cure her. He babbled on about Annie questioning the medication she was asked to give Mrs Ackland.'

Supplied by Sir Bernard Crompton.

'Annie wanted to call the doctor. And he couldn't have that because it would reveal her illness. He said his wife had had an affair with a serviceman and had contracted syphilis.'

Pascoe's pencil froze.

'It was a dirty lie and I made him admit that. He couldn't wait to spill it all to me then to avoid another beating. Bullies don't like it when you stand up to them, and Ackland was the worst of the species — he bullied women.' Fallows took a deep breath and his eyes flicked to Miss Enys. 'Ackland was the fiend who had infected his wife. After he admitted it, I killed him. I struck him with my stick. There was this fury inside me. This man was a coward, a predator and a murderer. And I was angry with myself. I had done nothing to find my daughter until it was too late. I let her down in life; I wasn't going to in death. After he was dead, I shot him in the head.'

Ryga looked at Miss Enys. Fallow, seeing it, added, 'I had the gun during my army days. I threw it in the sea.'

A long silence followed, broken by a gentle cough from Pascoe. 'Whose idea were the five pieces of rock in each man's pocket?' he asked.

'Mine, Sergeant,' Miss Enys answered. 'Stupid and petty. I don't know why I did it.'

Ryga said, 'They represented the lives Ackland had ruined: your sister's, Logan's and his wife's, Annie's and Mr Logan's son's. And Crompton's five pieces of rock?'

'The same. He was complicit in all their deaths.'

'How did they get into Crompton's pocket?'

Fallows said, 'I put them in his dinner jacket before I left the boat at Fishguard.'

Ryga knew that wasn't the case. David or Sarah had put them there, but Ryga didn't think Marjorie Enys or Fallows were ever going to admit that. They'd do their best to keep the Bergmanns out of this. In truth, the five pieces of rock in Crompton's pocket represented Phyllis Ackland, Charlotte and Jory Logan, and David and Sarah Bergmann.

'But why?' asked Pascoe. 'I know it represented the deceit practised by those two men, but it made us curious and even keener to begin an investigation.'

Fallows answered. 'It was another thing linking the two men, like the telegram and the evening dress. And it was appropriate, given their deception. No one might ever discover its meaning anyway. They might never have found Ackland's body — only, I made the mistake of not dragging it back into the tunnel.'

Another lie, thought Ryga, but didn't say.

'If anyone did wonder about the stones, perhaps they'd shrug it off, or think the two men being in Cornwall had been discussing minerals and looking for a way to exploit the apatite for gain. It can be a valuable mineral.'

As Ryga had discussed with Miss Wargrove.

Wearily Fallows said, 'It's over now. I killed Ackland and that's all you need to know.'

Defiantly, Miss Enys added, 'And I helped him. We're the people you need, Inspector. Neither of us will change our story.'

Ryga knew that.

CHAPTER TWENTY-SIX

It was early light when Ryga and Pascoe finished. Victor Baxter aka Fallows had been charged with the murder of Ackland, and Marjorie Enys with being an accessory. Edna, returning home, had watched in tears as her employer had been taken away in the car. Pascoe and Ryga had taken statements at the station. They hadn't deviated from what they had already been told. There was no reference to what Logan had done, none to Charlotte and her condition, and nothing about Sarah going on board Crompton's boat or David Bergmann's swim to the shore from it. Pascoe had asked Ryga why he didn't press for the latter. He'd said because he didn't think it would stand scrutiny when and if it came to court. They had a result, they had confessions, they had enough evidence to convict Fallows and Miss Enys, both of whom said they would plead guilty and leave the judge to decide their punishment. Later that morning, Marjorie Enys would telephone her solicitor, who, she said, would represent them both. Ryga hoped the judge would be merciful and spare Fallows the noose.

Ryga had telephoned Street at his home, who said he would inform Major Tweed of events. There were still the inquests to resume. Ryga would return to London on the night train the following day, or rather that day, then travel back to Cornwall for the inquests. He'd asked Street what was to be done with the *Patricia Bee*.

'We'll leave that for the solicitors to sort out.'

Ryga had telephoned the Bergmanns and told David what had occurred, including Jory Logan's death, which he had heard about anyway. 'There's no need for you to do anything further, Doctor,' he said. 'Crompton's blood tests might show he ingested or was given a drug by a woman who was seen going on board and, possibly suffering from the effects of it, he took the boat out and subsequently had a seizure. Alternatively, it could come back negative.' Ryga knew Pedrick would keep his silence, as would Silas.

'I—'

'And there will be no need to mention Charlotte Logan's illness.'

'I don't . . .' He inhaled. 'Thank you, Inspector.'

Enough people had suffered.

Ryga didn't wish to return to the *Patricia Bee*. He'd have to at some stage to collect his holdall and murder case, but not yet. He also needed sleep, but he could get that on the night train. He'd survive until then. He'd done so before on little to no sleep for hours and days, both in the camp and on duty. He told Pascoe to go home and asked Chief Inspector Jerram for the use of his car, one last time.

His heart was weighed down with sorrow for the victims of Ackland and Crompton, including their killer and Miss Enys. Old Silas's words rang through his mind as he drove across country to Tregarris House.

'Here comes the chopper to chop off your head. They hang people now.'

'Only the guilty ones.'

'I doubt that, mister. And some don't deserve to be hanged.'

'Even if they're guilty of taking another person's life?'

'They might see it as justice.'

He didn't condone what they had done but part of him said Ackland and Crompton had got what they deserved.

He drew up outside Tregarris House. What would happen to it now? Who had it been left to in Logan's will? It wasn't his concern. It wasn't a happy house.

He struck out on foot to the clifftop where he'd last spoken to Logan. The sun had risen. The day was still and the sea stretched out endlessly before him. The body had long been removed to the mortuary. Only the rocks, sand, shingle and seagulls remained. He couldn't help thinking that if he hadn't come here, Jory Logan would still be alive. He tried hard to let go of that last image of a tormented man with sad, anguished eyes, leaping to his death.

He stood, gazing into the distance, thinking of the past, his past. It couldn't be rewritten. This case had, like the one before it, played with his emotions, conjuring up the ghosts of the war. They'd never leave him, he knew that. Giving up the job he loved and returning to sea was running away. Life had to be faced, no matter how tough it became. And for Jory? Well, it had become not so much tough — Jory could deal with that — but pointless, which was far worse.

He removed his hat, his eyes steadily on the horizon. 'Hope you're now at peace, Jory,' he said aloud. 'You deserve it.' The wind stirred around him as though answering. In its gentle caress he heard the words Jory had spoken: *I don't know what's out there . . . and there's only one way to find out.* Ryga took a deep breath. He didn't know what was out there either, but there was work to do and a future to make here. Replacing his hat, he squared it firmly, turned and made his way back to the car.

THE END

THE JOFFE BOOKS STORY

We began in 2014 when Jasper agreed to publish his mum's much-rejected romance novel and it became a bestseller.

Since then we've grown into the largest independent publisher in the UK. We're extremely proud to publish some of the very best writers in the world, including Joy Ellis, Faith Martin, Caro Ramsay, Helen Forrester, Simon Brett and Robert Goddard. Everyone at Joffe Books loves reading and we never forget that it all begins with the magic of an author telling a story.

We are proud to publish talented first-time authors, as well as established writers whose books we love introducing to a new generation of readers.

We won Trade Publisher of the Year at the Independent Publishing Awards in 2023. We have been shortlisted for Independent Publisher of the Year at the British Book Awards for the last four years, and were shortlisted for the Diversity and Inclusivity Award at the 2022 Independent Publishing Awards. In 2023 we were shortlisted for Publisher of the Year at the RNA Industry Awards.

We built this company with your help, and we love to hear from you, so please email us about absolutely anything bookish at: feedback@joffebooks.com

If you want to receive free books every Friday and hear about all our new releases, join our mailing list: www.joffebooks.com/contact

And when you tell your friends about us, just remember: it's pronounced Joffe as in coffee or toffee!

Milton Keynes UK
Ingram Content Group UK Ltd.
UKHW010641020624
443038UK00003B/5